DOCTOR WHO

THE BLUE ANGEL

PAUL MAGRS AND JEREMY HOAD

BBC

Published by BBC Worldwide Ltd,
Woodlands, 80 Wood Lane
London W12 0TT

First published 1999
Copyright © Paul Magrs and Jeremy Hoad 1999
The moral right of the authors has been asserted

Original series broadcast on the BBC
Format © BBC 1963
Doctor Who and TARDIS are trademarks of the BBC

ISBN 0 563 55581 5
Imaging by Black Sheep, copyright © BBC 1999

Printed and bound in Great Britain by Mackays of Chatham
Cover printed by Belmont Press Ltd, Northampton

the blue angel arrives with thanks to…

Joy Foster, Louise Foster, Mark Magrs, Charles Foster, Peter Hoad, Rita Hoad, Jonathan Hoad, Rachel Hoad, Nicola Cregan, Michael Fox, Lynne Heritage, Pete Courtie, Brigid Robinson, Paul Arvidson, Jon Rolph, Antonia Rolph, Steve Jackson, Laura Wood, Alicia Stubbersfield, Siri Hansen, Paul Cornell, Bill Penson, Mark Walton, Sara Maitland, Meg Davis, Ewan Gillon, Amanda Reynolds, Richard Klein, Lucie Scott, Reuben Lane, Kenneth MacGowan, Georgina Hammick, Maureen Duffy, Vic Sage, Marina Mackay, Jayne Morgan, Louise D'Arcens, Julia Bell, Lorna Sage, Ashley Stokes, Steve Cole, Jac Rayner, Pat Wheeler, Kate Orman, Jonathan Blum, Dave Owen, Gary Russell, Alan McKee, Phillip Hallard, Nick Smale, Helen Fayle, Mark Phippen, Lance Parkin, Anna Whymark, Chloê Whymark, Stephen Hornby, Stewart Sheargold…

…and companions on the bus past and future…

Welcome to Valcea, everybody…

Love,
Paul and Jeremy

Spring 1999
Norwich

Contents

Chapter One
Door's Stiff. Frozen...?

Door's stiff. Frozen?

I haven't been out the back for over a week. It's been too wet. Soaking. Chucking it down constantly. I've barely been out of the house. Sent the others out for shopping. I've kept the central heating on and hidden myself away. Only thing to do.

But I want to check on the garden. See what damage has been done. All that planting and transplanting and the tender loving care we gave it at the end of the summer. I want to see if the weather has ruined it all.

Today there's no rain. Too cold to rain. The sky is full and grey, the colour of Tupperware. Someone's put a Tupperware lid over the town.

Our garden is tiny, walled in by bushes and redbricked walls. You can't even see into next door's either side or over the back. We have a secret garden. In the few sunny days we've managed to have here, I sat in a deck chair and read, bang in the middle of the lawn. I sat for hours while Compassion set about making us a path from fragments of flagstone she found in the shrubbery. She can be a good little worker when she wants. She dug out a curving shape for the path and dug it quite deep. Filled it with the rubble and dust from chipped plaster that we had bags and bags of after we did the downstairs walls, and then she put the paving stones on top. Scooped the earth in and, hey presto, we had a path. She made it a curve so as not to disturb me from my reading, in my chair, in the middle of the garden. So it's in a kind of S-shape or, as Fitz has pointed out, a reversed question mark.

Actually, it's more than cold today. It's absolutely freezing. The grass is silvered and I can't smell the honeysuckle at all.

That's when I crouch to examine the herb garden, expecting

1

the worst. The rosemary is dead, I can see that at a glance. Black in my hands, the needles like blades. And – worst of all – the bush that we moved to a place where it would be in shelter, treating it so carefully, so solicitously, even Fitz pitching in to help – the wild thyme has been split right down the middle. Its branches are snapped. In two halves, both lolled flat on the ground. Quite dead.

I straighten up and sniff the air and realise that it's going to snow. This idea makes me shiver and that, I suppose, is because I've been dreaming about snow rather a lot lately. It's figured everywhere – every scene I can recall having dreamed just recently. As if the seasons changed sooner in my nightmares.

There is a bang then as the window two storeys above my head is flung open. I look round to see Fitz glaring down, his palms on the wet sill. He isn't even dressed yet. In the T-shirt he slept in, his hair tangled up, unwashed, a furious look on his face. Three days' worth of stubble.

It was all some time ago. Now the worst had passed and this was his quiet time. He hadn't had a funny spell in ages. He was still learning to be calm, however, and not let his mind tick over too quickly. His Doctor had warned him about the dangers of that. His private Doctor to whom he paid out vast sums of money. That Doctor worked from a Georgian town house by the North Park, across town.

– One Doctor to another, eh?
– Indeed. I hadn't thought of that.
– Well, sometimes we all have to see a specialist.

And with a flourish, his private Doctor wrote him out an indecipherable prescription, at which he stared, all the way down the street, back into the centre of the town. He didn't know what he was taking, but the Doctor seemed to think these funny green pills were just the ticket.

2

- I should be more curious. Don't you think, Fitz?
- Oh, probably.
- I used to be more curious, didn't I?
- You used to be insatiably curious.
- Hmm. I thought so.

He could still remember the things he said then, at the time he was having his funny spells. The things he went around saying in the thick of it all. But he couldn't remember where he had been, what he had done, exactly who he had said these things to. Still the words came back to him, thick and fast, his irrepressible words of warning. His gift of the gab, his sixth sense, his gift for being seventh son of a seventh son. He had the knowledge and wanted to pass it on. His words had the ineluctable force of truth and he had to let them out. But people never listen. They told him these words were lies, just his lies, and none of them convinced anyone.

That had made him more anxious than anything.

Anxious was exactly what he wasn't these days. He had learned to calm down.

- Is the garden wrecked, Doctor?
- My herb garden's looking a little shabby.
- It's nearly winter. The whole lot would die then anyway.
- No, no, no, Fitz. It would be all right. I'd see to it.
- But it's too late now.
- The thyme is split completely asunder.
- What?
- The wild thyme. Dead. Lolling on the grass.
- It's too cold to hang about here all day. I'm going back to my book.

He remembered telling everyone – who? – about the men who were made out of glass. Whose hearts were scarlet and could be seen, pulsing, alive, through the sheeny see-through skin, muscle,

3

sinew of their chests. These hearts, it could be plainly seen, had faces of their own – malign and watchful faces. These men of glass sat in golden chairs which ran on wheels and shot bolts of fire at those who stood in their way.

The Doctor was convinced – swore blind to anyone who would listen – that they were coming here. Heading to this world out of revenge. They were coming specifically after him.

It is winter now and this is my new house. In the mornings the windows are mapped in careful lines of frost. I suppose you could say I laze about. I like to cook. I spend a lot of time in the kitchen.

My watchword is optimism.

We've painted the kitchen bright orange, and all the crockery and utensils are cornflower blue. I had crates and crates of kitchen things, far more than I'd ever need. I can't remember actually buying any of them. These blue things were bought in Italy, in Florence, and I don't remember when I was there. A side effect of the green pills, I imagine. One of many. Very strange.

I cook and I put on the same CD again and again, shuffling and repeating. It's the incidental music from all the Bette Davis movies between 1938 and 1953. I like a little drama.

I live optimistically with my lodgers, Fitz and Compassion. I call them my companions. That's what they're like. Compassion isn't very well. She's been having funny spells too, just lately. Fitz is languid, somewhat sarcastic. Sometimes he looks at me quizzically, as if there's something he wants to ask me. We have a floor of this new house each. I don't mind sharing. The attic is full of my boxes. I can't be bothered unpacking all that stuff yet. Maybe I'll do it on Christmas morning, and pretend someone has sent me presents.

Fitz has been up there, poking around among all my books. He's a great reader, it turns out. Lately he's been poring over an ancient leather-bound volume he found in a trunk in the attic. A warped and frangible text that he says is called the *Aja'ib*.

He spends all day reading that.

I think… I think it was my grandfather who brought that book back from the East. I'm sure that it was. My mother passed on to me all my grandfather's things. When Fitz has finished with the book I'll take a look at it and find out.

At least the dreams that the Doctor was having were under control. That was the main thing. His private Doctor in the Georgian house by the North Park told him not to worry. Ever. There was nothing at all to be anxious about. Indeed, sometimes his Doctor would phone him in the middle of the night – just when the dreams were becoming perplexing – and murmur a few words of consolation. The Doctor thought that was very good value indeed. He felt he was being monitored all around the clock. That his welfare was being seen to.

He has a healthy imagination – that's what the Doctor tells himself. But one that needs controlling and tempering. That's all it is.

– And you don't want any more episodes, do you?
– Oh, no! No more episodes for me!

Funny thing is, his private Doctor even infiltrates the dreams that he does still have and gives him words of advice there, too. Is nothing sacred? His private Doctor is an avuncular presence. A deeply lined face and a shock of silvery hair. He wears frilly shirts and bow-ties to work, his opera cloak flung on to the consultation couch. A touch of the old Empire about him. We'll crack this little problem, Doctor. Nothing to it. Have more pills. He speaks winningly and sometimes he hypnotises his patient, spinning a kind of golden pendant in his face. He sings a sort of nursery rhyme – half familiar, terribly exotic.

The Doctor believes he is getting his money's worth.

He hasn't had an episode in ages.

* * *

These men of glass lived in a city called Valcea, which, the Doctor would insist, he had visited. An impossible city of glass, set up at an incredible height. He had gone there and visited the Glass Men and learned how brutal and sadistic they were. Their city had black-and-white parquet floors, which the Glass Men's golden chairs couldn't leave at all, because they seemed to run on something akin to static electricity. Something like that but, at any rate, this circumscription meant that the world – the real world – was safe from their incursions. The Glass Men were too precious to endanger themselves by leaving Valcea.

Yet, having foiled their plans that first time – their plans to destroy the Ghillighast, the race with whom they shared their world – the Doctor returned home. Soon he learned that the Valcean Glass Men were working on schemes to make themselves more powerfully mobile, so they could transport their avarice elsewhere.

They had discovered the means to motivate themselves, and could detach their glass city from their world and set it free, to float like an iceberg detaching from its mother berg in the frozen north. The city of Valcea was free to swim across vast expanses of murky space, to come to Earth after the Doctor, to come to this world. And he knew they were coming after him.

At the height of his queer, excitable spell, the Doctor had taken to alerting everyone – friends, relations, the authorities, people on the street – that the Glass Men were coming, and it was all his fault. He had led them to this world. Curses on his travels and his endless curiosity!

Any day now. That is what he suspected.

But the pills his private Doctor gave him calmed him down, calmed him down, calmed him down.

Chapter Two
The Ladies Were Having a Day Out...

The ladies were having a day out. It was the worst day of the year they could possibly have chosen. They set off first thing that morning in Maddy Sharp's off-white Morris Minor and even before they'd left town the snow was three inches deep with no sign of letting up. But they weren't to be deterred.

Big Sue was wedged in the back seat, gazing at the clogged sky. 'I reckon we should turn back now, Maddy. This is madness.'

Maddy didn't like to talk when she was driving. She fixed her elderly friend with a quick glance in the rear-view mirror. 'Look, Sue, we're out now. It was enough of a job getting out this bloody morning. And it's Christmas. So cheer yourself up.'

Big Sue was wearing a knitted tea-cosy hat, mustard-coloured. It was clamped down over her wig, which, in the dim light of the morning, looked as if it had been dyed indigo. Sue was using the mirror to check both hat and wig were straight. She tutted at Maddy for her stubbornness and sat quietly sulking for a while, sucking her teeth.

Beside Big Sue, the boy stared serenely ahead. He made no comment about Maddy's determination to get them to the mall in all the snow. He had every faith in his mother. She wouldn't let them down. Maddy gave him a quick smile, which he returned automatically, and turned back to the task in hand. Every time she looked at the boy she felt stronger. It was strange. He made her feel brave.

Secretly, though, as they rumbled through the undisturbed snow on the route out of Newton Aycliffe and rolled on to the country road that would take them to the A1, she was wondering if the trip wasn't foolhardy after all.

The radio had promised Snow Chaos this morning. And here it was. Listeners had been warned not to leave home unless the trip was vital. Maddy had been doing her hair in the living room with hot tongs and she turned off the weather report before it could finish. That was when the boy came downstairs, wearing the blue, diamond-patterned tracksuit she had bought for him from the market. He gave her a strange look for turning the radio off so abruptly. And in that moment Maddy just knew that she and her little party had to go ahead with the planned shopping trip today. Somehow she knew how disappointed the boy would be if she didn't make the effort.

'I think it's nice,' said the other woman in the back, Nesta, who was daft and skinny and glad to be rid of her kids for the day. 'I think it's like a proper magical Christmas adventure, seeing all the countryside like this.'

Big Sue grimaced. She wasn't keen on Nesta's company at the best of times. Nesta had this habit of getting herself involved in whatever was going on. She was a scrounger, too, always knocking at the back door, asking for milk or sugar. Begging off a pensioner! It was the pits, really. And Big Sue had seen Nesta stocking up on ciggies and cider at the small shop round the corner a couple of times in the past week. Big Sue thought Nesta was letting her kids do without. Nesta was meant to be living on the breadline, but she was keen as any of them to get out to the mall to do some shopping.

Big Sue looked across and watched Nesta staring entranced at the snow. They were pulling through the winding country roads outside of Chilton now. They hadn't been out chucking grit on the roads yet. You could feel the Morris Minor's tyres sliding on the fresh snow, and Maddy was wrestling at the wheel. This was going to be a stressful drive, and there was Nesta looking entranced out of that window. She was probably singing

Christmas songs to herself. She was that type. Never lived in the real world all her life. The usual trials and tribulations just passed her by.

Big Sue was tutting when she realised that the boy was, in turn, staring at her. He was looking straight into her face with those wide, bright-blue eyes. An honest, searching gaze. His hair had flopped into one of them. There wasn't the slightest expression on his face. She looked away.

Sometimes Big Sue found that the boy gave her the heebie-jeebies. She couldn't help it. Usually she got on really well with kids, even the awkward teens. But this one, Maddy Sharp's new son... well, there was something not quite right about him. He looked blankly at everyone, staring unashamedly into their faces. Everyone except Maddy Sharp, of course, his adoptive mother. On her he bestowed the most sickeningly sweet and loyal smiles. Maddy in turn glowed with pleasure. So you couldn't really tell Maddy you thought there was something wrong with him. You just had to be happy for her. And Big Sue was happy for her friend. The boy had done her a power of good.

Soon they were on the motorway. It was easier here, pushing on in the wake of the lorries, letting them clear the snow ahead, churning it into toffee-coloured mush. They could stay on the motorway now until they reached the Mall. No more winding roads. Maddy allowed herself to relax a little.

Half an hour and they would be there.

It was as light now as it would be all day. Everyone had their headlights on. You could feel the day turning, slipping back towards twilight already.

'Everyone all right in the back?' she shouted over the noise of her motor. The car rattled and roared and it was freezing inside. She glanced back and checked on her neighbours and her son. They grinned at her – Big Sue nervously, Nesta dreamily and her son enthusiastically, as if he couldn't think of anything nicer than being taken out shopping in a blizzard by his mum.

She called him Icarus because that was what he had asked her to call him. It was one of the few things he had brought from his earlier life, one of the few things she knew about him.

He was sixteen and, in many ways, he was much the same as any other sixteen-year-old lad. There was, perhaps, a trace of something foreign in his accent. He spoke English as if it were an acquired language, sometimes lingering on words as if they were unusual to him and to be savoured. He turned them over as if he were turning pebbles and seashells over and over in his palms on the day she first saw him.

That had been last summer, at the height of the summer, in fact, on Marsden Bay, the beach at South Shields where Maddy had taken herself off for a sunny afternoon wandering on the sands. One of the perks of being on her own – she could take off whenever she wanted for a day out.

Marsden Rock was a vast, natural edifice about a hundred yards out from the cliffs. The size of the Albert Hall, perhaps, and the same shape, its ceiling crammed and noisy with a thousand gannets and gulls. You could walk out to the rock when the tide was out, and here were dripping arches and tunnels that led deeper into the rock, the water sloshing and lapping around the fallen shale. It didn't pay to wander too far into the rock, of course. You could get lost and before you knew it the tide would be in.

Maddy poked around in the rock pools and balanced on the piles of stone, looking for bits of driftwood and interesting shells that she might use for a still life.

She was arty – that was how the other women round her street described her. If you went round her house, you'd see her setting up a new still life, or rolling out a fresh load of lining paper, on which she daubed spectacular renderings of scenes from the Bible, usually the Old Testament.

The other women from Phoenix Court thought she was a bit

funny, doing all this stuff – all these apocalyptic scenes, these volcanoes and destruction, all this mayhem. But she certainly seemed to enjoy her painting. They'd seen her work herself up into a right old state – thrashing the paint on; splashing out the colour. Big Sue – though she thought Maddy's paintings possibly blasphemous – said she thought the enterprise seemed quite therapeutic.

This summer gone Maddy had decided to branch out into sculpture and she was going to use natural materials. So she went poking around on the seashore and started to gather a host of gnarled and salt-washed objects.

She peered into the first chamber of the Rock and found it swimming in water, which reflected gorgeously, hypnotically on the dank, overarching ceiling. A circular space, like a womb.

And there, sitting on a rock in its centre, was the boy. He gave her quite a start. Already he was grinning at her. He was naked.

Maddy took fright. He was a big boy, after all – a teenager. He shouldn't have been sitting there like that, where just anyone might walk in. She started to back away.

Then the boy's voice came to her, echoing in the cavern. But it was as if the natural room were her own skull and it went resounding inside her head, and still the boy kept on grinning, showing each of his perfect teeth – and his lips weren't moving at all.

'Please don't run,' his voice said. That curious, halting tone. The odd, almost neutral accent. 'I can't do you any harm. You were meant to find me.'

Suddenly, despite the summer heat, Maddy felt chilled, as if this cavern had trapped the bone cold of the sea. 'What does that mean?' she asked.

'I've been waiting for you here, Maddy. I'm here.'

'Who are you?'

Instead he answered her in a way that stopped her breath for a moment or two, that made her head swim and her fingers grab the smooth wall beside her.

'Your son, Ian, didn't he die at five? Hadn't he just started school? Wasn't he like an angel, Maddy Sharp? Wasn't Ian your angel boy?'

She was starting to sob. Again she asked, 'Who are you?'

'How old would Ian be now, Maddy?'

Of course she knew. She knew precisely how old he would be now. She knew everything she was missing.

She looked at the boy as he stood up and started walking through the shallow green water towards her.

'Aren't I that age? Aren't I exactly like your son would be?'

She had a picture in her head, one she took with her everywhere, of how Ian should look now. Each year she had aged him, watched him grow towards maturity. She had looked at the boys that were Ian's contemporaries and tried to keep him in line. Only she knew that image in her head. Yet here it was before her. This boy.

'I've been waiting for you, Maddy Sharp,' he said.

She said, 'You aren't Ian.'

'No.' He was standing quite close now. His skin was pale, quite beautiful in the light. He didn't seem at all chilled. 'I'm not your son. But I could be.'

Once more she asked, 'Who are you?'

'I could be better than a son to you, Maddy Sharp,' he said, and took her in his arms.

And, once he was home and installed in her council house and given a room of his own, he'd settled in to the extent that Maddy could hardly believe that he hadn't always been there, and the neighbours had accepted him and didn't think it odd that Maddy should suddenly adopt a cousin's child and they understood because she'd had a lot of tragedy in her life. It was only after a week or two that the boy who wasn't her son, but who pretended to the outward world he was, told her his name was Icarus.

* * *

When they drove into Gateshead the traffic was thicker with others who had decided to hang the weather and go Christmas shopping anyway. But the snow was thicker, too, and they were at crawling pace, but they could see the lights and the low, flat, expansive roofs of all the shops in the dark valley ahead.

The ladies stared at the statue on the hill as they passed it, cooing and craning through their windows. It was a massively tall man with wings, rusted orange by now and white all down one side with plastered snow. The Tyneside Angel. It turned out Nesta had brought her camera with her, a cheap Instamatic, and she flashed up at the colossus as they swept by in its shadow.

The flash filled the car and made Maddy swerve and swear. 'Will you watch out, Nesta?'

'Sorry, Maddy.'

Maddy said to the boy, 'Will you take that thing off her while I'm driving?'

With a smile he pulled the camera out of Nesta's hands.

'No need to snatch…' she said. Then, 'Hey!' when she saw that he was opening the back of it and touching the taut black film inside with his fingers. Even Nesta knew that had ruined her pictures.

'Hey, you silly lad,' Big Sue barked. 'You've gone and…'

But Icarus wasn't listening. He picked at the slippery, shining spool until it had all come free and was tangled in his fingers. The empty camera dropped into his lap. He stroked at the film, each blank frame, with the tips of his fingers. Then he started to breathe on it, short gasps of frosted air.

'Hey,' Nesta shouted. 'Your bloody son has broken my film!'

'What's he done?' Maddy asked distractedly. She was concentrating on the road, but she felt a glow of pleasure that Nesta had called him her son.

'I said –'

'Hang on there,' cried Big Sue. She was staring at the strip of film in the boy's hands. He showed it to all of them. He looked pleased with himself. And there, frozen in each still frame of

Nesta's thirty-six potential exposures, was the perfect image of an angel. Far brighter and clearer and much more extravagant than the statue she had attempted, so clumsily, to shoot.

And soon they arrived at the shopping mall.

They parked in the red quadrant and Maddy tried to construct a mental map so she could find her car again. It was almost dark now, with a purple cast to the light. No stars at all. They wrapped up well, even though it was about a hundred yards to the main doors of the place. And inside it would be warm, air-conditioned, perfumed, and full of the crush of Christmas shoppers.

Except that wasn't true. They would find that out when they got inside. Things had already started to go wrong in there.

But let them find this out gradually. And leave them for a moment as they lock up the Morris Minor, fasten up their coats and scarves and check they have everything they need before going inside. Let's leave them for now beside Maddy Sharp's Morris Minor, which is parked in the shadow of a red double-decker bus.

No one in their party has remarked on the strangeness of this vehicle's presence. Or that fact that the bus is labelled quite clearly as the number 22 to Putney Common.

The ladies are thinking about different things. Nesta is thinking about the bright lights and the shopping; Maddy is thinking they can't leave it too late before turning back; Big Sue is wondering what trick the boy did with that film, and the boy is thinking...

Well, the boy is thinking many things. And among them, in fact, jostles the thought of this errant red bus. He knows exactly what it is and who has brought it here.

Chapter Three
Captain's Log. Stardate Etc., Etc. . . .

Captain's Log, stardate etc., etc.... Dispense with the formalities. Dispense with the protocols. Dispense with the captain while you're at it, why don't you? I've had it.

Computer. Coffee. Hot. Strong. Black.

I want that bloody Doctor off my ship and I want it now. One mad medic is enough for any crew.

This is Captain Robert B. Blandish recording.

I'm in my oval office, just off to one side from the bridge, where everyone is, as usual, getting on, quietly, calmly, with the task in hand. So efficiently. They're good, my crew. Very professional. Trained to be so. And it's my number two, Garrett, watching over them, and he's very good too, especially at maintaining that particular cool equilibrium on the bridge while the *Nepotist* is in flight. But he hasn't quite got it yet – that slick sense of command that comes only with experience.

Me, on the other hand, I've got that innate sense of leadership that instils loyalty in my crew. OK, so I cause scenes. But I'm only the captain. Who cares? I'm just the one who has to command three hundred and seventy-nine souls and make sure they return from this tour of duty intact. I'm the one who has to report back to the Galactic Feds. Oh, there's not much pressure on me. Oh, no. I've absolutely no right to be blunt and courageous on my very own bridge. And if I ever do I should be packed off to my little oval office just off the bridge to bring my report up to date.

It's not the same since that damn counsellor visited. 'It's more productive to engage with the feelings people have in order to motivate them with respect and sensitivity.' That's what I should do. It's soooo obvious. Well here I am. And I think it's more productive if I give the orders and people obey them instantly without question.

You see, the thing is, I'm used to having the *Nepotist* to myself. She's mine. My responsibility. Everything we engage with, well, it's my fight, it's my show. Even Garrett – that appeaser, that charmer, that backstabber in embryo – realises that fact. There are few things I'd deny Garrett, it has to be said – what with his expertise in most areas and all – but there are parts of my life that are sacrosanct. The *Nepotist* is mine and mine alone.

Even with Galactic Fed VIPs on board, swishing around in their oh-so-space-age gold and silver lamé frocks with their high collars and their ever-so-exotically-alien physiognomies, even then, when I have to wine, dine and wheedle, I'm still the big cheese on board. I still get to fire phasers when I want. I still get to fly as fast as I want. I still get to fight hand to hand with whichever warmongering bastard wants to meet up with me – and me alone – planetside, as they so often want to. It's still me. And I definitely get the first choice of the ladies, whatever colour they are. I've got a reputation to keep up.

But I can't help thinking things are slipping out of my hands. Just the last few days or so. Things aren't the same.

Then, two days ago, we came to Valcea. The City of Glass, hanging in space within a strange and erroneous region of… nebulosity, my second-in-command Garrett called it, with one of his rather prim and humourless smiles. Valcea, the City of Glass. That's where we are, in stationary orbit around its outer rim, drifting helplessly beside it.

And, what's more, a day ago, the Doctor arrives. In he swishes in his velvet coat, and starts interfering big time. Should have had him thrown in the brig.

Computer. This coffee stinks. Something stronger. Thaurian whisky. Now.

Meanwhile the bridge of the *Nepotist* was as hivelike in its activity as its commander Captain Robert B. Blandish supposed it was. The deck crew were sitting in their usual semicircle, at their consoles and desks, with lights blinking, flashing spasmodically, claiming their attention; these tiny controls and devices and levers they would tweak and adjust as necessary. A very highly trained and practised crew. No rush here, no matter what the situation. And the crew of the *Nepotist* had seen a good many of those. And they knew how to behave with the utmost decorum whenever their captain was in his chair.

They were all, as usual, focused on the viewscreen at the front of the chamber. A vivid wide-screen affair, size of a private cinema, except the *Nepotist* wasn't equipped with one of those filmic wide screens. More of a two-way telly, really. It showed them the inscrutable gleaming westernmost side of the glass city Valcea, suspended in space. A kind of dirty, contaminated space here, though, full of errant bits of matter and fragments fallen off other worlds. Nebulosity, Garrett had called it – a hazardous region for the ship to proceed at more than, say, five point nine. But Blandish had demanded more and more speed, damaging the hull and shields *en route* and then – typically – they had hit upon this unquantifiable obstacle, this blue-green gleaming city in space – an inscrutable, impossible edifice just hanging there and now holding them ineluctably by unseen devilish forces, and their journey was delayed hopelessly now. It didn't even respond to their scans or probes. Garrett knew Blandish's crossness was mostly directed at his own self, and his demanding that they cross this patch of queer nebulosity post-haste, for the sake of saving a day's travel to their next port of call. But there was nothing to be done now. They wouldn't be getting to Peladon and its revolting miners and hostaged royal family and VIP Feds or anywhere near it in the foreseeable future, and the situation (code A) would just have to wait.

Here they were. Stranded.

Chief science officer, second-in-command, all-rounder and prodigy Mr Garrett didn't share his commander's impetuous dislike and distrust of their recent visitor. He rather hoped the Doctor might provide the key to this whole somewhat baffling affair.

Garrett turned in his rather plush swivel chair and asked their communications expert, Belinda, to call the city again.

Belinda gave him a look. She was a big, Scottish woman squeezed into regulation tight velvet minidress, harassed and uncomfortable, her own workstation a tangle of leads and dismantled circuitry. Hers was the messiest and least efficient station of everyone on the bridge, but the captain was fond of her, so there it was.

The look she gave Garrett wasn't quite as fond. There was no love lost between those two. She had the idea that he thought of her as a kind of receptionist and she wasn't far wrong. She thought of the irony that she felt trapped by a glass ceiling and rampant tokenism in her job and here she was, trapped in space by a glass city.

'They are deflecting all calls at the moment, Mr Garrett,' she said primly. Garrett was sure she was eating as she said this. She had a mania, it seemed, for sugar mice.

'Hail them again. Do it on every frequency. Tell them we will send a delegation down to the city to find out what's going on if they do not respond immediately.' Garrett had had enough of waiting about. His captain's impatience had at last rubbed off on him.

Belinda returned to the task in hand, with a sigh, swallowing.

'Mr Timon,' Garrett called the chief security officer on the bridge. Instantly, a tall, calm black man appeared at his side. 'Would you fetch our visitor, please? I think we might need his help.'

Timon nodded and, with a quick glance at Belinda, left the bridge. Garrett was sure those two were lovers, though nothing had been said. He didn't think it did much for morale on the bridge, that sort of thing, between senior officers. He wouldn't let that sort of thing go on when he had his own ship.

It was Timon's job to know where everyone was aboard the *Nepotist* at all times. No easy feat, within its miles of corridors and its scores of decks. Especially when it came to those loose canons, the visiting dignitaries and the occasional strange interlopers, such as the Doctor, who refused to be contained. Already, in the Doctor's first twenty-four hours here, he had appeared and made a nuisance of himself in almost every department. Timon had tried to keep a tighter reign on his whereabouts, but the Doctor was infuriatingly able to pop up everywhere. He knew far more about the running of the ship than Timon thought possible or desirable. He wasn't the sort of guest they liked having aboard at all.

The Doctor's own craft – a tiny object, the size of a wardrobe – was in a docking bay, where it had first manifested itself. Timon knew for a fact he hadn't been back to it yet. He was happier involving himself in the affairs of the *Nepotist*. Captain Blandish thought it would be simpler if the Doctor just decided to take himself off again, but Garrett disagreed, thinking the Doctor may actually be able to help out somehow. Almost despite himself, Security Officer Timon was inclined to chime in with this thought. Belinda, too, though Timon wasn't pleased by her enthusiasm. That was simply a case of her fancying him, as she tended to do with most new faces turning up on board.

Timon went straight to the recreation deck, where the Doctor had last been seen. He must make the Doctor wear a comm badge.

Three settees arranged in the corner. Bright-yellow velvet plush, focused around a brown smoked-glass coffee table. The three guests had been served coffee and between them they had emptied the bronze pot and now they were waiting rather listlessly as crew members of the *Nepotist* wandered by, to and from their various activities here on the recreation deck.

To Fitz it all looked horribly energetic. Various bipeds went strolling by with squash rackets, towels draped over one shoulder. Others rushed back and forth, gabbling, from something called the hollow deck. He couldn't work out what that was at all, but it sounded awful.

Two very excitable Alpha Centaurans settled to a game of multidimensional chess at a nearby arrangement of sofas. Fitz couldn't believe how ridiculous the acid-green hermaphrodites looked. The Doctor hushed him a number of times as he snorted with laughter at the appearance of various crew members.

'This is really like being in outer space, Doctor,' he said, snatching up his cigarettes and fishing out the last one. 'I mean, this is really a *proper* spaceship.'

The Doctor was cross with him. Since arriving on board Fitz had done nothing but be sarcastic. But to Fitz this was a self-determined show of sarcasm. He almost felt he had to be like this, as if it made him more himself. Fitz Kreiner *was* sarcastic; that was the kind of fella he was. Always had been, always would be, no matter how messed around his head may be. Aboard the *Nepotist*, Fitz was trying desperately to revert to type.

Compassion had drifted off into a bit of a trance.

Not many laughs there, Fitz thought, not for the first time. Under the lights, bright and oddly unlike any kind of natural lighting at all, her skin seemed different from everyone else's. There was a peculiar cast to it. She had her auburn hair tied back and was wearing an outfit that the Doctor had suggested – a glittering, gauzy affair that didn't look too out of place in the... whatever century it was supposed to be.

Fitz looked at the Doctor – languid, yet alert, propping his chin on one palm – and wondered again if all of these adventures were just something the Doctor had made up for them. This was too much like outer space to be real. There were even great slabs of glass in the walls with the stars swirling and shifting by.

'Doctor,' Compassion said suddenly, 'I think I'm fed up now. Waiting around. I think I want to know what's happening now.'

She blinked solemnly at him.

Idly the Doctor flicked at his cravat. She was urging him, quite politely, into action, with a rather determined undertone to her voice. (What a peculiar voice, too, Fitz thought.) But she also sounded as if she didn't want to offend the Doctor.

The two of them were playing out some kind of power game. And Fitz Kreiner, once again, was just the spare prick at the wedding.

They were joined by Timon, the security guard.

Fitz wanted to laugh at his tight-fitting security guard's outfit, his gold badge of insignia, the bright-blue blaster gun holstered at his hip.

'Timon,' said the Doctor smoothly, with a warm smile. 'We've been missing you. Is the captain ready to see us again?'

Timon flinched at the Doctor's overfamiliar tone. 'Second-in-command Garrett is waiting for you on the bridge.'

Compassion was straight on her feet. 'Good. The sooner we –'

'Sorry, ma'am. Just the Doctor was asked for.'

Her reply was scalding. 'Just the Doctor?'

'He is the leader of your... delegation, is he not?' enquired Timon.

'He is not,' retorted Compassion. 'I –'

The Doctor butted in. 'Ah, we're all equals here, Timon. All for one and... um... so on. Wherever she goes I go. And so does Fitz.'

'Not necessarily,' said Fitz, but he stood, nevertheless, and straightened up his layers of garments, in which he had been sitting slumped. He got a sudden flash of envy at the Doctor's easy elegance. He thrust his hands in his coat pockets and found a number of half-smoked Woodbines and was pleased.

'Very well,' Timon sighed. 'Perhaps you can all help with this situation.'

'I'm sure we can.' the Doctor grinned, and looked at his two, rather nonplussed companions as they followed him from the pastel-shaded, potted-plant haven of the recreation deck.

Chapter Four
He Met Her That Afternoon...

He met her that afternoon in a café in town.

This was the extent of their involvement these days. Perhaps every three weeks or so they would get together for a longish lunch in this upstairs café with its whitewashed walls, scrubbed wooden tables, its pitchers of iced water and its home-made ice creams.

In recent months it had become a somewhat busier place. Less calming, because of the advent of the computer terminals. It was now an Internet café and neither the Doctor nor his friend, Sally, could approve of that.

Today she was waiting at their usual table, bang in the middle of the spacious back room, gazing out over the town through louvred shutters. Such windows, they had often said, ought to look out upon a much more picturesque town. Bell towers and pretty churches; a green slow-surging river. Instead, a market town, grey municipal buildings, car parks and endless exhausting traffic.

Still, they made the best of it. These regular lunches were, after all, an attempt to rekindle and reflect upon their youth – a youth spent together. And it was, perhaps, the force of that nostalgia that transformed the venue for both of them.

He shrugged himself out of his long green coat and hung it where the waiter told him.

They knew him in this place now. He rubbed his hands warm and ruffled his long dark hair back into order.

She hadn't seen him yet. She was feeding her Jack Russell brown sugar lumps from the bowl on her table. The dog had a chair all to himself and the Doctor smiled to see Sally talking to her pet, and listening, as if he could reply.

She looked like a smart, professional woman. Perhaps forty – chic in a cream linen suit and silk blouse. Her hair was glossy and dark and she was smoking as she concentrated on feeding and communicating with her dog.

There was just a hint of eccentricity about her. Her notebook was open on the table, as it always was, with the black pen uncapped beside it.

Briskly the Doctor made his way towards her, the bare wooden boards creaking pleasantly as he stomped along.

What did she call that Jack Russell again? Something ridiculous. He should remember. He'd bought it for her when it was a puppy, quite some years ago. He never thought she would get so attached to the irritable, straggly-looking thing.

– You're having mozzarella?
– Why not?
– I couldn't eat it.
– Oh, one of your little prejudices. Why ever not?
– Because, Sally, I believe they make it from the curd of buffalo milk.
– Don't be ridiculous.
– It's true!
– You make things up.
– That's true, too. But they definitely use buffalo milk.
– I'll ask Canine. He'll know.
– Canine. I forgot. I knew you called him something silly.
– It's not silly. It's what he is.
– Anyway, he can't talk.
– He can talk to *me*.

Funny that I can be so intolerant of other people's eccentricities. I mean, that afternoon Sally started to get on my nerves. Maybe it was just that we were getting bored with raking

24

over the past. There are only so many times you can go over the old days. Yes, we had some laughs and we got into some scrapes, but do we really want to churn them over endlessly?

As I recall, however, that afternoon we did try to move on to other topics. These were no more entertaining though. The awful thought crept up on me: perhaps Sally and I had outgrown each other.

I talked a little about my private Doctor, and told her about my medication and how my Doctor even phones me in the dead of night. Sally seemed singularly unimpressed.

She wanted to talk about her writing. She wanted to talk all about her plans.

– But you always hated science fiction. I remember giving you books, forcing them on you, years ago. In the 1970s. You just laughed at them. Said you didn't need your mind expanding, thank you very much.

– Oh, well. I was younger then. I knew my mind, I thought.

– Michael Moorcock, Brian Aldiss, J.G. Ballard, Edmund Cooper, Edgar Rice Burroughs… I bought them all for you!

– It was like you could see something in them that I couldn't. I just couldn't get the hang of that stuff. Stepping into other worlds. Other lives, other dimensions, what-have-you. I didn't want to know there were alternatives. When I was that young, I didn't like to know anything that wasn't real.

– They were books, Sally. Of course they weren't real.

– I mean realistic. With realistic things happening in them.

– Oh, that.

– Anyway, the point is, my taste has changed. Those kinds of books seem realer to me now.

– I suppose, especially after the lives we've lived.

– Exactly.

And she liked the way he would throw back his head and laugh. He'd let his hair grow much longer. There was something almost carefree about him. He wasn't knotted up with anxiety as he had been in recent years. She was starting to remember why she enjoyed being with him. She felt a surge of enthusiasm again for their friendship. A daring spark of desire.

The waiter brought more coffee and soon she was reeling with too much caffeine. The waiter brought some sausages for the dog, left over from lunchtime. Canine wolfed them.

– So I ditched the thing I was already writing. My novel. My realistic novel. I'm saying 'realistic' like it was a dirty word now, aren't I?

– You haven't ditched it! Sally… you've had that on the go for years…

– And it wasn't going anywhere. I'd outgrown it. I started writing this other thing. It's almost done.

– Can I see some of it?

– That's what's in the bag. A present. It's the whole thing so far. I'd love to know what you think.

– You haven't given me anything in years.

– I lost a lot of confidence.

– You?

– Absolutely. But now… I feel like I could write anything. Take my characters anywhere. It's freed me up. Well, you'll see.

– What's it about?

– That's hard to explain in a few lines.

– You'll have to. For the blurb on the back…

– My agent says she's already got publishers worked up about it. On the strength of the first few chapters. But wait till they see the rest… It's quite mad.

– Tell me about it.

– It's in two parts. The first half is a story about an arid world. A desert world ruled by a Queen who sits in a vast jar of jam. Don't laugh.

– I'm not!

26

– And the second half of the book is wintry. Like today. It's about an everlasting winter and a city of glass that travels through space. This city comes to our world and rests just inside our atmosphere. It is ruled by a godlike being called Daedalus... and he invents these Corridors – a labyrinth of passageways through space and time...

– Who's the hero of all this?

– There's a woman. But you're in there, too.

– I am?

– Someone a bit like you.

– Write about what you know, eh?

– The woman is called Iris and she can travel anywhere in the cosmos in a red double-decker bus...

– Sounds like my kind of woman.

– Oh, really?

– Iris, did you say she was called?

– A joke, really. She's like this woman who lives next door to me.

– Also called Iris?

– Yes... but, Doctor, what's...?

That was when he had his funny turn.

There was the most surprising and sudden pain in his left leg. It felt like a burn, but one that originated from within.

He cried out, seized by the shock of the pain. He slipped sideways from his seat, and fell on to the polished wooden floor. He knocked the milk jug and his cup from the table.

The dog barked, affronted. Sally jumped up and the waiter came running.

The Doctor passed out and

came to, moments later, with his concerned friend looking down at him.

There was something quite wrong with his left leg. It was numb from the knee down. He didn't dare touch it yet. He would look at it when he got home. He would go home now. He wouldn't talk about it any more. He would act as if he'd had a twinge of cramp, so as not to alarm Sally. But it wasn't cramp.

He brushed off her concern.

He put down his funny turn to the pills his private Doctor was making him take.

Then he was getting up to be gone, taking her manuscript with him. He clasped it to his chest, rustling the plastic bag, and trying to mask the wince he made as he put his weight on to his leg.

- Will you come to dinner this week? You can meet Fitz and Compassion.

- I'd love to. Who's Compassion?

- She's only just moved in. A new friend. Sort of.

- Compassion. Honestly, Doctor. These women you hang around with…

Chapter Five
It Might Have Been Any Time of Day . . .

It might have been any time of day. Once the ladies were inside the shopping mall time outside could be conveniently forgotten as they, like all the other shoppers, surrendered themselves happily to the brightly lit, perfumed, air-conditioned halls and walkways and amphitheatres. There wasn't a scrap of natural lighting here, nor of air – and all the potted palms and Christmas trees were triumphantly plastic. The water in the many fountains and pools that glistened and rumbled beneath the busy escalators had a golden quality to it, as if that, too, were somehow artificial.

'Stay close by, girls,' Big Sue said, as they braced themselves for the crowds. 'We don't want to get separated in here.'

'That can spoil your day, that,' said Nesta gloomily. 'You spend the whole time looking for each other and, before you know it, it's time to go home.'

They were standing by one of the entrances to British Home Stores. Each of them was itching to be off to her own favourite departments. Really, though, Maddy was in charge, since she had driven them through the perilous snow, and by rights it should be up to her where they went first. This was the kind of democracy the ladies operated by.

Maddy was preoccupied just that minute, however, with her son, who was drifting off into the department store already. He took no heed of the others' careful plans.

She called after him and he ignored her. She watched the back of him, disappearing into the push and crush of the Bhs *parfumerie*. She shrugged and laughed to the others. 'He's seen something that interests him, obviously.'

Big Sue and Nesta exchanged a look. Maddy let that lad get

away with murder. It was as if, Sue thought, Maddy felt that, if she reprimanded him properly for his behaviour, he would just wander back out of her life. But that was no way to bring up a wayward son, Sue thought, letting him have his own way all the time. Maddy was just making more problems for herself in the future. Big Sue bit her lip though, and nodded.

'Well! Your Ian's gone and made the choice for us. Come on, Nesta… follow us!'

Maddy smiled gratefully and led the way after her son.

They found him two floors up from the *parfumerie*. The ladies had been dogged in their pursuit, jumping on escalators behind him, hunting through the forests of racks and hangers in Ladieswear. They caught up with Ian at last in the music department.

'I didn't know he was interested in music, Maddy,' said Nesta, looking round.

'Neither did I,' she said.

And there he was. On a podium among a whole set of podiums, he was standing poised above the many keyboards of a rather complicated-looking electric organ. He was testing out several sounds and, it seemed, had the volume turned up full. Maddy winced. He'd make a show of her.

Ian was in a world of his own as he flipped through a book of songs from the sixties and settled on his choice. Then he flipped a switch and the machine began pumping out a slowed-down bossa-nova beat. Then his fingers went to work, ranging over all of the keys and playing, note perfect, a Cilla Black song that all the ladies half recognised as they rushed up to him.

Ian's face was solemn at first, as he wrestled with the complications of the tune, the first few tricky bits. Then he appeared to relax into it, and he started smiling. He looked completely serene.

Nesta and Big Sue started to applaud, then clapped along, keeping time with him, delighted that they had something to praise him for. Maddy glanced about nervously, waiting for the manager to come over and give them a shouting-at. There was indeed a salesman, in a black suit, hovering beside a display of golden saxophones and things, pink and green lights bouncing festively off all their intricate keys and nodules. But the salesman didn't look very cross at the commotion her son was making.

What was that song? She would have to ask him afterwards.

And then Maddy looked round behind her as the song reached its rather melancholy climax and there, perched on the seat of a glossy black baby grand, was a woman some years younger than herself, dressed rather slinkily in a kind of catsuit affair, with her head in her hands, weeping buckets at the song Ian was playing.

Maddy could never stand to see someone upsetting herself. She drifted over to the poor woman, taking in the details of her eccentric outfit. She was wearing yellow plastic boots that came up to her knees, and it really was a catsuit, of the sort Maddy hadn't seen in years, since the sixties in fact. It was pink and purple, extremely close fitting, and fastened right up to the neck. The weeping woman had masses of honey-blonde hair, which covered her face as she sobbed and heaved.

'Excuse me...' Maddy patted the stranger's shoulder. The metallic stuff of the catsuit was oddly warm to the touch.

The woman took her gloved hands away from her face and looked up. Her mascara had run, bleeding black down her inflamed cheeks. Her eyes were terribly puffy and her lipstick was smudged. But she was beautiful. Almond-shaped eyes, heart-shaped face, slightly upturned nose – all the clichés of sex-kitten beauty applied. She had, thought Maddy suddenly, a look of the young Jane Fonda about her.

'Yes...?' asked the stranger.

'You looked upset,' Maddy said. 'I thought...'

At this moment Ian finished his rendition of the nostalgic Cilla Black number with a grand flourish and silence fell for a second with a crash, and then the other ladies, a small crowd which had gathered, and the salesman himself started clapping enthusiastically. The stranger in the catsuit applauded likewise, her green eyes gleaming.

Then she said to Maddy, 'I'm not upset really. Just that song… caught me unawares. Made me nostalgic for a second.'

'I know.' Maddy nodded. She herself who was known to become very morose whenever she heard 'Goodbye, Ruby Tuesday'. 'Everything you regret, every lost chance, the end of your youth…'

The stranger nodded tearily and thrust out her hand for Maddy to shake. 'Thanks for your concern, anyway. I'm Iris.'

'Maddy,' said Maddy. 'That was my son, Ian, playing the organ, by the way.'

'You've got a very talented son.'

'Yes… I didn't even know he could do that.'

'A very good-looking son, too,' noted Iris approvingly. Across the way, the others were trying to cajole the boy into playing for them again. 'He's quite beautiful.'

'Beautiful?' For a second Maddy thought the word sounded odd. But, when she looked at Ian, there was a kind of glamour radiating off him. Glamour also in the older sense – that of witchcraft, of a kind of spell about him.

'I don't think he'll play another song for them,' Maddy said, breaking the moment and watching the boy move away from the instrument.

'My nerves won't stand it anyway.' Iris smiled. 'I feel quite wrung out.'

'Mum?' Ian came towards them. 'You aren't cross at me, are you? For playing?'

Maddy hugged him. 'Course not. It was fabulous. Here, look, you've got a fan. This is Iris…'

Maddy turned then, back to the woman by the baby grand, but when she did she caught her breath and blinked.

Iris had slunk away.

Chapter Six
I Used to be a Lot Bigger...

I used to be a lot bigger. Perhaps I'm not used to being this slender and perhaps I never will be. When I'm in crowds – like this one, Christmas shopping – I still tend to turn sideways and I get the urge to cry out, 'Coming through!' preserving my bulk against the masses. Now, of course, I needn't bother. I can squeeze through the tightest of crushes blithe as a spirit.

When I was the old me I used to exaggerate my size. I loved being a big woman. I would wear layer upon layer of cardigans and coats. It was always freezing aboard the bus. It was full of draughts and, when I drove it through the night on long hauls, the window panes would rattle and let in the freezing air. I also used to wear those disgusting woollen stockings. I found those again recently and couldn't imagine wanting to wear such things. What had I been thinking of? Practicality, I suppose. The old Iris was nothing less than a practical dame. Sometimes the old me seems like an entirely different person. An awful, pushy, tasteless person. A funny old aunt of mine.

The two of us met up, I seem to remember. In the Death Zone, a breezy bleak place, and we were brought together to solve something and the two of us looked at each other with wary disdain. And the other Irises, the other five, all of whom were somewhat hazy to me, looked on with their own appalled reactions. I can see that scene now, the seven of us with all our friends in that freezing mausoleum at the climax of our adventure together, and I can see it through seven pairs of eyes. Though I don't think this particular me has been there yet. Which means I have to brace myself to be scooped back there at some point, someday soon, and live it through again. Ah, me.

* * *

These days I wear these tall boots in black, yellow, red or silver. Colossal heels. Not exactly practical for the scrapes I get myself into.

But they do turn heads.

One other thing I used to be – in the days when I was large, elderly, obstreperous and Valkyrie-like: I was in love.

It was something I felt quite definite about. Its pressure was as insistent and unmistakable as my own two good hearts. Today I feel ambivalent about my erstwhile object of desire. Funny, to change like that.

But… I haven't seen him in a while. How will I feel when I see the Doctor again?

I know it must happen someday soon. There are plans of mine afoot that will bring us into certain contact and, I fear, conflict.

Ambiguous as my feelings might be about that mysterious traveller in the region where time and space are one… I do still feel obliged help him out now and then.

I can't let him fall into danger when I see a way of letting him out. He doesn't know it yet, but he's gone breezing into a terrible situation. One of the worst yet.

And, if I can just shunt him along into safety with a harmless little nudge, then so be it. I know he hates being tampered with, timelines and all, but I can't help it. He's safe. Confused but safe.

And that leaves me to deal with the rest of it.

This is where it starts. With that boy, the one who played us that tune. That has to be him.

But that song he was playing. I hadn't expected that. A song from the sixties, by Cilla Black. 'Love's Just A Broken Heart'. How would the Doctor react if I told him that was Our Tune? In it, Cilla recants her love for her perfect fella, tells him that they are worlds apart now and that she has been warned off him. He's had too many lovers in the past, he's seen too many things. Now they are worlds apart and she can have nothing more to do with him. It gave me quite a start to hear that boy playing it – such an obscure Cilla classic – on the organ. It quite caught my breath and, when I was meant to be acting like a proper double agent, there I am bursting into tears sitting by a baby grand piano in Bhs.

It's ten to three local time. Soon that first wave of shoppers will be leaving. Maddy and her small band will be tiring and thinking of turning back home. Outside, the snow has piled up ceaselessly and, with every hour, the journey home becomes a more terrifying prospect. They have had their lunch (sandwiches and tea in Marks and Spencer's café) and they have spent all of the money they brought with them. Maddy will have told herself that three o'clock is her limit. Her nerves are frayed, and she's feeling tired. Three o'clock is her limit and that's when she will tell the others that it's time to go.

So now I have to slip myself into position. Because at three o'clock it will all start to happen.

The electricity will fail, the lights will flicker and dim. The exits and entrances will seal up. That's when our disaster movie starts up. We'll be stuck inside our *Poseidon Adventure*, our *Towering Inferno*, our very own *Earthquake*.

Except it won't be any of those things. It'll be hundreds of people trapped inside the frozen interior of a shopping mall. And beasties outside slavering – slavering to come in.

Five to three. Got to get to the exit.

Red Quadrant: here I come.

Oh, so much zippier, this new body.

Tearing about in my knee-high boots…

Chapter Seven
When They Come it Will be Across the Waves...

When they come it will be across the waves.

Washed clean by the waves, washed supple and bright, gleaming gimcrack, crazed with veins of light.

The Men of Glass will be clean, naturally, with only a slight rinse of salt and silt and sand caked on their cool skin.

Their chairs, metal, will be covered with barnacles, encrusted, deep-sea ferns and weed choking their spokes.

Quite a struggle for them as they manoeuvre clumsily out of the surf and up beaches, crunching their gold-rimmed tyres on shells. Crunch, crunch, crunch.

White in the winter sun, only their hearts untouched by frosty salt water. Their hearts the sea has left warm, pumping red, vital, grimacing. Unaffected, unassuaged by the currents and cross-currents they have traversed.

The faces on the hearts clenching in anger, like fists.

They leave the sea behind them and now they are here.

From the bottom of the sea, from the back of beyond, from, perhaps, some other world.

And yet, we are always told they come from such a great height. A land far loftier, far more remote than any height we will ever attain.

It is winter and we have been brought into the dangerous orbit of the Glass Men.

Their wheelchairs glisten and settle on the sugar-soft sand of the beach.

Weary conquerors contemplate the infinite grains.

Look back at the expanses of water.

'Come...'

'Come on…'

'Come on up. Time's over. We'll finish up the job.'

'We must…'

'We must head…'

'We must head on.'

'Not…'

'Not much…'

'Not much daylight left.'

'This is…'

'This is how…'

'This is how we seek shelter. We cannot stay out in a storm.'

So fragile. So caring of each other. So delicate with the glassy perfection of their collective selves.

They wheel themselves up, achingly, cautiously, on to the mainland.

'There…'

'There is…'

'There is a fresh wind. Quite pleasant really. Drying out like this.'

The Glass Men pretend to have sensation.

Fake their responses to the stimuli of this new world.

But they have no nerve endings. Or their nerve endings were frozen and cauterised when they were turned to glass.

Still, they pretend to register these sensations. A game and a complicity that pleases them.

They each of them hum and whistle, pleased with the chilling draught that comes in behind them, off the sea.

Here they are now.

They have arrived.

Chapter Eight
At Last the Captain Deigned to Come Out...

At last the captain deigned to come out of the relative sanctuary of his oval office. As the doors swished open he tugged his mustard polyester top straight and glared round at the assembled heads of department. No one turned to look at him. They were all fixated on the image of the glittering city of glass suspended on the viewscreen before them.

It was like a wedding cake, an ocean liner, a mountain of ice. And it had to be dealt with. The Feds wouldn't be pleased with an anomaly like this hanging about. It was Captain Blandish's sworn duty to smooth out ructions such as this...

He stepped up to the raised dais and his cushy captain's chair. The small huddle of officers noticed him at last and Garrett whipped around. 'Captain on the bridge,' he noted with just a hint of that insufferable sarcasm of his. Beside Garrett, tapping away at a bank of sensors and looking perplexed, was the Doctor.

'Who gave that man permission to carry out a scan?' barked Blandish.

'Captain, Captain, Captain...' grinned the Doctor, hurrying over. He had loosened his cravat and to the captain's eyes he looked crazy. His two unauthorised companions were hanging about, staring at the city on the screen. The scruffy-looking man they called Fitz was talking to Belinda and she was gazing dreamily up at him.

'Captain,' said the Doctor, grabbing his hand and shaking it. Blandish snatched his hand back. 'I'd like to take a... um, party down there, to the city. See what's going on.' There was a gleam in the Doctor's eye.

'Mr Garrett,' said Blandish in a carefully controlled tone. 'Do you realise how much a sensor scan like that actually costs? You're letting an untrained man dabble with our most sensitive and expensive –'

'I am well aware of the cost, sir,' purred Garrett. He gave his captain a swift glance up and down and produced the small and incredibly complex calculator on which he habitually computed the *Nepotist*'s budget. Every laser fired, every minute calibration and acceleration, every transmat operated, Garrett would plug it all into his Ship's Kitty. 'But the Doctor knows precisely what he is doing. I saw it as a necessary expense.'

The Doctor beamed.

'If people are going down there,' said Compassion suddenly, 'I am coming too.' She was looking at the city rather strangely. 'You will need my help. I'm hearing all sorts of interesting things. I'm more useful than this –' she nodded curtly at Belinda – 'communications person. I'm picking up messages that she never would.'

The Doctor frowned at her quickly. Of course. Her earpiece. He tried to signal her to keep quiet but she went on.

'I am going to come with you. Obviously.'

Fitz snorted. 'Well, I'm not. I'm going back to the TARDIS.'

'Neither of you is coming,' said the Doctor, rather sternly. 'You can wait here on the ship. I'm taking the TARDIS.'

'No, you're not,' Blandish put in smoothly. 'You're transmatting down with me. I'll head the away team and I'll consent to let you advise.' He glared at the Time Lord. 'And no funny business.'

Minutes later Belinda was dashing into the corridor, heading for the lift. She had a bag to pack, her hair to wash, and she had to change into planetside gear. She had been chosen, as communications expert, to join the team. She was thrilled.

Timon, too, had been picked by the surly Captain. This was usual. Blandish went nowhere without his heavily armed Timon. Timon took it for granted. Already he had gone off to put on his regulation red top.

Compassion and Fitz had been packed off to the Doctor's TARDIS. Fitz eagerly, Compassion seemingly in a fit of pique. As soon as they were off the bridge the Doctor had seemed to forget their very existence, applying himself to the matter in hand, evidently itching for the off. He bristled with curiosity, Belinda could tell.

By the time she got to her cabin she was huffing and puffing with exertion. She flung open the door.

Inside there was the usual strewn mess and gentle, coloured lighting from the lava lamps placed at intervals around her bed. Something was wrong, though. As the door whispered shut behind her she knew she was not alone in her room. For a second her heart leapt up and she wondered if Garrett had at last taken the hint and gathered the import of the various sly winks she had shot his way while they were on the bridge. Maybe he had secreted himself in here.

Then she became aware of a point of green light on the wall, about a foot above her headboard. It grew in size and intensity and Belinda was rooted to the spot, staring as a green shape started to materialise before her. Emerald smoke and fumes, coruscating lights. Someone trying to connect with the communications expert and, well trained as she was, she held her breath and waited until the message came through.

It was the head of an elephant. A peculiarly malevolent-looking creature with ears stretched wider than her headboard. Its tusks thrust two metres into the room, threatening to skewer her. Its eyes blazed with fury. It bellowed at her soundlessly and green fumes rolled around it. She was reminded of Ganesh, the Hindu god, who was said to always take this form. Garrett was the anthropological expert on board ship and for more than one reason Belinda wished he were there.

Then the apparition spoke. 'Your coming here will set events in motion. You do know that, don't you? It will be the step that makes the War inevitable.'

He tossed his gargantuan trunk at her with a snort of derision. He trumpeted down the intimidating length of it and the sound made Belinda's ears burn. It was the fanfare for the beginning of a war. Then the elephant's head faded away.

She didn't tell anyone about this. She was sure the eminently practical Blandish would prevent her coming on any planetside missions if he suspected she was going doolally.

The transmat room was clinically clean. They had to step through a number of locks and barriers to get anywhere near it. The Doctor had never seen so many precautions taken with such a device – he who had been zipped and beamed and shot across the galaxies and through time by such a ramshackle assortment of rather hazardous means. But the crew of the *Nepotist* dreaded anything going wrong with the transmat. They said a little prayer before shooting off anywhere. They evidently took to heart the alarming possibilities of disaster and prayed that their bodies, once dissolved and transported, would reassemble neatly and properly at the other end. They found it all traumatic and, of course, it was fearsomely expensive. As the away team prepared themselves, going through the ritual solemnly – to the Doctor's bemusement – Garrett was totting up the cost of the sortie on his Kitty.

'Nothing ventured, nothing gained…' smiled the Doctor, hopping into the odd bathlike arrangement from which he gathered he would be beamed. Blandish, doing likewise, scowled.

They had to lie in these empty baths, one of them in each, and wait as the engineers in the gallery did their stuff, hovering over controls with crossed fingers.

The Doctor had never seen such an arrangement before. Usually, he mused, as he lay in the cold, dry tub, humanoid species invented upright contraptions to beam themselves from: stand on a luminous disk, walk into this cupboard-type contraption, and so on.

He shrugged and settled himself down to be transported.

Actually, it felt just like being swept down the plughole. There was even a disturbing gurgling noise. He steeled himself and looked forward to being reconstituted.

And then, the five of them – Garrett, Blandish, Timon, Belinda and the Doctor – were standing in the midst of a mild snowstorm, standing up to their knees in fallen snow. It was dark with the pitch-dark of space all around them, and the sleek lilac shape of the *Nepotist* looming above them.

Ahead was the grand shining spectacle of the City of Glass. Its turrets, minarets, its baubles and towers. And now they could see its glints of lights burning and they fancied they could see shapes flitting about in those thousands of apertures. Inside, the natives of this errant land were aware that they had visitors.

'We're here,' breathed Blandish, as if he couldn't quite believe it.

The Doctor rubbed his hands for warmth and grew expansive.

'It's like... the Emerald City! The City on the Edge of Forever! It's... Valhalla!'

And he set off at a run, stumbling through the snow.

Chapter Nine
This is a Story About Winter...

This is a story about winter.

You've guessed it already, of course.

It is the kind of winter in which you will never be warm enough, no matter how you wrap up. You will still shiver down to your bones. It's the kind of winter that settles itself in and intends to stay. It will be unshakeable, sealing this town off from the outside world, forcing the cables and gutters and pipes that keep the building fed, clean and alive into a stifling, deadly, icy torpor. Everything will be made brittle and dead.

There are always animals in the winter.

Creatures who, needing to survive, take their chances and creep closer to the town and its bewildered, unwary inhabitants.

The townspeople sit by meagre fires, burning anything expendable that they can lay their chilled fingers on.

At the Doctor's house Compassion urges the burning of the Doctor's books.

His library will keep them warm through many days. He has so many thick, dry volumes they might feed the flames through the whole festive period.

Compassion claims – quite modestly – that she has an infallible photographic memory – she has illimitable recall and she will gladly remember everything they consign to the grate.

Fitz is appalled by her attitude. He won't hear of it. He carries on reading his way through the Doctor's books. He carries on with his reading of the arcane *Aja'ib*.

– It is the sensible thing to do. You can't get fuel anywhere. We will freeze.

- It's barbaric, Compassion. It's ridiculous.

- Have you seen the attic, Fitz? It's crammed full with dusty old things. He never looks at these things. He never will. He says he will, but have you ever seen him sit down and read anything?

- Maybe he doesn't have to. Maybe it's all in his head. Maybe he has illimitable recall, too.

- I don't think so. I think he's even forgotten how to read. He doesn't know what books and papers he's got up there. It's as if they belong to someone else. He wouldn't miss anything.

- I would. I'm telling you, if you touch anything of the Doctor's…

- What, Fitz? Are you threatening me?

- You've not known him – or me, not really – long. You're still new around here.

- That doesn't mean I have to freeze to death.

- You're not going to touch any of the Doctor's stuff. Look, he's having a hard time of it just now. You can see – even *you* can see – he isn't a full shilling. Don't take advantage.

- How would you ever know, Fitz? I could be up in that attic at any time. Any time you're not paying attention, or you've braved the cold outside. I could be up that silver ladder, poking my nose in anywhere. I could burn anything from his messy old library just to keep my feet warm and you'd never know, would you?

- I'll just have to trust you, Compassion. Won't I?

- Think about it. I might already have burned things. This fire now could have come from the Doctor's precious volumes…

His living room was deep violet, so it was dark, too dark for reading in. It was here that the Doctor and his lodgers came to sit by the fire and talk through the long evenings. It was here he described his lunch with Sally and his subsequent funny turn. His companions made concerned noises about this and he waved their compassion aside.

There were two fish tanks in here. One was stocked with angel fish, lit baleful blue from beneath. The fish were languid, silver, haughty, swishing about and watching the human inhabitants of the room as if they were the specimens to be kept an eye on. The other glass case contained lizards, which crept across and across their small space of sandy rubble and stopped every now and then to sigh. The largest was a green, spined creature that Fitz couldn't put a name to at all. The Doctor, however, could, and he called this lizard Gila. Its eyes shone with what Fitz thought was a malevolent pink.

This living room was quiet; only a golden clock ticked on the mantle above the fitfully burning fire.

The Doctor talked quietly that night about Sally and how she had given him her book to read and how he would take it to bed with him that night.

He also said he had invited Sally for dinner, one night soon, and his current lodgers might meet this long-time friend of his. They acted pleased at this. The Doctor was in a strange, pensive mood, however, and soon he drifted off to bed.

– He's acting strangely.
  – I told you. He's not himself.
  – Neither are you, Fitz.
  – How would you know? How long have you known me?
  – Not long. I can't remember.
  – No. I can't either, Compassion. Isn't that odd?
  – Probably.
  – And I can't remember coming here. I don't know how any of us came here.
  – No.
  – Doesn't that make you worry, Compassion?
  – I'm going out.

Compassion was full of energy. She was restless and bored. Her limbs tingled and stung with potential, with a kind of bristling irritation that she knew would be assuaged only by exercise.

47

She walked, she ran, she tore around the town.

It was deserted outside. The streets were laminated with a terrible black frost. All the trees were sealed in ice.

There was hardly a sound and, above, the stars were invisible, as if they were no longer there.

It made Compassion want to scream.

There was something out there, calling to her. Something that belonged to her, or that she belonged to. It would tell her what her future would be.

This town was keeping her down. These people she was living with were constricting her.

The winter that encroached all around them was the epitome of the stifling sense of frustration that imposed itself upon her. She could feel her anger mounting as each day went by, and so she went running out into the night.

If anyone had observed her, they wouldn't have thought she was exercising. Nor would they have thought she was running into the grateful arms of whatever destiny beckoned her.

They would have imagined that she was fleeing something. As she ran, skidding on the thickening ice in the North Park, Compassion looked stricken.

Late that night she paused for breath by the bandstand in the park. It was wrecked – seemingly held together by the rime of ice that coated its ceiling and struts.

The park was pitch black. Not the best place to stop for a rest. She leaned to catch her breath.

There was a slight rustle in the trees beside her. Just the breeze. But there was no breeze tonight.

There was the call of an owl.

And then it was upon her.

Something the size and weight of a large dog hurled itself upon her, barrelling into her chest and knocking her flat on to the hard path.

She grunted and fell, winded.

The creature stank. A rancid, foxy smell.

It slavered and drooled and she could see its teeth as it wrestled with her.

She felt those teeth nipping, almost playfully, at her coat. It didn't bite hard. It didn't bite into her skin.

It was playing with her. It had wanted to frighten her.

They had fallen on to the black and white squares of the giant chessboard by the bandstand.

As they rolled and struggled they knocked the giant chess pieces aside, sent them scattering across the paving stones.

Toddler-sized pawns were sent sprawling as Compassion clasped the stinking creature, pulling and ripping at its matted coarse fur.

There was a yell then, cutting through the night.

A man's voice, hoarse, commanding, speaking some weird foreign-sounding language.

Instantly the dog thing stopped toying with her and jumped back.

Compassion sat up and watched it scamper back off into the bushes.

She was left alone with whoever had shouted.

She stilled her breathing and listened.

Someone scraped a match somewhere on bricks. The scrape of the sulphur on stone was the most sinister thing Compassion could imagine. She tensed.

There was a flicker of soft yellow flame nearby. She could almost feel the heat from it. It wavered and approached.

In the slight glare of the flame there was the deeply lined face of a man. He had silver hair and wore an expression of concern as he hurried up to her.

He was in some kind of cloak, old-fashioned, velvety stuff. He said, helping her on to her feet, 'This is a foolish time for a young woman to be out in the park.'

Compassion merely grunted.

'That creature wouldn't have harmed you. I think you scared it as much as it scared you.'

'What was it?'

'Something rather like a fox. Something halfway between a fox and a rabbit. Didn't you see?'

The man blew out the match and promptly lit another. 'Poor things. They are being driven into the town from the country. They're feeling the winter far worse than we are.'

'Thank you for...'

'That's quite all right. I suggest you get yourself home. No bites? No twisted ankle?'

'I'm surprisingly resilient, thank you.'

Compassion was already moving away across the park, leaving the man in the opera cloak. His face seemed to hover in the match light, receding behind.

'Goodbye, my dear,' he called.

Compassion hurried on wordlessly.

She found herself negotiating a kind of maze of box trees before she was out of the park. Here there was a scant, brief glare of moonlight and she could see that the bushes were all holly, studded with the ripest of scarlet berries.

Enough roaming around for one night.

She thought about crawling under the duvet back at home.

Suddenly the Doctor's house didn't seem quite so unalluring.

Chapter Ten
The City of Glass Was Raised Up...

The City of Glass was raised up on a bed of stone.

It was only as the small party who'd beamed down from the *Nepotist* came within a mile of the place that they realised this.

The black rock was riddled with caves, each of them lined with ice blistered and cracked like mouths and throats plagued with ulcers.

The team were spoilt for choice... which cave to take?

Captain Blandish picked one of the hazardous apertures quite at random and determined this would be the one.

'But how do you know?' the Doctor teased.

'Instinct,' grunted the captain. 'When you've been on as many missions as I have, you learn to listen to your gut feelings. And right now my guts are gurgling pretty insistently that this is the one.'

The cave mouth glittered with ice, drawing them in. 'Quite,' said the Doctor. 'I bow down to your greater um... instincts and experience.'

'Huh,' said Blandish, and scowled at the Time Lord, who was now egging everyone up the glassy slope.

'Captain!' Belinda was panting a little with effort and irritated by the fake fur of her snorkel hood. 'Captain, communications with the ship are breaking up. Once we're inside the cave we won't be able to speak with them at all.'

'We're being jammed,' the captain growled.

'Indeed,' said Garrett, who was peering into the pale cavern.

Timon brought up the rear, blaster drawn, looking somewhat nervous.

The Doctor led the way. Blandish let him. Let him handle the danger. If anything leapt out at them, let the Doctor get it first. It would be no loss.

* * *

As they pushed along, their sheepskin boots started to fill with meltwater. It was becoming wetter as it grew darker, and yet there was a definite sense of walking up into the Glass City of Valcea. Perhaps they were succeeding after all, in creeping up on the inhabitants unsuspected.

Captain Blandish was quietly excited. He tried not to give his feelings away as they inched up the sheeny tunnel, but his mind ran with images of what they might come across in the city above. It was his explorer's instinct taking the helm. This was the reason he was Captain, after all.

Garrett made them pause while he felt around in his backpack. Then he produced torches for them all. They were lime-green tubes, stuffed with luminous gel. He reminded them all how expensive these things were and to be used only in the most vital (and dark) of their expeditions.

The Doctor peered at the torch he was handed, his face a ghastly green in its baleful light.

'But these are Ffenitrite bulbs!' he gasped. 'These have been outlawed for years... even in your time!' When he used that phrase 'in your time' he couldn't keep out a note of accusation. Belinda was at his shoulder.

'What's wrong with them?'

'They're alive! There are living creatures trapped in here! These devices are barbaric.' With that he threw his own torch down on the frozen ground, where it exploded in a brief flash of green shards.

'You idiot,' Blandish burst, shoving him back.

All five stared down at the wreckage of the Doctor's lamp. In among the broken glass there was a host of writhing luminous worms. They seemed startled by their sudden liberty.

'Now, don't the rest of you get any ideas and copy this stupid bastard,' Blandish warned.

'No fear,' shuddered Belinda, moving away from the Ffenitrite worms.

'Happy now, Doctor?' Garrett asked him sardonically.

'Yes,' he said, and stomped off ahead, leading the way into the dark.

Chapter Eleven
They Call Me Big Sue . . .

They call me Big Sue.

She of the self-knitted woolly hat and the unbecoming lilac wig.

She of the swollen legs and varicose veins.

She who was too tired for all this about two hours ago.

Oh, I know what they say about me, right enough. I know that everyone round our street believes that I killed my husband. Roasted, basted, served up and eaten with three kinds of veg one Christmas fifteen years ago.

I'm a kind of witch woman, you see. The people I know accept me as that. Wise woman of the community.

So when things start to go awry it's to me they look to for explanations. Like when Maddy Sharp discovered her angel boy on the beach, back in the summertime, it was to me and me alone that she confided the true nature of his advent.

To everyone else he was a cousin's child she had merely taken in. But Maddy came to me with the truth.

I told her, 'Look on it as providence. That boy is everything you ever wanted. Don't make it more complicated than it need be.'

It's not many people who get their heart's desire.

Now I wonder if I gave her the right advice.

It's only since her Ian – or Icarus, as I know she calls him when they're alone – came to live among us in Phoenix Court that things have started to go wrong.

He's working a terrible karma on the place, that child. And this is particularly evident today. I'm sure if we'd left him at home we wouldn't be in the pickle we're in right now.

* * *

55

Look how he sits there, on the bench across from us, by the fountain and the Christmas trees outside Marks and Spencer's glittering domain. He is so serene, even though half the lights are out and the doors are frozen solid; stuck, wedged and jammed; and shoppers are milling, sounding shriller and shriller.

And you can feel hysteria mounting on the air, heaped on in shovelfuls, stoking the fire.

Icarus looks around with interest. Unlike the rest of us, he doesn't flinch when the Tannoy crackles into life and tells us not to panic.

The exits will be freed shortly and the lighting restored.

'Even the woman with the microphone sounds panicky!' says Maddy Sharp. 'What do you suppose is happening?'

Beside her, Nesta is eating her way through a selection box of chocolate bars for comfort. The plastic tray is laid out on her lap. 'I bet we're snowed in,' she says. 'We'll have to lie down and sleep here all night.'

It's not often that Nesta figures out a situation this fast. And this time I think she might actually be right.

We're all wishing we hadn't come out shopping today.

The Tannoy crackles again just then, and the microphone woman hastily clears her throat and she speaks rather hesitantly, her words bouncing down the dim boulevard: 'Again, we ask our customers and visitors not to alarm themselves... And the automatic doors will be opened quite soon...'

Her voice starts to crackle and pop and break up, as if she's talking to us from a very great distance.

'Even if we do get locked in overnight,' says Nesta, 'there's enough food and everything in Marks and Spencer's. We needn't starve.'

Already Nesta is looking greedily back at that shop.

Maddy is suddenly tearful, slumped on the bench. I'm

surprised at her. She's moaning, 'I just want to go home…'

Icarus – or Ian – gets up then and walks to her. Takes her in his arms.

The Tannoy voice says, 'One of the exits… broken… outside maybe… local… police… emergency wishes… Green Quadrant… services… Now we have… exit… You may… quietly… leave…'

The crackling is much worse. The crowd around us mutters its complaint. Many start to drift off towards the Green Quadrant. They look relieved.

The security men here in the Red Quadrant, prising at the frozen exit with crowbars, are giving it up as a bad job.

The Tannoy woman bursts out again: 'There is a way out through the Green Quadrant!'

There's a general push and shove of exodus in that direction.

'Shall we go?' asks Maddy hopefully.

I'm tempted to say no. We don't want dragging along pell-mell with the rest of them in that hysterical push. We should stick to our ground and leave by the exit of our own choice.

'Green Quadrant!

'Green Quadrant!

'Green Quadrant!'

And then, when we are left almost completely along in the frosty Red Quadrant, the tannoy woman bursts out into distorted laughter.

'Where… you must watch… broken glass… ice… and Mister Fox… slippery… is waiting…'

'Mr Fox?' asks Nesta.

Ian looks alert at this. His head is cocked like a budgie's. 'I don't like this.'

There is a draught coming in. An icy wind. I feel it first in my bones. The stiff breeze is getting stronger. The cold so much colder.

Winter stealing in.

* * *

57

We are joined by one of the few who elected not to run off with the mass of shoppers. It is the woman Maddy was talking to in the Piano Department. The young woman in the boots and the plastic catsuit.

She descends upon us, all concern and kerfuffle.

She seems to be glad to have found us.

'You were right to stay here,' she tells us, running her hands through her hair. Her nails, I notice, are painted metallic green. 'We have to watch it now. They've let whatever is outside… in.'

'All there is outside is a car park!' Maddy Sharp retorts. 'And my car!'

The woman shakes her head. 'That's not all.'

Chapter Twelve
The Doctor Advances Blithely . . .

The Doctor advances blithely, humming a tune. Behind him Captain Blandish clutches his blaster and Belinda keeps her head down. Garrett has his eyes peeled and watchful for his precious Captain's back and Timon brings up the rear with his handy phaser cocked the whole time that they advance slowly up the dripping incline.

Belinda, almost glad of her snorkel hood now, because she can see and hear next to nothing of this terrifying place, has started to mull over that curious manifestation in her cabin. It's not something she has told the others about yet. A triumphantly livid green elephant's head, stuck like a trophy through her cabin wall. Best keep mum about it. Unless anything crops up down here that has to do with elephants. Then she can tell them. They will thank her then. She'll have provided information at exactly the right moment. That's what Captain Blandish likes. He doesn't like his head cluttered with irrelevant plot details. Cut to the chase, Belinda, he always tells her. I can store things in my head only one at a time. She's Chief Communications Expert. She has control over the release of information in any given escapade and Captain Blandish hates too much information. He throws up his hands and wails.

Now Garrett, on the other hand, is a sucker for information. The more she can give him, the better. Just now, he has stowed away his precious Ship's Kitty in his anorak and he's whipped out his nifty recording device, which gives off alternately lugubrious and chirpy sounds as it records. Garrett is analysing the rock walls around them and drawing up list after lovely electronic list.

'Captain,' he says, in that purring, fascinated tone of his, 'I have good reason to believe that –'

59

Captain Blandish, true to form, flings up his hands. 'Ssh,' he whispers harshly.

By the light of the cruel and pale-green Ffenitrite bulbs they can all see that the Doctor has stopped dead in his tracks.

Then he turns. 'Back up! Quickly! Company!'

The Doctor starts to bundle them off down the way they have come.

'But there's nowhere to hide...' Timon tells him.

And the Doctor finds them another corridor in the rock. Belinda could almost swear that it wasn't there before. The Doctor behaves as if he'd expected it to be there. He flings himself into another steeply inclining tunnel and the others have no choice but to hurry after him. They're making such a lot of noise. I couldn't hurry soundlessly, thinks Belinda frantically, if my life depended on it...

Behind them they can hear wheels. The groaning and splintering of ice under pressure.

Screeches of unoiled springs and gears and pulleys. The unnerving shushing of blades on snow.

As they hurry, stumbling, the noise behind them increases in pitch and determination.

'It's like being chased by a bobsleigh team!' the Doctor gasps. Belinda imagines he's enjoying this.

The noise of pursuit alters in pitch.

'Whoever they are,' mutters Timon, 'they've found which way we went. We could stand and fight...'

'We don't know who they are yet,' Blandish points out reasonably as their cramped tunnel starts to ring with the approaching noise. There is also a kind of chiming sound.

'Here,' the Doctor calls from ahead. 'It widens out up here.'

They stumble and hurry to the source of his voice, Blandish cursing him again for smashing his light.

They discover an antechamber, somewhat brighter than the

tunnel they have left. Its floor is dusted with snow, oddly, and the space is ringed with rocks.

The Doctor urges them all to hide.

Which they do, not needing to be told twice, as the creatures making the ominous sounds of pursuit emerge into this dim and frigid arena, to stand for all to see.

They are the Glass Men of Valcea in their shining bladed chariots.

The Doctor hides with Belinda and she stills her breath, realising that he stilled his some moments ago. Timon is ready to open fire and Garrett is, naturally, fascinated while Blandish, clutching his first mate's thigh, is quietly appalled.

The Glass Men stand, or rather sit, two metres tall in their shining chariots, and their shoulders seem to be the width of a car. Their most impressive feature, of course, is the fact that they are built *entirely* of glass, and the uncertain light of this place is drawn to them, suffusing them, filling up their hollowness.

From their hiding places, the members of the *Nepotist* team can see the glinting red eyes, and the burning coals of the hearts that beat stolidly in their glass chests.

'There isn't any reason,' says one.

'There isn't any point,' adds another.

'There isn't any cause for alarm,' finishes the third.

Glass Men always come in threes.

'We picked up your transmat...'

'We detected your transmat...'

'We overheard your particles as you beamed to our city.'

'We know,'

'We know you,'

'We know you are here.'

All of which provokes the Doctor, bursting with curiosity, to jump up from his hiding place and dash out on to the slippery floor.

'Well, in that case,' he beams. 'I shall be delighted to introduce everyone.'

The Glass Men smile at him and look him up and down.

Chapter Thirteen
Someone Has to Take Charge...

Someone has to take charge in these situations. When they do, everyone else has to trust them. Usually, of course, it's me who does the taking over.

Other times you have to let the experts in.

Nesta says to me, 'Sue, Iris seems to know what's going on. Let's listen to her.'

Maddy has gone funny and compliant. She hangs on this strange young woman's every word.

That boy is staring at Iris oddly.

And Iris decides to lead us, not in the direction of the exit in the Green Quadrant, but upstairs, and we trek up an escalator that appears to have packed in for the night.

As she brings up the rear, Nesta shouts up to our new leader, Iris, 'But... what is it that's gone wrong? Is there a bomb?'

'Worse than that,' says Iris cheerfully.

The upper level is quite deserted. All the doors still stand open, the shops inside lit. The weirdness of this quietens us all.

'It's like the end of the world,' breathes Nesta.

Even the Tannoy has gone dead.

But that's a godsend.

There is a glass ceiling above a fake pavement café in the fake Roman Emporium.

Iris leads us straight to this and we glance up at the frosted, figured glass that's supposed to let in at least some natural light.

'You're not expecting us to climb up...?'

The glass ceiling is covered with snow.

When we look, there are feet all over the glass.

Shuffling feet, scratching feet, stirring in the snow.

It's hard to make anything out.

Big feet, hopping and scratching about and… when we stare, it becomes apparent that these are not human feet.

They're birds' feet, clawed and three-toed and…

Oh, massive.

Stamping on the glass above our heads.

Iris swears. 'Come away from here.'

We duck away, through the pillars of the fake Roman Emporium, dodging the fake marble bric-a-brac, the gimcrack antiques, and then, as a terrific scratching noise sets up, there is a rending crash, due, I suppose, to the concerted effort of all these outsized feet.

As we stumble and run I manage a backward glance.

I see feet and claws and ice and feathers and shards.

I actually see the glass dome caving in and bursting into shards of ice.

On our heads it comes crashing, breaking down like glass and ice on the clean, clean marble floor.

There is a swift thumping down of wings.

Icy bodies beating snow and shards away from themselves.

The owls are beating snow from themselves and thumping down in the shards of glass and ice.

We hear shrieks and the glass smashing down.

They thump down with aplomb. Perfect in their plumage.

'Run!' screams Iris.

So we run.

After what seemed like hours Big Sue had to pause.

'We've drawn the short straw,' she huffed. 'Again.'

'What?'

'I said, we've drawn the short straw. Every other bugger's managed to get out in time. When they all ran off. Oh, hang on, I'll have to stop. I'm not built for all this dashing around.'

They found themselves in a decorated grotto. There was a

cottage at one end, with a golden sleigh outside.

Santa didn't appear to be at home.

His reindeer were in attendance, however, woven from white and silver twigs and roped in fairy lights. They appeared to guard the small cottage and the path leading to it. There was even a small humpbacked bridge over the fake stream.

Big Sue thought that was a nice touch. She could imagine the kiddies being led by their parents towards Santa's house and how exciting that would be for them. It wasn't very exciting at the moment.

The lights were shorting out, fizzing and sparking around there. There was a terrible whistling draught and real snow was starting to drift in heaps on the plastic stuff.

And somewhere at the back of them, though they hoped they had given them the slip, were those creatures.

But Big Sue wouldn't think about those now. She concentrated on getting back her breath.

Iris was talking. 'All we have to do is find a way to the bus. And then we'll be safe.' The young woman hardly had a hair out of place.

Listen to her, ordering everyone about. Her new companions were gazing at her mutinously.

In a curious tone Maddy said, 'We've placed all our lives in your hands, Iris.' She looked the stranger straight in the eye. 'Whoever you are. I don't understand any of what's going on. But if you think you've got a way out of here, I'll follow you.'

'I don't follow any of this either,' Nesta broke in. 'What are those things we're running away from? They looked –'

'Owls,' said Iris simply. 'They're on the hunt. They've broken into the mall by the simplest and most direct method they could. They're obviously starving.'

'But they're huge!' gaped Nesta. 'I've not seen owls like that before.'

Iris was glancing back down the way they had come. 'I think *I* have. Someone's let them through.'

'From where?' Big Sue asked.

'No more questions now,' said Iris curtly. 'We have to keep moving. They'll have our scent.' She started to lead the way again, her boots squeaking shrilly.

'Our scent!' groaned Big Sue unhappily.

Iris had some sympathy for the ladies under her care, especially for Big Sue. Panting and galumphing along in panic, striving to keep up with the younger ones. Not so long ago Iris had been almost as large and as elderly.

They kept their talking down to a minimum as they crept back up on to the upper walkways searching for a safe exit.

They paused and looked down again upon the chintzy boulevards and they could see the things swooping through the main thoroughfare, the massive heads cocked on powerful necks, listening.

And the great wings beating very slowly. And the vast eyes of the owls – eyes the size of tea plates – glaring unblinkingly into the fronts of shops for their quarry.

The ladies held their breath and kept their positions.

When the coast was clear they picked up their figurative skirts and dashed on.

'They never caught our scent after all!'

'No, Sue. Thankfully. It must be the perfumed air of the mall. Probably it's saved our lives.'

Big Sue tossed her head, as if she didn't believe a single word Iris said to her. Then she put on an extra, surprising burst of speed as if to prove she wasn't finished yet.

Snow was coming into the mall. It was inches deep on the tiled floors by now. It had crammed on to the escalators, into the glass lifts between levels; it had frozen the fountains and pools and gummed up shop doorways. It was growing darker and darker, a baleful blue that seemed intent on staying. Snow began to stream and rush through the air towards them, blizzarding from an unknown source, but one, they instinctively knew, that ought to mean freedom.

They pelted on in that direction, but they were soon forced to slow down frozen and stinging in the onslaught.

Iris decided it might be quicker at ground level after all.

Nesta pointed out the nearest escalator, though it looked like they may have to slide down it.

This they were about to do when the air suddenly split with an inhuman shriek. There was a profound beating on the air that knocked out Big Sue's hearing for a few moments. She thought she'd burst her eardrums and she fell heavily on to the snow as a great white shape dropped into their midst.

She got an impression of black claws and a blur of pristine feathers, then she ducked and hid her head under her arms. She felt herself being hurled and pushed into drifts of snow.

The owl toyed with them, diving down and plucking at them, tearing at their clothes and their hair. It rose to dive once more.

It could carry one off for the eating, it knew. This teasing and pecking at the howling creatures was a kind of testing out. It wanted the pick of this noisy crop.

Ian dragged his mother back towards the shelter of the shop behind them.

The door was locked and he kicked at it. Maddy was yelling something about not leaving the others.

She stared in appalled fascination at the monstrous bird.

Nesta appeared to have given in.

She lay prostrate before it on the whipped-up snow, her anorak ridden up around her neck and her shoes hanging off.

Feebly she kicked her legs in the air as the owl hovered to ransack the plastic bags of shopping that lay scattered around her.

Their contents were ripped apart and flung back to the ground. Nesta moaned and shivered as the owl elected, at last, to examine her.

The shining talons grasped her by her anorak and they dug in with tiny, tiny ripping noises.

The owl beat its wings and started to lift, and her body sagged uncomplaining and began to leave the ground.

There were further terrible tearing noises.

Nesta started to regain her wits and she was thrashing on the air, flailing her limbs, but it was too late.

The owl bore her off into the twilit air. She struggled less as he took her higher, until they were both above the silver Christmas trees and just beneath the translucent dome of the ceiling.

The owl screeched out its triumph and rose and rose, gathering power and speed, until it burst open the thin glass skin of the roof.

With an almighty crash, the glass and more snow and darkness dropped in, punching out a hole to let the outside in.

The wings trembled and heaved once more and Nesta sagged in torpor.

And then they were both gone.

'Nesta!' Maddy screamed after them.

Iris grasped her by the arms. 'She's gone. Come on.'

'But what are those things?'

Iris was reaching into one of her high-topped boots. 'Time for that later,' she said grimly and produced a small, rather elegant pink blaster gun. 'I forgot I had this on me. Come along.'

Ian had stepped forward and he was staring up at the hole in the ceiling. Snow settled in his hair, on his face and in his eyes, and he never flinched once.

'They're after me,' he said.

Big Sue turned on him. 'You? What makes *you* so important?'

Iris glanced at them. 'The boy's right, actually.' She sighed. 'The sooner we find my bus, the better.'

'What's all this about a bus?' Big Sue looked rather wild and shaken by this point.

'My TARDIS is in the car park. Somewhere. We'll be safe there.'

'TARDIS?' said Big Sue. Her eyes were out on stalks.

'That's what I said.' Iris had gone over to the mirror-panelled walls of the emergency exits.

Locked and frozen solid, of course.

She stepped back, levelled her blaster and fired a slim pink beam of concentrated energy.

The glass panels misted over like mirrors in a bathroom. Then they cracked and fell in.

Beyond, there was a staircase, thick with snow and ice.

Maddy took Big Sue's arm. 'We have to trust her.'

'But…' stammered Sue. 'She's got… a ray gun!'

Iris smirked and blew on the thing to cool it before slipping it back into her boot.

'You better believe it, honey.'

'And she said she had something called a… a TARDIS!'

'I know,' nodded Maddy wearily.

Iris was losing her patience. 'Look, if you want to see your rotten, good-for-nothing pal Nesta ever again, and if you want me to actually save your scraggy old arses, then I suggest you follow me. Now.'

The ladies had no choice.

'That means you, too, Angel boy,' she told Ian, with an arch look.

Chapter Fourteen
The First Thing You Notice...

The first thing you notice upon seeing the Glass Men of Valcea close up, is how small they actually are. Many are fooled into believing them less of a threat because of this.

Not so the Doctor who, though he appeared affable and informative towards these new hosts of the away team, was still ferociously on alert. Though he chattered happily, hands clasped behind his back, all the way up into the City of Glass, causing the members of the *Nepotist* crew to mutter, he still didn't trust these curious creatures at all.

The second thing to notice about the Glass Men was the fact that they had thin metal rods projecting from the backs of their wheelchairs which connected with the metal grilles of the ceiling. Every ceiling was constituted of this mesh, even those in the tunnels. The ends of these rods brushed the black mesh and caused showers and flurries of blue sparks whenever the Glass Men moved even the slightest inch. There was a fair bit of noise and fireworks around them and their glass skins shone all the more because of it. They were accompanied by a rich stink of ozone, a crackling, staticky smell.

'Rather like,' the Doctor suggested to the unimpressed Garrett, 'when you pull a jumper over your head and it gets stuck.'

There was also an aroma of charring meat, like fat burning off a wodge of pork at two hundred degrees Celcius. The Doctor tried not to attribute that smell to the hearts of the Glass Men. Those hearts, which were the only organic components on display. Up close you noticed the faces of those convulsive organs. Squinting, malign.

None of this malevolence came through in the things that the Glass Men actually said.

'You will find nothing...'

'You will find nothing untoward...'

'We have heard of you, Doctor. You will find nothing untoward here.'

The Doctor grinned. 'You make me feel like a social worker.'

Captain Blandish was immensely put out that the Doctor's reputation for valorously involving himself in the affairs of others had preceded him, whereas his own had apparently gone nowhere.

The Glass Men were behaving towards the intrepid Captain as though he were just one more companion of the Doctor's.

As the ground became easier going, more level and shiny, and they found themselves walking on sheets of polished chrome, their pace picked up. Soon they were strolling through pleasant corridors shot through with light from stained glass. The Glass Men seemed to go in for Art Deco, the Doctor noted approvingly. Here and there, on polished podiums, were exquisitely wrought-glass objects. He assumed they were abstract rather than figurative, but it was best not to make hasty decisions about such things.

'I'm afraid I haven't heard of your people at all,' said the Doctor, fiddling with the grey silk of his cravat and generally titivating himself in preparation for the coming inevitable interview with the big cheese. 'Should I have?'

'But you were...'

'But you were here...'

'But we know you because you were already here, Doctor,' said the third of the Glass Men.

'Well... it's possible. My memory's terribly shaky these days. Especially just lately, I've been...'

'Doctor,' Blandish barked. 'Could we hurry this up? We need to –'

The Doctor whirled round to face him. 'Captain! I'd forgotten you were there.' He frowned and his face darkened. 'What's the matter? Isn't this exciting enough for you? Not enough guns?'

Blandish sighed. 'I want to get back to my ship. We should find out what's blocking our communications and –'

'Ah yes.' The Doctor turned back to the patient Glass Men.

'Daedalus will…'

'Daedalus will answer…'

'Daedalus will answer all of your questions.'

Garrett put in, 'I believe, Captain, that they are referring to their Supreme Commander.'

Belinda tutted. 'Of course they are!'

Blandish stripped off his fur-lined anorak and his subordinates followed his lead. 'Timon, keep us covered.'

'Yes, sir.'

'First you must…'

'First you must rest…'

The third Glass Man blinked. 'I will show you to your rooms.'

And all the way there Belinda was thinking. They must keep rooms ready for unexpected guests. How hospitable of them. I could do with a nice lie down. A little drink of something.

I hope when they say rooms they don't mean cells. But no. They've been far too pleasant and polite for that. There doesn't seem to be any danger here at all.

So that's all right.

They showed Belinda to her room first. She bounced into it happily, a symphony in peach and chintz with a four-poster bed and a minibar. As soon as the others were gone and the automatic door shushed shut she stripped off her work uniform (all that hugging red velvet constricted her terribly) and tried on the satin dressing gown she'd discovered flung over the *chaise-longue*.

There was an *en suite* bathroom with a verdigrised tub she could happily drown in. The taps were green dolphins and someone had drawn her a bath already. As far as Belinda was concerned, the Glass City of Valcea was perfection. It was heaven.

As she was about to dunk herself into the pink froth of bath foam there was a knock at her door.

It was Timon, still dutifully clutching his blaster.

'I don't like it,' he said.

Belinda tied her dressing gown tighter. 'You'd better come in. You know Blandish warned us about fraternising too much.'

Timon cast an anxious glance behind him and stepped into her boudoir.

'I'm having a bath,' she said, and went back to the *en suite*.

'I think they're buttering us up,' Timon said. 'I think –'

He stopped in his tracks as Belinda let her dressing gown slip to the carpet. She hopped, somewhat inelegantly, into the tub, slopping warm water on to the floor.

'Come on in and join me,' she said. 'You can brief me in here.'

The Doctor had a four-poster bed, too, in the rather sumptuous room they had allotted him. He didn't feel as if he needed to rest at all and he found himself pacing up and down on the emerald shag pile. He was starting to wish he'd let Compassion and Fitz come along. They'd be better company than the others.

He flung himself down on the feathered mattress and, realising the source of his discontent, cried out, 'I've got no one to talk to! No one to banter with, bicker with, complain to, show off to, explain things to! No one to mystify and perplex! What an existence!'

He put in a quick mental check on the TARDIS. Not a communication necessarily, just a kind of reflex action, to check if it was still where he had left it, on board the *Nepotist*, with his young friends still inside. Rather like patting your pockets to hear your keys jangle. But the reassuring answering echo wasn't there. The TARDIS wasn't within his hearing.

He jumped up off the bed. It had to be Compassion. It had to be. Fitz wouldn't be stupid enough to interfere with anything. Compassion had taken the opportunity, once he was out of the way, to... to what, exactly? He only knew the way she looked when she watched him operate the controls of his vessel. She looked – and the Doctor blushed to think it – avaricious, almost

74

lascivious, as his hands roved expertly over the needles and dials and intricate mechanisms...

Oh, maybe he'd imagined the whole thing. After all, that girl had some peculiar unresolved problems. But she'd deal with them. He'd help her.

And another thing was certain. He had absolutely no idea where his ship was. In the old days he might not have minded too much. But he had been younger then, thinking nothing of truly horrifying escapades he would balk at now. And the three years he had spent in prison on Ha'olam, not all that long ago, had made all too plain to him the folly of thinking he could go his own way in the cosmos unimpeached. He couldn't depend upon the idea that the TARDIS would always be there to whisk him safely elsewhere. In fact, several times he had been seriously stranded – the kind of stranded that made him want to tear out his hair and start to appreciate how most creatures (those, that is, that lived their lives in an entirely linear fashion, whose lives didn't habitually adopt the form of an endlessly complex temporal weave of fugue and counterpoint) must feel much of the time.

A screen was opening up on his bedroom wall with a squeal of polished glass and the Doctor shook himself out of his mood.

One of the Glass Men appeared – one of the nicer ones that he recognised from his capture, he thought. His capture. Interesting automatic phrasing, Doctor. You really don't trust these fellows at all, do you?

The Glass Man said, 'Doctor, I've been hunting around for evidence for you, in the library.'

'Evidence? Of what?' Then, thinking he'd sounded rather abrupt, ameliorated that with, 'Please – tell me your name, first.'

The Glass Man looked flattered by his courtesy. 'My name is Marn. I went looking for photographs or film stock from your previous visit.'

'Ah.' The Doctor smiled. 'My previous visit.'

The image of Marn was replaced suddenly with a sequence of

grainy black-and-white photographs. They were of varying quality and were accompanied by a crackling, shrieking tape recording of many voices raised in anger, gunshots, lasers, and the noise of glass walls coming down.

'Many tapes in the archive have, unfortunately, been wiped,' said the Glass Man over the top. 'Those deemed not useful for Further Edification. I have, however, managed to reconstruct this for you.'

The Doctor stared at the pictures, and tried to filter some sense from the cacophony of the soundtrack.

He could make out a burly man in a shimmering waistcoat and a Napoleon hat. He wore an eyepatch and had a lavish black moustache and he seemed to be bellowing at the top of his voice. This person was brandishing what appeared to be an elephant gun. More pictures followed, in which this orotund aggressor was fighting it out with what appeared to be giant owls. They were a blur of brilliant plumage and talons. The eyepatched mustachioed man was accompanied by a black boy in a silver, figure-hugging spacesuit and... the Doctor squinted hard and almost swore aloud at this next image.

He was accompanied, also, by – he groaned – Miss Iris Wildthyme in her body number three. Which the Doctor remembered all too well – a body based on Shirley Bassey in her prime, famously possessed of a rather conspicuous beehive, evening dress with feather boa and considerable prowess at championship darts. In the pictures she was wielding a harpoon gun.

'That's not me!' burst the Doctor. 'I've no idea who that fat man is!'

Back came Marn on the screen. 'He called himself the Doctor. The words TARDIS, Time Lords, Gallifrey, companions were all bandied about. He arrived and departed in a blue flashing box. Is that not you?'

'I suppose so.'

'But you don't recall these events?'

The Doctor shook his head. 'It's not unusual.'

Marn shrugged and smiled, showing his transparent teeth. 'Never mind. Perhaps Daedalus can help out with your memory. He will see you within the hour. Perhaps you could prepare yourself?'

The Doctor lay down heavily and closed his eyes.

From across the deceptively refractive measures of time and space between them, Iris was attempting to hail him.

Hail there, Doctor! Old friend! Beloved!

How about a hand down here?

Chapter Fifteen
One Night I Decided I Needed to Get...

One night I decided I needed to get out of the house. I went off across town again, skirting through the snow-choked streets. It wasn't that late but it was pitch-black and you couldn't hear a single car or bus on the roads at all. As winter deepened the town was becoming quieter and quieter.

In such circumstances some people were succumbing to cabin fever. The silence would make them claustrophobic and they would claw the walls to get out. Not that there were many places they could go.

I rather liked the quiet, however.

I went to a bar I knew, under the archways down on the greasy docks. Fittingly enough it was a bar like a ship inside. Being in there, squashed among the surprisingly large and energetic crowd on a Friday night, was just like being a crew member. The music was crashing and loud and they all sang along. We should have been heaving oars. We should have been scaling the rigging.

Three barmen worked busily behind the pumps and the optics and it was as if they were operating the complex, arcane machinery that kept us propelled and afloat. The biggest of the barmen, his arms bursting with tattoos, even wore an eyepatch. I looked, but he didn't have a hook with which to pull his pints. He had a bottle opener and he wielded it skilfully to open my bottle of ginger beer.

How easy it would be for this whole ship to break itself free from the rusting, disused, frozen docks, to crack away from the brittle cold crust of the town and to float off down the big river. The river wasn't frozen solid yet. If we heaved ourselves free of the docks, we could sail away to warmer climes.

As the night went on, with singing and cabaret and general

drunken revelry, it wasn't hard to imagine that we really were pulling free of the frozen world.

What is it about this new life of mine that makes me think like this?

I never used to think like this before. I never used to come to bars like this before.

What happened to me? And why do I say new life?

It's as if I've lived several.

You were sick of being different from everyone else. You were tired of being nothing like human. You had had enough of taking the whole world – the whole of several worlds – in your two hands.

Time's Champion, my arse. That's what Iris said to you. She laughed in your face.

Time took you up as her Champion? You were forced to roam the universe and it was your job, just your job, to sort out the whole shebang?

Do me a favour. Do yourself a favour.

So let's say you found yourself wanting to be a little more human. That's what happened to you. All that knocking around with human beings, just run-of-the-mill people... it must have rubbed off.

You began to want the things they wanted. You'd had adventures, sure... but not ordinary adventures. When human beings had adventures it was usually another person who set their heart beating that bit faster. What set their adrenaline flowing were things you had never experienced. Never experienced, Doctor. That's why Iris shook her head in sorrow at you.

A virgin, in many ways, Doctor. You were Time's Champion and each new adventure was newer than the last. Your cosmos a dark and complex place. But in the human run of things, in terms of the most vital experiences, you were a virgin.

* * *

I've talked to my private Doctor, him of the opera cloak, pince-nez and ruffled shirts. I've told him about my memory losses and the peculiar voices I hear even outside of my dreams, but he pats my back in a chummy way and tells me not to fret. My life will come back to me. I mustn't push it. But shouldn't my Doctor be trying harder? The money I'm paying him!

Sometimes I get paranoid and suspect that he's treating me all wrong.

How little I remember. I have to take things on faith. The things in my dreams can never have been true, obviously. Things like the Glass Men of Valcea, the Keys of Marinus, the City of the Damned, the Mad Cacti of Zolpha Thura... So I listen to my good private Doctor anyway and must trust him.

I remember being in San Francisco and it was New Year. I kissed a woman in a park. She was dressed in some satiny stuff and the trees were strung with fairy lights. I kissed her. Quite impulsive for me, jamming my face right into hers, feeling her relax into me. I hardly knew the woman.

I kissed her because she'd given me back part of my memory. She had restored it to me with just an inadvertent word. I wonder if I could somehow find her again and she could tell me more?

Grace, Grace, Grace, she was called.

Is San Francisco the place I come from? Is that where I belong?

Oscar Wilde once said anyone thought missing will be found, eventually, in San Francisco. As he said it he was fiddling with the exquisite cuffs of a new white silk shirt made in Paris for him by the same woman who made mine... No, that can't have been.

At any rate, now I am in the northeast of England, in a rather sordid bar down by the docks on a Friday night. Adventures have begun in far less surprising places.

Chapter Sixteen
The Back Stairs...

The back stairs, it turned out, led to a corrugated-iron door which had frozen solid. The ladies were left breathless on the dark landing while Iris got to work again with her ray-gun thing.

'We're almost out,' Maddy hissed.

Big Sue wasn't as easily consoled. 'But Nesta's gone. And we don't know what's out there yet. It could be anything.'

Ian spoke up, startling them. 'The owls probably won't eat your friend. I wouldn't worry about that.'

'Eat her!' cried Big Sue, although the thought had already occurred to her.

They were interrupted by the noise of rending metal as Iris succeeded in shearing a great hole in the emergency exit. She let out a yell of triumph. 'Home and dry!'

Snow blew in from outside. She stomped out into the dark and the others followed.

They were back in the car park. But this time there weren't many vehicles and there were no lights. The last time they had been here it had been murder even finding a parking space. Now the snow was over four feet deep and it was almost completely untouched.

The sky was black and they couldn't see a single star. As they pushed and plodded on, so relieved to be out in the open again that they hardly complained about the snow, they looked around. They couldn't see any familiar landmarks at all.

'From here we should be able to see the lights of the town, at least,' said Maddy. 'Where are the tower blocks? The lights on the bridge?'

'Whatever knocked the power off in the shops', said Sue gruffly, 'must have done the same to the town. It happens in winter sometimes.'

'Not like this.'

'Mum's right,' said Ian. 'There is something else at work here.'

'Look,' Big Sue shouted at Iris over the noise of the wind. 'Where are you leading us now? We just want to find our car.'

'I'll never get the car through this snow!' Maddy burst out. 'It was bad enough getting here.' She had visions of them trapped in the snow, freezing in her Morris Minor. She didn't even have a shovel in the boot. For a second she was starting to wish they'd stayed inside the mall. At least there was food in there.

But the owls were in there too.

'We're going to my bus,' said Iris firmly. She was ploughing determinedly ahead, seemingly knowing exactly which direction to take. She was wading; the snow came up to the golden belt of her catsuit, and way over the flared tops of her boots. Yet she didn't appear to feel the cold at all. 'We'll all be safe on the bus. And we can have a nice drink and a change of clothes and we can all warm up.'

'Her bus?' asked Big Sue. 'Why's she got a bus?'

'There was a bus beside our car,' said Maddy. 'When we arrived.'

'It was the number twenty-two to Putney Common,' said Ian flatly. He seemed to move quite easily through the snow, treading down a less hazardous pathway for the ladies. 'Was that yours?'

'That's the one!' Iris beamed.

Then they heard the shrieking from behind them again. The hooting and shrieking that had become all too familiar while they were trying to escape from the mall. The owls were out here too. And they didn't sound any less frightening in the open air. Big Sue looked up in alarm, terrified at the idea of those creatures lurching out of the blackness, sweeping down to gather her up just as they had done to Nesta.

'Where do they come from?' she asked. She was startled when Iris provided her with an answer.

'A small rocky world called Ichor,' she said. 'It's in the Enclave.

And, if I'm not very much mistaken, so are we.'

'What?'

Iris stopped to look up at the sky. 'If you look, none of your usual... um, stars and constellation things are there any more. And it's not just the weather. Look. You can see other stuff forming there. It's very interesting, actually.' Iris sighed and moved off again. Really, she was never half as interested in the scientific explanations for things as she pretended to be.

'Well, where are we?' demanded Big Sue.

Suddenly Ian was looking rather frightened. 'Enclave?' he muttered. 'Enclave?'

'I'm more bothered about those owl things,' said Maddy.

'There's more than owls here!' said Iris cheerily. 'If I'm right – and I generally am – then there are going to be all manner of beasties and nasties hanging about here!'

'Oh, Christ,' said Maddy.

'Which is why we have to find the –'

Visibility was very poor here outside. There wasn't an awful lot to see. But in that instant, as Iris trained her rather feeble pen torch into the oncoming snow, she caught a sudden glimpse of cherry red. She hurried on, practically dragging her companions after her. 'It's here! It's here!' she yelled, and, sure enough, rising out of the dense frozen air was the reassuring shape of her bus. 'We're safe!'

She kicked back the snow a little way to clear a space in front of the hydraulic doors. The others pitched in to help, and soon they had enough room for Iris to get to the complex locking arrangements. She produced an odd-looking key from around her neck, jammed it in the lock and immediately the lights aboard the vehicle coughed and flickered.

'That's no ordinary bus,' Maddy said.

Each of the windows was lit golden now and, from outside, it looked like heaven. There was a whole array of furniture in there. 'It looks like an antique shop, Iris!' said Big Sue, peering in to see shaded tasselled lamps, a *chaise-longue*, and shelves and shelves of ornaments and books and maps.

'Antique!' said Iris. 'Some of that stuff is beyond priceless!' And with that, the double doors shooshed open.

As the ladies clambered aboard, they stamped snow from their shoes and Iris made straight for the driver's cab. She shut the doors with a deft flick of the relevant switch, and activated the bus's various tremulous instruments. 'I was right. We are inside the Enclave.' She pulled down what looked like a 1950s television set from the ceiling of the driver's cab. It was snaked in tubes and wires. Its picture flickered and resolved to show reams of alien script and a kind of diagram that looked to Big Sue like a knitting pattern.

'There's my car!' Maddy shouted. She was further down the bus, kneeling on the *chaise-longue*, and staring out of one of the windows. Indeed, there the Morris Minor was, with snow almost as high as its windows. She sighed. 'We won't be going anywhere in that tonight.'

'Plenty of room aboard the bus!' Iris yelled. 'Not as transdimensional as some, but we've got everything we need here.' She hopped out of her driver's seat and hurried down the gangway to the staircase.

'What is this thing, exactly?' asked Big Sue.

'I told you. It's my TARDIS.' Iris reached for a small cupboard door set into the staircase and yanked it open. Inside there was a black telephone. It was rather dusty and she tutted as she picked up the receiver, checking that it was still connected. She dialled a twenty-digit number from memory and the dial lifted itself neatly off, displaying a more complex set of controls underneath. These looked almost organic, pulsing with life. Iris gritted her teeth and stabbed at the quivering matter several times. Then she put the receiver down. She pulled a face at Big Sue. 'I hate using biotech stuff.' She rubbed her hand on her catsuit. 'But when needs must…'

'Who were you calling?' asked Ian. Big Sue didn't like the way that boy seemed to have a better grasp of the situation than the rest of them had.

'An old friend of mine. Someone whose help I think we could do with at this point. He's already caught up in this.' Iris became suddenly brisk. 'All right, girls. While we're waiting, I think it's time for a drink. Sue, the drinks cabinet is over there. It isn't locked. Do me a very stiff gin. I'll be changing upstairs. Back in a mo.'

As she stood watching over the busy and perplexing lights of the six-sided control console, Compassion was slowly rubbing her hands. It was a tight, nervous gesture. Not that she would have told Fitz she was at all alarmed at what was happening. She wanted him to think she had everything under control. And really, she did. The TARDIS was working quite smoothly, it seemed, with none of the lurches and bumps and terrible protesting rackets it went in for with the Doctor at the helm. This was quite an efficient flight, it seemed, and it was all down to her. She made an effort to stop nervously flexing her fingers, and smoothed down the satiny material of her overalls.

Fitz had sat himself down in the Doctor's chair and he showed no attempt to hide his anxiety. With each new sound from the TARDIS console he jumped and, at one point, smashed the teacup that had been resting unnoticed on the arm of the chair.

He glanced around at the shadowy, cavernous room and thought, not for the first time, that it was a forbidding place. Somehow, with the Doctor in it, you forgot about that. The curious statues, the bats, the cloying cobwebs just seemed like eccentricities, like harmless affectations. Jules Verne stuff. Now though, with the Doctor left behind, and his two inexperienced companions hurtling headlong into the vortex, the TARDIS console room seemed like a terrifying place. Anything could go wrong. They could tear themselves to pieces trying to materialise again. They could wind up anywhere with no hope of getting back. They could smash the whole caboodle into smithereens.

'You haven't got a clue what you're doing,' he snapped at Compassion.

'I'm not doing anything,' she said. 'The ship is flying itself. Simply responding to a summons.'

'But we can't just leave the Doctor!'

'We already have,' she said.

'We could have at least left him a note, or something…' Fitz grumbled.

'He left us, remember? He went swanning off down to that city with the others and didn't think for a moment about us.'

'That's no reason to steal his TARDIS.'

'It's hardly stealing, Fitz. The TARDIS just took off by herself. Look at it this way: we're carrying on the Doctor's good works without him.'

'You needn't sound so sarcastic.'

She smiled at him and he didn't like the look of that smile.

He gave up talking to her then, and resigned himself to his fate. You could never have a really good argument with Compassion. You couldn't wind her up. She wasn't his ideal companion for whatever horrible scrape they were getting themselves into.

He could always refuse to leave the ship, wherever they landed. He could just sit here and refuse to move, until everything was back to normal, normal service was resumed, and the Doctor came breezing in, blithe as you like, and offering little or no explanation for what had been going on.

He could just sit here. But he knew he wouldn't.

Compassion was itching for the off. And wherever *she* was going, *he* was going. Because, if anything happened to her, he'd have even less chance of piloting the TARDIS safely. Compassion at the controls was bad enough, but Fitz at the controls was a horrifying prospect. Though he'd hardly admit it, Fitz knew his own limitations.

The soothing air of the ship's interior was shattered then by a certain wheezing, groaning noise that told them both they were arriving relatively safely. At one level he was relieved to arrive in one piece. At another he regretted they couldn't just stay in limbo. Limbo wasn't such a bad place, surely.

He jumped up and strode over to the brass railing that fenced in the console. 'Well?'

Compassion was staring at the viewscreen that was meant to tell them all manner of things about where they had landed. She was squinting and frowning. 'It's very confused. It's giving me at least forty-three different types of information.'

'We can't have landed in forty-three places at once,' Fitz grinned. Then his face fell. 'Can we?'

'There's one word recurring throughout all of this,' said Compassion. 'Enclave.'

Fitz nodded. 'So you can't tell me anything sensible, then?'

Compassion glared at him.

'Who sent the SOS thing, anyway?'

'I suggest we go and find that out.' She looked down at the console. '"Breathable but Brass Monkeys".' She blinked. 'What does that mean?'

'Does it really say "Brass Monkeys"? Let me see.' Fitz looked and burst out laughing. 'Oh, he's a one, all right. It means, Compassion, my love, we'd better wrap up warm.'

Fitz strode off to a distant hatstand, where he seemed to remember having seen an incredibly long multicoloured scarf hanging. He'd thought at the time that might come in handy some day.

The boy, Ian, sipped on a tepid Coke and perched himself on the edge of one of the brocaded sofas. He glanced around the interior of the bus and his mind was churning over with a thousand things. He knew he was coming closer with every minute to what might be termed his destiny. He knew his father was reaching out to him. Their paths were about to cross again.

He could feel a tingling down his back and in his shoulder blades, as if a ghost had crept up to him and pressed both chilling palms against his bare flesh.

His mother and Big Sue were upstairs, on the top deck of the bus. Iris had explained there was a wardrobe up there, containing a wide selection of outfits. They could take anything they took a fancy to. They were bound to find something to fit them. But they should fetch something warm and durable. This little adventure wasn't over by a long shot. The ladies didn't question any of this. They were relieved to go upstairs and change out of their freezing, mussed-up clothes. And they were pleased to busy themselves with something as ordinary as getting changed.

Iris was left with her stiff gin and the boy. She threw him a pair of jeans and a thick jumper. 'You can have these. They used to belong to a friend of mine. David. He travelled with me for a bit. He was about your size.' Then she opened a locker in the ceiling, rooted around, and discovered a pair of red patent-leather boots. 'These were his, too. Or they may have been Nigel's.' Ian took them gratefully.

Iris sat herself down on her *chaise-longue* and lit a cigarette. She watched the boy struggle out of his wet things, changing, quite unabashed, in front of her.

Iris had ignored her own instructions to wear something warm and sensible. She was in a gold and cream embroidered kaftan. A souvenir from the couple of years she had recently spent in New York during the late sixties. The kaftan and the cigarette holder she was using were gifts from the novelist Jacqueline Susann. Iris had been helping her out with her novel, *The Love Machine*, and Jackie had showered Iris in presents. Iris found she could think better when she was wearing this outfit. The catsuits she reserved for action and adventure.

'You knew I would be here to save you, didn't you?' she asked Ian archly.

'What do you mean?'

'You're part of all this, aren't you, little Ian?'

The boy shrugged.

Iris shrugged back and pulled a face. She wouldn't beg him for information. Stroppy little devil. She'd find it all out soon enough. She always did.

The silence outside was shattered by the arrival of the TARDIS. The dark-blue police-box shell settled down with its usual trumpeting aplomb, sharpening and filling out and solidifying and finally squashing aside the snow till it rested in a patch fully four feet deep. The snow still falling started to settle immediately on this novel construction, lining the frames of its panels and windows. But, had anyone been around to observe quite carefully, the first few flakes sizzled and melted as they hit the wood of the box.

The door opened and Fitz, swaddled in his new scarf as if he were wearing bandages, took one look outside and swore. 'It's horrible!' he complained to his companion behind him. Compassion told him to get a move on. Because he blocked her way out she was trapped, for a moment, on that queer interstitial bridge between the interior and exterior dimensions of the ship. It was a very odd, brightly lit patch, that, and it made her feel queasy. Nobody else seemed to comment on that peculiar interface and Compassion said nothing herself. It must be something to do with me, she thought. She filed that information away for possible future use.

Fitz flung himself into the snow. He trampled down a kind of path, getting himself covered in the process. Compassion followed at a more sedate pace, locking the doors behind them.

'Where do you suppose we are?'

Compassion ignored him, craning her neck to stare at the dark sky.

Fitz turned to look back at her. Those hamster cheeks. Her

freckles. He had a sudden compulsion to push her over in the snow.

'Look,' she said simply.

He looked up to see the slow-moving lilac underbelly of a vast space craft directly above them. It glimmered with tiny lights. 'It's the *Nepotist*,' explained Compassion helpfully.

'We haven't come far,' he said, though, secretly, his heart leapt at the thought of that. They hadn't travelled to the other end of the universe after all. The Doctor could still come and sort them out. He shivered and gathered in the ends of his stolen scarf.

Compassion took him firmly and turned him around. What Fitz saw when he looked in the direction she indicated took his breath away and crystallised it in front of his face.

The City of Glass, Valcea, on its floating podium of silver rock, rested serenely in the night sky above them. From down here they had a much more spectacular view than they'd had from the bridge of the *Nepotist*.

'It's huge!' Fitz breathed. He blinked. 'But what are all those lines?'

There were silvery threads running off from the city, radiating in all directions from the glass turrets and spires. The silver lines described arcs and loops across the black sky, some of them vanishing into nothing, into the far reaches of what was presumably space, and others touched down here, on to the snowy landscape where Fitz and Compassion now found themselves.

'What are they, Compassion?' he asked.

'I think...' she said. 'I believe they are Corridors.'

There was a scream then. It came tearing excitedly through the whipping wind and the snow.

'Doctor!'

Iris picked up her floor-length skirts and perched on the doorstep of her bus. She wished she'd put on something more sensible than sandals.

She stared, awestruck, at the sky – the lines and lights, the cat's cradle of silver she had watched materialise across the heavens only minutes ago. And she stared at the majestic towers and struts of the city, which, likewise, had made itself manifest, blocking much of the tundra's horizon. Where that had come from she had no idea.

Iris had been much more pleased with the arrival of the police box shortly afterwards. She flapped her arms inside her kaftan and waved at the two figures that emerged from the interior of the ancient box. Then she put down her ciggie and her gin and tonic and waved them again, with greater abandon this time. 'Doctor!' she screamed across the open fields of snow.

Behind her there was another scream. The ladies had come downstairs, newly kitted out, and they had seen what had appeared in the sky. Ian was silent on the matter.

Iris began to gabble. 'It doesn't matter! He's here now! It doesn't matter!' And in one part of her mind she was berating herself all the while for not being terribly feminist. But bugger it, Iris thought. She was ecstatic to see her old friend.

Here he came, galumphing through the snow in one of those endless scarves, seemingly just as pleased to see her, too. Which was a novelty. Behind him came a quite frosty-looking dame.

'Doctor?' Iris asked uncertainly as he dragged off his balaclava.

'At your service, madam,' the man grinned, with the most elegant bow he could muster.

Chapter Seventeen
Over the Years, Sally . . .

Over the years, Sally had had what you might call her share of odd neighbours.

When she lived with the Doctor – twenty or so years ago – that had been when it started, with a whole host of eccentrics beside them. A shifting population of headcases and free spirits. As if she and the Doctor had consciously attracted such types. And, in the years following their separation and their living apart, even when she and the Doctor had, for a while, not even lived in the same town as each other, Sally still found herself with interesting and sometimes disturbing types dwelling nearby.

The past two years, with old Iris in the basement flat next door, had been the strangest experience so far.

These were terraced houses, like the one the Doctor lived in, only this was the other side of town. The side of town where kids kicked about on the street till all hours of the night and you could assume an elderly woman living on her own wasn't in the safest of situations. So Sally had kept a determined eye on the old lady who, it seemed, ventured out from behind her net curtains only during the night; wearing four layers of baggy, multicoloured cardigans and a shapeless, green, felt hat.

Sally's own basement flat shared a slimy stairwell with Iris's and it was here that their paths often crossed, most often when Sally was leaving home in the morning and Iris was returning from whatever nocturnal business she got herself into. Sally had given up the temptation to ask her what she did overnight. The woman must be over seventy. It couldn't be anything too exciting. Iris would just tap her cold beaky nose wryly and shuffle past, a rakish gleam in her eye. But the two women had fallen into the habit of going round to each other's flat for a cup of tea. Iris was very fond of Battenberg cake, and Sally kept up a regular supply of the pink and yellow stuff, which she herself couldn't abide, though Canine seemed partial. The real reason Sally liked Iris, of course, was that the old woman seemed to see nothing strange in talking to the terrier. Indeed, she often did so herself.

Sometimes Sally could imagine herself turning out, in old age, to be just like Iris. Sometimes she relished the idea, other times she dreaded it. There was something about the old woman that made you feel you'd met her before.

'In some previous existence!' the old woman would cackle, kicking up her surprisingly high heels.

What had intrigued Sally about Iris in the first place was the rusting and wheelless vehicle that she seemed to be responsible for, which she kept in the communal garden at the back of their terrace. It was a double-decker bus. God knew how she'd come by it and she refused to be drawn on the subject. She referred to the tatty article as 'she'. Its paint had almost completely flaked off, and its windows were dark and some of them cracked. Grass seemed to grow through its floorboards and tangle inside with wild flowers, pressing and flaunting against the dirty panes. For the past two years the neighbours had been complaining in droves about the bus. The council had been called in; they had tried and failed to have something done about it. No one but Iris would claim any responsibility for the thing and, according to her, it wasn't going anywhere. It would be impossible to move, anyway: it was wedded to and rooted in the soil. It would have to weather away and rot very, very gradually. It was as intractable and stubborn as the old woman herself.

What Sally found especially intriguing was the fact that no one ever asked what was to her the most obvious question: how had the bus got there, into the communal garden, in the first place? This garden backed on to more gardens and the back of the terrace beyond. There were no convenient alleys down which it could have slipped from the main road. It wasn't a small bus by any means. Simply, one night, two years ago, when Iris had arrived, the bus had come with her, smuggled snugly into the matted undergrowth of a neglected garden.

This had set Sally's imagination running.

She had invented a bus and an Iris of her own.

She had come up with a reason for what they may be doing here. And so she had written a rather long book.

Of course, she never told the old woman what she had made out of the raw material of her peculiar life. Sometimes she wondered what Iris would say if she knew. Sally had hardly told anyone about the - still, even to her - preposterous book she had laboriously constructed over two years, all about the bus and Iris. Telling the Doctor that afternoon in the café had been a sudden, decisive moment. What would he make of such a fantastic cocktail?

To Sally now, the bus and the Iris she had invented for herself seemed to inhabit a quite different space from the very real Iris and the hulking wreck of a bus next door. Yet she got them confused now and then. As a general rule, Iris was very unforthcoming about her past. Sally was understanding about this, as if she already knew what it had consisted of, through what she had extrapolated and created by herself. And, somehow, the old woman colluded with that. She felt respected.

They sat by the hissing blue and orange of the gas fire. The curtains were drawn against the night.

They listened to the weather reports on the radio and it seemed that tonight would be the worst one yet. A time for battening down the hatches.

Iris pulled a shawl around her shoulders and a tartan rug over her knees. She plumped up a cushion and found, wedged behind it, down the back of her armchair, a strange-looking electronic device that neither she nor Sally could fathom. It looked like a kind of egg whisk. The old woman frowned and popped it on the dresser, to be examined later.

Just now she had to tell Sally something.

They were both drowsy in front of the faulty gas fire. Their heads were spinning slightly from topping up their tea with whisky. When Iris talked she just let her voice run on, losing the sense of the words. She knew there was something in particular that she had to warn Sally about. Something about the book Sally had talked, only vaguely, about writing and which Iris knew she had finished now and given to some great friend of hers. Iris knew she had to give her young friend some kind of warning.

But it was as if, in the heady, cramped atmosphere of the basement flat – which smelled only slightly of damp – the words were speaking through her. As if she were turning into something.

Or, rather, *tuning to* something. She was being used as a medium, voices thrumming through the fibre of her ample being.

Did Iris have that gift?

I have to warn you, my dear, and it isn't about the council.

Dear Sally, you have been treading on ideas, my ideas, about which you know so very little, but somehow you have hit upon the answers directly.

How can you hit on the answers so directly? If I was to read what you have written about me, all the while would I be shaking my head?

There is a kind of correctness here. Correctness in these astute suppositions and where they come from. Do you know this quotation, dear Sally? This line about, beware of treading and trampling all over my dreams? For this is what you have done and I must ask who exactly is escorting you over this hoary old dangerous ground.

You must be far more than you appear to be. You must know far too much about me. Yet so unassuming you look, my dear, but as innocent, I suspect, as wily Mr Fox: feathers stuck on his champing jaws, and in his oily muzzle. I took you on as a friend;

gave you tea, my hospitality… but you… you understand too well and you write all of this about me…!

And you must not! Do you hear me? You must never give all this material away. You think I started a war, and all the pointers point that way. And I prevented a war from being averted. These are secrets that some would give a great deal to set their hands upon. They are very great secrets indeed. Indeed I did prevent the ending of a war. I do have to warn you.

Now we must pray, to guard us both.

But shush, don't be frightened.

Your actions have been all wrong, but we will make them right yet. At least, here in the Obverse we have that chance…

Kneel with me, Sally.

Of the Glass Men of Valcea, I will say only this.

They are real. I know they are real, because I have seen them. They have that quality of realness about them that draws their malign presence ever closer by the mere act of thinking… writing… believing them.

Danger? Yes, we all are.

Now pray with me, child.

And pray you have not brought the Glass Men very much closer by the rashness of your actions.

Chapter Eighteen
He Wasn't Huge...

He wasn't huge. The Doctor found himself thinking that size wasn't the issue here. Daedalus was no larger than, say, an ordinary Earthbound elephant. An Indian elephant, say, with the smaller ears.

The thing was, no one had given them fair warning of what to expect.

When the Glass Men came wordlessly to collect their guests from their luxurious rooms, there was no word of warning – not even for the sake of manners – so that the *Nepotist* crew members or the Doctor wouldn't gasp in surprise at their first glimpse of the ruler of Valcea. Obviously, Garrett pointed out smugly afterwards, it must have been evident that their party consisted of fairly seasoned explorers. The kind of people to whom an elephant was no great surprise.

The room was lit by jade and emerald flames which licked and lapped busily in braziers set into custard-yellow walls. The shadows thrown were alarming and the visitors had to squint, at first, to get the measure of things in the throne room. Belinda seemed the most apprehensive of the lot. On the walk through the chrome-floored city, she explained breathlessly to the Doctor how rare it was for her to be picked to go down on one of these missions. Usually she was the one left on the bridge, at the other end of the phone, so to speak. She was full of admiration for the blasé manner of her commanding officers, Garrett and Blandish, and even for her beloved Timon, who between them didn't appear to give a fig for the grandiosity of this inner sanctum of the Glass City of Valcea. Belinda wished she'd thought to go to the loo again.

The Doctor, she noted, was strolling along as she spoke to him. He didn't seem unduly upset at the situation either. But he murmured a few consoling words about how he was sure Daedalus would be nice and friendly really.

And then this. The awesome mass of the creature himself. Quite green, with ivory tusks thrust out and a trunk of formidable proportions, draped quite elegantly over his robes. Despite his bulk, Daedalus sitting on his throne managed to give off a powerful air of casual elegance.

Belinda was still coping with the shock. She had seen this creature before. She had seen him in that vision in her cabin. She knew she should have told the others, but they'd only have laughed at her.

Daedalus had colossal hands. His fingers were quite long and tapered, terminating in fine, blade-like nails that had grown and curled like his tusks. As he spoke he rattled these nails together, shearing them against one another like sabres.

'Come closer,' he rumbled, and the party advanced beneath the flickering torchlight.

Belinda heard Timon give an involuntary gasp at the sight of the mouselike creatures that were scuttling in and out of Daedalus's robes of state. In one sleeve, out the other, down his collar. They were nibbling at him and cleaning him, she supposed.

'I think we have a small misunderstanding,' the creature said smoothly.

Blandish came into his own here. 'There's no misunderstanding as I see it. This whole city, this world, whatever it is – your world, whoever you are – shouldn't – be – here.' His teeth were gritted and he was using his most impressive tone.

'I do hope, Captain, that you aren't going to be tiresome. I've seen your sort before, you know.' Daedalus's eyes were a scorching orange. They were like ancient amber.

'You are breaching Federation space,' Blandish went on. 'This – apparition – of yours – is tantamount to an act of war.'

'Hmm.' Daedalus clenched his cultivated fingers and the nails rasped together.

'We of the *Nepotist* patrol this sector, maintaining the equilibrium. It's a very delicate balance. You have no idea what you're messing up here, blundering in like this. If our neighbours get wind of this incursion of yours, they'll assume it's a Federation plot – they always do – to invade their precious borders, and –'

'Oh, pipe down, Captain. If you will let me explain…'

'Explain! You take us prisoner! You sever connections with our ship! You refuse to let us transmat back aboard and you –'

'You cannot be allowed to return to your ship.'

At this point Garrett glanced backward and took a look at the ring of Glass Men behind them. They seemed composed and still, but there was an underlying sense of menace. He looked at Timon and gave him the nod. Timon swallowed.

'Captain,' said the Doctor. 'Perhaps I might intervene?'

'I think we've heard enough from you. This isn't your battle.'

'I hope it isn't any kind of battle. If you let Daedalus speak, you may just find that he wants to be here even less than you want him.'

'Thank you, Doctor.' Daedalus smiled.

The Doctor looked pleased. 'Well, I don't see any point in shouting all the time.'

'Indeed.' Daedalus settled himself more comfortably on his throne. 'But you're quite wrong, Doctor. I fully intend for Valcea to be here in this position. And what is more, I know precisely what boundaries and treaties and strange local customs I am infringing by bringing my world here. I'm not as hapless as you may think. All of it is deliberate.' He winced and made a jabbing gesture with one talon, neatly extracting one of the mouselike parasites from within his robes. He snapped its neck with a quick twist of his fingers and flung it into a nearby brazier.

The Doctor was surprised. 'Then I think Captain Blandish has a right to know your reasons for being here.'

'Thank you, Doctor,' said the captain grimly. He tugged his velour top straight. 'Well?'

'There is someone I need to find,' Daedalus began.

At which point Garrett's patience snapped. He wasn't used to moments like this. With a cry of 'Now, Timon!' he wrenched out his own blaster and started taking wildly inaccurate pot shots around the throne room, smashing ornamental glass vases and scorching chunks out of pillars. One of the Glass Men themselves was taken off guard, bursting into fiery splinters with a screech. Timon, meanwhile, yanked Belinda out of the way and flung her to the ground, and she took the Doctor with her. He disappeared under her considerable mass as Timon made his own assault on the room. Blandish dove for cover and Daedalus roared at the Glass Men, 'Do not kill them! Do not kill them!'

The Glass Men activated their own weapons. Some, in the heat of the moment, and out of their highly developed sense of self-preservation, started firing back. The armrests in their wheelchairs discharged gouts of terrible flame. Timon's firing arm was caught and he went down with a cry.

'Tell them to stop!' Belinda howled from the floor.

Blandish was furious. 'Garrett! Who gave that order?'

Garrett was beyond speech. His face was clenched in absolute hatred as he discharged bolt after bolt of energy.

'Garrett!'

The noise was deafening. Over it all came Daedalus screaming, 'Isolate them!'

And, from the metal grille of the ceiling, three distinct pillars of flame descended with unseemly haste – a cool, lambent flame not intended to kill but to disable. They fixed on Garrett, Timon and Blandish and held them immobile in their separate spaces, and suddenly the throne room was almost silent again. Apart from Belinda's horrified whimpering and a distant squealing of disturbed mice.

'That was very, very foolish, Captain,' said Daedalus.

Blandish fought hard to overcome the paralysing effect of the green flame. He ground out his words. 'Garrett – acted – of – his

- own - accord. He's - been - experiencing - emotional - conflicts - of - late…'

'Oh, dear,' said Daedalus. 'You don't appear to run a terribly tight ship, Captain. I expect the people who belong to me to do exactly as I tell them.'

'Belong to you?' asked the Doctor, getting to his feet and brushing down his coat and trousers. 'People don't *belong* to you, Daedalus, no matter who you are.'

Suddenly Daedalus seemed irritated with them all. 'I think you'll find that they do, Doctor.'

'Oh, I see,' said the Doctor breezily. 'Another one.'

'Another what?'

'Another tyrant. Another evil despot intent on jiggery-pokery.'

The elephantine ruler bridled at this. 'I shall ask you to take that back.'

The Doctor shrugged. And then his voice hardened. 'And I'll ask you to free my friends first.'

'They're hardly your friends, Doctor. Captain Blandish can't stand the sight of you.'

He flushed. 'That's as maybe, but you can't keep them against their wills. It isn't on, Daedalus.'

'Would you set yourself against me, Doctor?'

'Oh yes,' said the Doctor, brightly. 'I've brought down better megalomaniacs than you.'

Daedalus tossed his trunk. 'Guards… be so good as to show the Doctor and his girlfriend back to their quarters, will you?'

'Girlfriend?' said Belinda, who was still shaken.

'The Doctor needs to learn a thing or two about my reasons for being here.'

'What about the others?' The Doctor was staring in concern at the frozen, flickering, living statues of Garrett, Blandish and Timon.

'If you've killed them,' warned Belinda rather shrilly, 'I'll… I mean, I'll…'

The ruler of Valcea stared her down with his blazing amber

eyes. He said, 'They are quite safe there. And out of harm's reach. Now leave me, all of you. I've got myself all worked up over this.' Indeed, his tough green hide was rippling with barely repressed fury.

'We'll talk later,' the Doctor promised as the Glass Men in their golden wheelchairs bunched forth to chivvy the Doctor and Belinda out of the throne room.

Marn was among the silent Glass Men accompanying the reduced away team to their rooms. The Doctor was in a contemplative mood as Marn's chair hissed and crackled along beside him. For some reason, Belinda thought, the Glass Man still wanted to make a good impression on the Doctor.

'I must apologise,' Marn said. 'You caught our leader in a tricky mood.'

The Doctor gave a tight smile. 'Well, I can't say I'm not disappointed. But people are often out of sorts when they meet me.'

'Daedalus isn't usually like this,' said Marn. He glanced sideways at his transparent compatriots before going on, but they gave no sign of listening in to the conversation. 'He's a man of great learning. A philosophical man. The last traveller we presented in the palace room, he just showed them his glass collection. He's got some lovely pieces.'

'Somehow,' said the Doctor wearily, 'I think he's got more on his mind than ornaments today.'

'Things haven't been the same just lately,' Marn whispered. The Doctor looked round at him and blinked. He could have sworn he'd seen the Glass Man's heart skip a beat.

'Go on.'

'No. I can't talk now. I'll come to you later.' They rounded the final corner and the Doctor suddenly got his bearings as they came face to face with his and Belinda's doors.

'I'll look forward to it.'

Marn gave a slight nod.

* * *

106

Belinda barrelled into the Doctor's room without being asked first and flung herself despondently down on his bed.

'We're going to be trapped here for ever!' she moaned. 'Or they'll simply murder us and no one will ever know!'

'Oh, nonsense,' the Doctor muttered, going through his pockets and organising the haphazard contents on his glass dressing table.

'We will, you'll see!' groaned Belinda. 'Oh, why was I so keen on coming down on a mission! With no Timon to protect me, and Garrett and the captain all frozen and hopeless...'

The Doctor turned to her. 'What do you want, Belinda? Someone to come and rescue us?'

Belinda sat up, shocked into silence by his switch of mood. 'Yes,' she said, with tears running down her blotchy, swollen face.

'It isn't going to happen,' he said gently. 'In this world we have to organise our own little rescues.' Then he grinned at her. 'And that's exactly what we're going to do.'

They waited until the City of Glass effected its artificial night. All of the lights in the citadel dimmed at once, as if controlled from some central source. The Doctor had spent an hour or two working on a strange device he had lashed together from the odds and ends in his pockets.

'It looks like a hairdryer,' said Belinda miserably. She was sitting on the end of the bed, where she had been spending the time smoking.

'If you've got nothing sensible to say, don't say it.'

She shrugged.

At last, once the lights had gone down, he jumped up and waved the hairdryer device under her nose. 'I'll need your help for this,' he said. 'You being a communications expert and all.'

'My help?' She seemed flattered.

'Why, absolutely.'

'But what are we going to do?'

'Free your friends and send them back to the ship!'

She stared at his invention and thought better of saying anything.

Marn had seen to it that the door wasn't locked.

The Doctor and Belinda stole cautiously out of his room, and found that the chrome corridor outside was still, barely lit and quite deserted.

'They've almost made this too easy,' hissed the Doctor. 'I'm used to much more complicated operations than this.' He led the way nimbly down the corridor, retracing their steps from the throne room the best he could. His sense of direction wasn't quite as hot these days. He'd had a number of bangs on the head in recent years and his equilibrium wasn't what it once was.

'Don't knock it,' said Belinda, panting over his shoulder and moving as delicately as she could manage. 'If they find us out and about like this...'

The Doctor was enjoying himself. 'Oh, I've had to crawl up ventilation shafts and hot chimneys. I've had to trawl though sewers and nip through cellars without waking Daleks up. I've been locked in warehouses with dinosaurs and I've... I've gone into all kinds of combat with giant spiders... haven't I?' He looked suddenly lost. 'Yes, I'm sure I have...'

'Enough, OK?' snapped Belinda.

Suddenly he froze. 'Back,' he gasped, and pulled her into a nearby alcove.

As they pressed themselves into the shadows, hardly daring to breathe, they listened to the spitting, crackling noise that heralded the appearance of a group of Glass Men. Seconds later a party of three rounded the corner. Each carried a kind of electric whip, savage hissing torture devices like cattle prods that they cracked on the air as they trundled along. Between the three of them, like dignitaries in a cavalcade, came a bunch of four forlorn and dirty creatures. They stood about four feet tall and were covered in glossy black fur. Broken and tattered wings hung behind them, dragging on the floor as the dispirited creatures were shepherded along by the Glass Men. The creatures chittered dolefully until the Valcean in front turned and lashed them with extra force.

Soon the dreadful parade was over.

Belinda and the Doctor stepped out into the corridor once more. 'What were those things?'

'Ghillighast,' said the Doctor thoughtfully. 'They've been taking Ghillighast as prisoners.' He seemed disturbed by this as he turned swiftly to go. 'Come on.'

The rest of their nocturnal trip to the throne room was unimpeded. As the Doctor launched himself at the impressive double door from which they had been expelled only hours ago, Belinda grabbed his arm. 'What if Daedalus is still in there?'

'I shouldn't think he is. Elephants may never forget, but they need their sleep more than you do.'

Belinda frowned.

He eased open the door and they shot in.

The room was even more eerily lit than before. Not least because of the three glowing columns of flame in which Belinda's friends were caught.

'No sign of Daedalus or the Glass Men,' said the Doctor, grinning. 'What did I tell you?'

Belinda looked too frightened to reply.

The Doctor hurried over to the trapped figures and set to work. He laid the hairdryer device on the ground, tapped it, and a host of coloured leads and wires spilled out. As Belinda watched, a series of dials and ratchets, each of them apparently clockwork, fanned out and extended around the machine. A sphere the size of a tennis ball rose out of this mess and opened itself, revealing three crystals, each a different shade of pink. The Doctor plucked one out and tossed it away. 'Broken,' he said. 'But two will do.'

'I've no idea what that's meant to be,' said Belinda.

'Well,' he said, 'it might look like a Louise Bourgeois sculpture, but actually...' And with this he produced a coat hanger from inside his jacket, twisted it roughly into the shape of a Yorkshire terrier and attached it to the mess of components on the floor. 'Actually, it's just what your pals need to set them free and send them home.'

'You mean this stuff –' Belinda indicated his handiwork with her boot – 'will stop the transmat blockage?'

'Like a good strong laxative,' he grinned.

'Go on, then.'

'I need you to talk to the *Nepotist*,' he said. 'You're the communications lady!'

Then he set the globe full of crystals spinning on its tiny clockwork axis. Almost immediately the wire coat hanger started to crackle and hum. As Belinda spoke rather self-consciously into the sphere and the crystals, the Doctor was laying out a loop of wire (it looked rather more like wool, Belinda thought) round and round the three columns of fire and the prisoners.

'This is Belinda hailing the *Nepotist*,' she said, with a small cough. 'Do you read me? I repeat, this is –'

'Belinda?' came a tinny, quizzical voice from the sphere.

'Doctor!' She almost fell over backwards in surprise.

He scooted over. 'Don't lose them! Get them to fix on our location...'

'Hello, *Nepotist*? Can you get a fix on our –'

'Got you loud and clear, Belinda. What's been happening?'

'Tell them to beam Blandish, Garrett and Timon up now,' said the Doctor. She looked into his eyes and they were a brilliant blue. 'I've lashed this up so that the transmat doo-dah will free them of all this awful flame stuff.'

Belinda hurriedly gave the ship his instructions.

'Sorted?' she asked.

'Sorted,' said the *Nepotist*.

Almost immediately the three figures in flames were suffused with a silver tinselly glow. The green flames leapt in alarm and rushed back into the ceiling. The three members of the *Nepotist* away team began to move at last, testing out their limbs and, almost just as soon, they faded into nothing.

'Ha!' cried the Doctor in triumph.

And then his hairdryer and all of its fiddly parts exploded in his face, leaving him to suck his blackened fingers.

Chapter Nineteen
He Was Meant to be a Man...

He was meant to be a man with a lot of old enemies.

In many ways this was his *raison d'etre*.

When they first thought him up, dragged him dripping and screaming from the deft weft of the Looms, it was already sorted out. His dance card was filled from the first with a rebellious host of fight-pickers, bone-pickers, quislings and terrorists.

Who would all, quite naturally, object to his standing foursquare in their way.

He had about him this air of insouciance. As if the cosmos were just his back yard. And because he came from that curious (yet unimplicated) race that invented the machines, the stolid wardrobes, that could travel - oh, anywhere, anywhere - he could step door to door and never really exert himself at all. Not if he didn't want to.

He did, of course. He exerted himself in the foiling and spoiling of plans of those who wanted nothing more than to step from door to door and treat the whole cosmos, the whole scintillating shebang, as *their* backyards. One they wanted to dig up and landscape to their own particular tastes.

For a number of years, as if flaunting his insouciance - this elegantly frayed tourist life of his - he traipsed about the place in his dressing gown and slippers. This infuriated even further those who had to make even and ever more effort in their travels and travails.

He was always good for rubbing them up the wrong way.

Daedalus, especially, was incensed by the way he could nip around and turn up anywhere in history, slightly late but unhurried, as if every grand scene he entered into were just another cocktail party, another casual lunch arrangement.

Daedalus worked hard to attain his own, never-quite-as-good

powers of blithe slippery. He trained with mystics and worse in unheard-of times and regions in order to gain the required skills for transporting himself in the blink of an eye. In the rational universe from which Daedalus originated, and where he tried his level best to wreak havoc (which he adored) there was very little room for mystics, of course. On arid, necromantic, apocryphal Hyspero he'd found a number of wizened enchanters and babblers, but they hounded him out. He was too pushy, too jump-the-gun, an all-round bad egg, in fact. Collectively they elected to transform him into a green elephant, as a reminder to keep his feet on the ground, to resist the temptation of flightiness. This rankled. For a man who loved elegance and had no joy in elephants, such a change-about was not one he welcomed.

Daedalus's native universe frowned on mystics and enchantments and put up with them only so long as they explained their doings and to-ing and fro-ing in terms of hard, ho-hum, empirical science. And chaos theory was no explanation. Neither were alternative timelines, or alternative dimensions, or, indeed, anything that offered the world 'alternative' as a pretext. The Time Lords of august Gallifrey kept umpteen files on the petty crimes committed by those who thought they could get away with it by appealing to the more mysterious and hectic nooks and crannies of invention. The Time Lords, pedantic guardians of Canonicity and Likelihood (the names of twin towers lording it over the north of their city) having invented every epistemological escape clause going, took a dim view of all such posturing. Posturing the Doctor himself – to their shame and embarrassment – was never above.

Daedalus packed his trunk and took himself off to the Enclave – a hidden boil, an abscess, an oddity secreted on the unexplored, unseductive underbelly of the workaday universe, to see what could be accomplished there. Here he fell in with races that neither the Time Lords nor anyone else knew very much about. He had heard whispers of them on Hyspero, and also tittle-tattle about the realm that the Enclave thresholded. This was the Obverse.

A mysterious region in which Time and Space are *not* only not one, but never have been and never will be. In fact, they are barely on speaking terms. Can't abide each other. And the Obverse is colossal. And none of our rules pertain.

And yet it was true and it existed and someone else filled in a few more details for him. A woman he had loved only briefly, during his years of ransacking colonial worlds. A woman called Iris, with whom he had had a child and who, in turn, loved the Doctor.

This is how it all works in spirals.

Like his Corridors – fashioned from Obverse physics, imported with no licence of any kind into the usual universe. He was using them without clearing, permission or copyright and infringing laws just about everywhere. He knew just how many injunctions he would incur and he relished the thought of them. He was a forger and a plagiarist and a shredder of contractual obligations and could it be only he who adored the idea of bringing mutually incompatible worlds together inside the same covers? Bringing them to bed under the same massive, lumpy duvet?

Like the Doctor, Daedalus wanted to be a man with old enemies. Old enemies would abound and he would languish in a self-engendered bliss of infamy, in the sure and safe knowledge of his own notoriety. And, because he had played around with everybody's universe, he had cuckolded most of existence. So half would love him, half would hate him.

And that seemed good enough to him.

Chapter Twenty
This is What . . .

This is what Big Sue would have to say about it afterwards:

'I'm not proud. I admit it. Well, what else would you say to an offer like that? The boy was offering us exactly what we would most wish for, given unlimited wishes and the potential to have them granted. What else are you going to say? Are you going to just say, "Get away with you, I don't want anything today, thanks"? "I don't believe in the supernatural nor nothing"? Of course you're not. No matter how odd it sounds, no matter how impossible, you're going to take a chance on it. It's a chance and a half, I say.'

She sat on the *chaise-longue* aboard Iris's bus, thinking it all through.

It was warm enough on the bus. Iris explained that for a long while the windows had been loose and, on one recent excursion, several had been smashed. Lately she had worked on making the vessel watertight and warm. The ladies should be pleased.

Big Sue, however, couldn't stop shivering. Something very odd was going on here. Her usual response to the traumatic or the unexpected was to knuckle down and just get on with it – get on with the usual routine of things, and let everything sort itself out. This was different, of course.

Maddy Sharp was sitting at the Formica table opposite her and she seemed to be in a world of her own, too. She would be thinking over what her son had told them, an hour or so ago. Really, thought Big Sue, Maddy had it worse than any of them. She had spent the time since finding and adopting Ian pretending that he was a normal child. So much of her happiness had been centred on that. Big Sue had known, though, known as well as Maddy did, that there was something peculiar about the boy – something faraway in his eyes, something almost malign about his presence. The events of this past day had drawn attention to his strangeness again and again. Big Sue was convinced he was mixed up in it all – the weather, those creatures, this odd woman with the bus, and even poor Nesta's disappearance.

Ian had taken both Maddy and Big Sue aside as they sat on the bus while Iris talked with the newcomers. Since the arrival of that man and woman the ladies had been left to their own devices. The excitable Iris had apparently lost all interest in them. She ushered her new guests on to the top of the bus for a hurried conference and left Maddy and Big Sue to Ian's mercy.

Not that he had much of that. He fixed them with his huge, luminous eyes and said, 'I have an offer to make. To you both.'

'Ian,' Maddy began. 'I don't think we need hear any more…'

He gave her a withering glance. It made Maddy shiver. Suddenly he seemed less like her child than ever. She wondered, not for the first time, what it was she had brought into her life.

'We don't want to be on this vehicle,' Ian said flatly. 'This woman, Iris, has done enough to get us out of the building. But we don't want to stay on her bus. She has a record, this one, of kidnapping people. She isn't evil, really, but she has been known to whisk people off against their will when it suits her.'

Maddy looked alarmed. 'She seemed so friendly… She saved our lives…!'

'If we stay with her, we'll get into far more trouble,' he replied.

Big Sue became practical. 'What do we have to do?'

'Get back to the car. Maddy's Morris Minor.' Maddy flinched as he called her by her name. He was growing more distant, more adult, by the minute.

'We'll never drive it in this weather –'

'We only have to go a little way. I know the way to go.'

'Go where?' asked Maddy. 'Home?'

Ian grew solemn. 'My father's home. We can be there in hours.

118

You must follow me.'

'His father?' said Big Sue. 'What *is* all this about?'

Maddy looked stricken. 'I really don't know. I don't know anything about his father.'

'It's true. He's waiting for me. All of this around us is simply to get me back.'

Big Sue shook her head. 'I don't know who you really are, son, but I'd say Maddy here has done quite enough on your account. She took you in and gave you a home. Why should she help you now? Sounds to me like you've been lying to her the whole time.'

Icarus shook his head. 'If you help me now, I shall reward you. I can't make this trip myself.' He was gripping himself, as if in pain. 'Mother... please... help me with this.'

Maddy couldn't help herself. 'Of course –'

Big Sue interposed herself. 'This reward. What is it?'

Icarus drew himself to his full height. 'If you come with me to Valcea, my father will grant you your youth again.'

Big Sue's mouth dropped open.

The upstairs deck of the bus was Iris's wardrobe, with a selection of outfits from every time and place she had ever visited. It was also her private office, in which she conducted her more delicate interviews and kept tied up any prisoners or hostages she had been forced to take. It was also where she kept her hundreds of hardbacked journals, detailing her various adventures down the years.

This new fella didn't appear to recognise the place at all. Nor Iris herself. And his girlfriend in the space-age outfit simply sat expressionless next to him. Her skin looked a bit washed out and unhealthy.

Iris sat composed in her kaftan and glared at them.

'It's a very dangerous game, impersonating the Doctor,' she reprimanded him. 'Especially to an old friend like I am.'

Fitz looked embarrassed, playing with the ends of the scarf. 'It

119

was a spur-of-the-moment thing. I didn't really think I'd get away with it.'

'I know the Doctor a million miles away!' she said. 'It's a hormonal thing.'

He pulled a face. 'Who are you, anyway?'

Iris became a bit coquettish. 'One of the Doctor's oldest compatriots. You might have heard of me. I'm Iris.'

Fitz looked blank.

'Iris Wildthyme. Transtemporal righter-of-wrongs, wronger-of-rights, meddler, artist, writer, glamourpuss and occasional Time's Champion. And very old flame of your precious Doctor.'

'He's never mentioned you,' said Compassion flatly.

Iris blushed. 'And who did you say you were, dear? Contrition or something, wasn't it?'

'We're travelling with him at the moment,' she said.

'And what about little Sam?'

'Oh well,' said Fitz. 'She's –'

'And where is the Doctor, anyway? Why are you two hopping about the place in his TARDIS?'

Something had struck Fitz. 'When you say "old flame", do you really mean that you and he…?'

Iris nodded smugly. 'We're terribly discreet.'

Compassion put in impatiently, 'The Doctor is currently involved in a mission on Valcea, the –'

'That dark horse!' laughed Fitz. 'Fancy hiding you away like this! I thought he must –'

'It's been going on for simply ages,' grinned Iris. 'People aren't meant to know.'

'He's with the crew of the *Nepotist*,' said Compassion through clenched teeth. 'The ship frozen above us right now. We seem to be in some region of collapsed –'

'Mind,' said Fitz as suavely as he could. 'I don't blame him, really, for hiding you away.'

Iris giggled. 'Whatever do you mean by that?'

'Well, I never thought a fussy old confirmed bachelor like the

Doctor would have someone fabulous like you on the side…'

Iris bridled slightly. '"On the side"? Fitz, darling, if there's anyone being had "on the side", then it's *him* not me! I –'

Compassion stood up abruptly. 'Can we stop talking and get on with this?' She towered over them both.

'Oh, do calm down, Compliance, honey,' purred Iris. 'Put your feet up. You look all peaky.' She settled back for a second on her creaky desk chair and surveyed them. 'Now, are you telling me that the good Doctor needs rescuing? Again?'

'It seems likely,' said Compassion.

'He's stuck with an awful crowd,' said Fitz. 'These militaristic fools from that spaceship.'

'Well, I certainly owe the old fella one.' Iris smiled. 'So let's get this show on the road.' She stood up. 'Just let me change into something slinkier.'

'Slinkier!' said Fitz. 'Far out.'

Compassion rolled her eyes.

When they came thudding down the bus's stairwell, moments later, with Iris in her lime-green catsuit, they were surprised to see the lower deck completely uninhabited. It was freezing down there. Snow had blown in and soaked the carpet. It was lying an inch thick on every surface in the driver's cab. Iris swore profusely and rushed to close the double doors, cursing the fact she had tried to save the ladies and the boy.

'Why would they leave?' wondered Compassion, more to herself than anyone else.

'And what were you doing with them anyway?' asked Fitz.

Iris ignored them. She was fiddling with the scanner and trying to get it to pick up their life signs. 'Bugger,' she snapped. 'They're out looking for their own transport. They're buggering off on their own. The idiots! And after I've offered to…' Suddenly she slammed her hands down on the dashboard. 'It's all down to that Ian! That's who's behind this! He's up to something…' She turned to glare accusingly at her new companions. 'That's because of you two – distracting me! Now I've lost them!'

'Oh, Iris,' said Fitz, shuffling forward. 'We're sorry…'

Compassion snorted. 'I don't see that we've got anything to –'

'Shut up, you little madam!' shouted Iris. 'I'm trying to get a fix on them.'

The windows of the bus were hopeless. They couldn't see a thing outside. As they watched Iris tinker at the controls there came a sudden howling from across the frozen wastes outside.

'Great,' muttered Fitz.

Ian found the car quite easily. He waded through the ever-deepening snow, cutting a way through for Maddy and Big Sue and all the while he attempted to ignore the increasing pain in his back and down his sides. It felt, despite the searing cold, like his skin was on fire.

When they came to the car, it was heaped with snow. He set about pushing and wiping it off. Big Sue pitched in but Maddy shook her head. 'We'll never get it going again. Let's just go back to the bus and –'

Ian swung round almost savagely. Maddy was taken aback to see his face contorted in pain and rage. 'No! We don't want that old hag involved! She was useful for a moment… but we can't risk her blundering in when we go to see my father…'

Big Sue had managed to wrench open the driver's seat. She cried out in triumph.

'But where *is* your father, Ian?' said Maddy. 'You still haven't explained where we're meant to be going.'

Now his face shone with a maniacal gleam. He pointed into the swirling darkness again. For the first time Maddy really looked at the night around them and she was shocked. She couldn't even see the shopping mall any more, or the car park around them. All of it had gone, had been swept up in this tumultuous bowl of ice and snow. And above, in the darkness, there was a great mountain of ice, alive and a-glitter with unearthly light. As she stared, it became apparent that this ice city extruded lines of silvered light. These wove through the dark, and some of them touched the ground around them. These lines moved and surged and some of them cracked like whips.

'What are they?'

'Corridors,' said Ian simply. 'Leading up to the City of Glass. To Valcea and my father. That's where we're going.'

Big Sue took her head out of the car, looked up and gasped.

'How do we…?' began Maddy.

And Ian pointed into the dark ahead, through the random clotting and blizzarding of snow. Maddy stared and saw that, several hundred yards ahead, one of those silvered cords touched the ground and it terminated in a huge aperture. It was lit from within. It looked to her like the channel tunnel, except that it sheared off into the night. She was silent with shock.

'Get in the car,' Ian snapped. Then he cried out and sagged to the floor.

'Ian!' Maddy caught him up. 'Sue, what's wrong with him?'

Big Sue helped her to bundle the boy on to the back seat of the car. His eyes flickered briefly. Sweat sprang out on his forehead.

They climbed into the front of the car and shut the doors and looked at him.

Sue said, 'There's only one thing we can do.'

Maddy stared ahead, then back at Ian again.

'If it's true,' said Sue, 'and his father really is at the end of that tunnel thing, then maybe he can help him. We can't.'

'So we just drive into that thing…?' asked Maddy. 'We give ourselves over to this madness…?'

Big Sue looked grim. 'If you care about your boy, I think we have to.'

Maddy faltered for a second, and then she gunned the engine. Immediately it sprang and coughed into life.

Chapter Twenty-One
The Doctor Rolled Over . . .

The Doctor rolled over in his bed, where he had been pretending to sleep for an hour or two.

'Doctor...?'

Marn had let himself into the room.

He was sitting in his chair and staring through the dark. In the dim light he looked quite eerie. His heart was pulsing a scalding red. He seemed agitated and reached out one glassy cold hand to shake the Doctor's shoulder.

'It's all right,' said the Time Lord a little irritably. 'I'm awake. What are you doing? How did you get in here?'

'It's almost dawn.'

The Doctor rubbed his eyes. 'I had the most amazing dream.'

Marn tutted. 'I don't believe you slept a wink, Doctor.' With that he touched a control stud on his chair and light leapt into the room. The Doctor blinked.

'Hmm?'

'I know exactly what you were up to all night, Doctor. And quite soon Daedalus will know, too.'

'Oh, really?' mugged the Doctor, hopping lightly from under the counterpane and starting to dress hurriedly.

'I was there. I saw you free the members of the *Nepotist* crew. What was that device you used?'

He shrugged on his coat nonchalantly. 'Just something I knocked together. The usual kind of thing.'

'Yes, I read the file on you, remember?'

The Doctor nodded.

'The thing is, Daedalus will be furious when he realises you've freed Blandish and the others.'

'That's his problem. I don't approve of people taking other people captive.'

'But don't you realise what you've done?'

The Doctor cricked his neck and winced. 'That bed's too soft. No, what?'

'Blandish is bound to try something stupid. He'll attack the city… or worse.'

'Exactly,' said the Doctor, marching for the door. 'Which is why I'm up at the crack of dawn.'

Marn wheeled into the corridor after him. 'Where are you going?'

'Straight to Daedalus.'

'You can't!'

'Watch me.'

Belinda was listening to the end of this exchange from her doorway. She opened it a little further and crept out, her mind working furiously. She knew her only chance was to stick with the Doctor, especially with her own people out of the way. But there he went – striding blithely back into the talons of the enemy, probably to own up to what they had done last night. He was impossible. And he'd obviously not given a moment's thought to Belinda's predicament. Belinda could think of nothing else. All night she had sat up in her regulation uniform, not even taking her make-up off, mulling over this latest disaster. She could imagine never getting back aboard the *Nepotist* again. Blandish wouldn't be fussed to organise a rescue team just on her account. He'd never thought much of her in the first place. She could imagine him just jetting off and resuming the mission to Peladon, relieved to be rid of her and the Doctor.

But she wasn't as easy to lose as all that.

Belinda knew that the best chance she had was in staying close by the Doctor. If he could send the others home safely, then he could send her, too.

Holding her breath, she slunk through the chrome corridors after him and his curious glass ally, Marn.

* * *

They didn't pass many other Glass Men on the way. Marn explained that most of his people spent the morning in prayer and contemplation. The ones that did pass them sailed by with serene expressions and very little interest.

'Tell me, Marn,' said the Doctor. 'How did the Glass Men come to be ruled by Daedalus? A creature of another race entirely? I mean, from what I've seen, the Valceans are fairly peaceful, unless provoked.'

'It's true,' sighed Marn. 'We are mostly concerned with spiritual matters – and the preservation of ourselves. As you can imagine, we aren't exactly built for combat.'

'Indeed.'

They were passing through a walkway of stained glass depicting moments in the history of the Valceans. As they walked, the Doctor took in the details of these momentous occurrences and decided that the history of the Glass Men was nothing to write home about. Much of it had to do with the finding of mineral deposits in unusual locations.

'But you will forgive me for saying that Daedalus seems quite different. He's something of a tartar, isn't he? When I accused him of being just another warmongering despot last night in the throne room, he seemed rather flattered and tossed that trunk of his about as if he was glad.'

Marn looked mournful. 'Daedalus believes that the entire Enclave belongs to him. By right as well as might.'

'The Enclave?'

'That's where we are, Doctor. This whole system. Don't you remember?'

'I haven't been here yet.'

They were standing before two huge glass doors, frosted with condensation. 'If you really must see Daedalus, he will be in his garden this morning. I warn you, though, Doctor… he won't be terribly pleased to see you.'

'He's a gardener, is he?'

The Doctor pushed his way in, eyes gleaming with impatience.

* * *

Blandish threw himself into his padded command chair with relief. Every eye in the place was on him. Back in the driving seat. Back in control. Even in the few hours he'd been back aboard the *Nepotist*, he still hadn't warmed up. Those weird flames in which he and his fellows had been trapped had chilled him to the very core. On their unexpected return to the vessel it had been some time before the ship's surgeon, John 'Forceps' Felixstoe, had allowed them out of sickbay.

Now Blandish was back on the bridge and ready for action. He ran his fingers through his thinning hair and barked, 'Put the city on the screen. Open hailing frequencies.'

'Um,' said Garrett nervously. Garrett hadn't been his usual efficient self since getting back aboard the ship. Something had shaken him down there. Blandish remembered his sudden panic attack in the throne room and it hit him: Garrett had lost his nerve. He looked haggard and pale.

'Sir,' said the officer. 'Belinda is still down there, remember? Would you like me to stand in for her?'

Wearily Blandish nodded, then caught a glance from Belinda's fancy man, Timon. The man was looking at him as if to say he hoped they'd make a point of rescuing her. Some chance. He wasn't risking his neck for that dithering, flaky broad.

The City of Glass materialised on the screen, stately, luminescent. Blandish repressed a shudder.

'I want a weapons report on the fire power necessary to destroy that thing. I want a costings estimate within the hour.' Once again Blandish found himself cursing their limited budget.

'Sir,' said Garrett, 'that would require my stepping back into my usual role. Do you want me to do both jobs at once?'

'Blast it, man! Of course I do! What's wrong with you, Garrett?'

Garrett stood up and looked at the floor. 'Permission to speak candidly, sir. In the oval office.'

'Very well,' snapped Blandish.

Garrett followed him into the poky room beside the elevator, making sure that the door was shut so the rest of the bridge crew couldn't eavesdrop.

'Well?'

'It's like this, sir. I recognised that creature. That elephant creature they called Daedalus.'

'Oh, yes?'

Garrett stared into space for a moment. 'On my homeworld of Nova-Kain Six, sir. A creature uncannily like this Daedalus attacked us with no provocation. He wiped out much of our civilisation. We were a peaceful world, sir. Dedicated to logic and mathematics.'

'I know all of that. Are you saying this Daedalus was responsible for the destruction of your homeworld and your being made a refugee? That he's responsible for your joining the FDP as a young ensign and dedicating yourself to the policing of the perimeter of Federation space?'

'I am, sir.'

'Then why don't we know this? Why isn't Daedalus known as a war criminal?'

'He disappeared, Captain. He vanished from the final confrontation on my homeworld. We thought he'd been killed.'

'And it turns out he's here...'

'It was suspected at the time that he had been helped by somebody to escape. Somebody we thought was working for the Federation in liberating Nova-Kain Six. It seems that this person really did succeed in getting the evil creature away.' Garrett slammed his fist down on the captain's desk. Blandish was taken aback by the unexpected show of emotion. He looked into his old friend's eyes, but Garrett was elsewhere, back in a personal past that Blandish could never share. In Garrett's face there was no hint that he remembered or even cared about the bond that he and Blandish shared.

'Who was this?' the captain asked quietly. 'Who was it that betrayed your people and helped this Daedalus to escape?'

Garrett ground his teeth. 'A mysterious traveller in time and space, sir. Known only as... Iris Wildthyme.'

* * *

Marn waited patiently outside the doors to the gardens of Daedalus. No Glass Man would wheel into those gardens for fear of his lives. Once more, Marn was overcome with admiration for the Doctor. He only hoped he hadn't delivered him up to his executioner.

After a while he became aware of the noise of heavy breathing. Someone was round the corner, panting and huffing. Then it came to him. He knew exactly who it was, hiding herself away and keeping tabs.

'Belinda?' he hissed.

She poked her head around the corner. Her hair looked wispy and wild.

'What are you doing here? Things have become somewhat delicate.'

'You're telling me!' she said. 'I just want to go home.'

Marn nodded at the double door. 'The Doctor is in there. With Daedalus.'

Belinda's eyes went wide. 'But he'll kill him, for what he did last night!'

'I trust in the Doctor's resourcefulness,' said Marn decisively. But then he realised that he didn't have quite so much faith in either his own or Belinda's. Abruptly he pulled his chair around and started leading the way down the corridor. 'Come with me. The Doctor can look after himself. We can't. We've got to get away.'

Belinda hurried after him, still breathless. 'But where, Marn? Where can we go?' She was whining now in the way that had worn down her captain's nerves and stopped him allowing her to come on missions.

'We', said Marn, trundling his chair at top speed, 'are going to enlist some support for the Doctor.'

And all the while as he made this decision and acted on it, he knew that things in Valcea would never be the same. He, Marn, was bringing about the end of the uneasy status quo between Daedalus and his conquered City of Glass.

* * *

The garden was an oasis of colour amid the pristine translucency of the city. It was to here, this verdant jungle headquarters, that Daedalus would retreat each morning and sit in his pool of mud. Under exotic, corseted trees several storeys high, the supreme commander of Valcea wallowed and hit upon brilliant new strategies and schemes.

The mud was cloying and black. It was like sitting in crude oil. In the interests of diplomacy, the Doctor took the strangely friendly lead that Daedalus offered him and sank himself in the filthy muck. Daedalus gazed at him dreamily.

'Very good of you to join me in my bath. My people have a saying. Something about if you can't sit in the mire with your best enemy, then... something, something...' He looked thoughtful. 'It's been so long that I've seen any others of my kind, I can't remember our most commonplace sayings.'

'I feel very much the same,' said the Doctor, coughing slightly in the sulphurous fumes. He stared down at the ruined nap of his velvet frock coat ruefully.

'Now, Doctor,' said Daedalus. 'We'll have some tea in a moment.'

'Tea?' the Doctor brightened.

'I hear tell it's the correct thing to offer you.' The Doctor shrugged modestly. 'Before that, I'd like you to explain what you did last night.'

'Oh, that...'

'I should be rather cross with you, you know.' The elephant's gimlet eyes shone with amusement. 'Much as your knack with bits of old junk impresses me, it isn't really on, to go round freeing someone else's prisoners.'

'I didn't think you'd mind, really,' said the Doctor, busking it. He stirred in the mud and was unsurprised to find that it held him fast. 'All those space people, crashing around and shouting. I thought you'd prefer to be shot of them. Especially that dreadful Captain Blandish.'

'That one gave me a terrible look when he walked in to meet

131

me. So did his little friend. Garrett, was it?'

'You're better off without them, I think.'

'Do you know, I think you're right?' Daedalus preened his coarse green hide with his prodigious fingernails. 'In fact, I'd go so far as to say that, actually, I really wanted you to send Blandish and the others back to their ship. And that, really, you have done me a very great service.'

The Doctor frowned in dismay. 'Have I?'

'Oh, yes. And what do you think they'll do now? Hmm? Now that they're back on board their lovely *Nepotist*?'

The Doctor gave a noncommittal shrug. 'Go home?'

'I don't think so.'

'They may. They may have had enough by now.'

Daedalus's voice became rather steely. 'I don't think they're that type. Shall we go and have a look, Doctor? Shall we see what they're up to?'

And with that, Daedalus muttered a command under his breath and the Doctor found himself and his host shimmering and coruscating and breaking up into the smallest particles possible while retaining some semblance of sentience as they were hurtled up through the glass ceiling of the city of Valcea, through a short hop of terrifying space and, in just a few seconds, found

themselves once more aboard the *Nepotist*. They arrived on the bridge, right in front of the viewscreen, with everyone staring in horror.

The Doctor realised he was still covered from head to foot in vile-smelling mud.

'Captain Blandish!' cried Daedalus triumphantly. 'How nice for you to have me aboard!'

Marn led Belinda up into a great gallery of glass. It looked out and down upon the vast, blue, translucent tubes that stretched off into space. He seemed to know where he was going, so

Belinda tagged along compliantly, awestruck by the sight of these strange appendages that the city had apparently grown overnight. Marn called them the 'Corridors', and told her hurriedly that they would be travelling down one. Belinda didn't relish the thought.

They came to a single chrome doorway and Marn set to work on the lock. His wheelchair activated a short mechanical arm which jabbed and prised at the arcane mechanism, sending showers of sparks into the air.

They were interrupted.

'Marn?' An elderly Glass Man wheeled up to them. They hadn't heard his approach because of the racket Marn was making.

'Dolac,' said Marn uneasily. 'What are you doing here?'

'I've got orders...'

'I've got orders to...'

'I've got orders to guard the entrances to the Corridors. Daedalus put us on alert last night. You know what these things are like. Anything could come out of these tunnels and get into the city. We have to keep a beady eye on them. The Corridors connect us with all kinds of undesirables.'

'Quite,' said Marn, playing for time as his chair worked busily at the complicated lock. 'Now, I've got a favour to ask of you, my old, old friend.'

'Oh, yes?' the elderly Valcean was becoming perturbed. He didn't like what Marn was up to with the lock.

'My friend here has to get away from this city. Both she and I are in rather a lot of trouble with Daedalus.'

'Really?' Dolac's glassy eyes narrowed.

'If he found us now, in fact, I believe he would kill us.'

Belinda was beside herself. 'Oh, get on with it, Marn!'

'You are going into this Corridor?' Dolac was incredulous.

'Yes. We are.' At this moment the lock sprang apart and the door started to rumble open.

'I can't allow this, Marn.'

'But Dolac... you know me! You knew my father and my

133

mother before that! You can't –'

'I have my instructions, Marn.' The old man's chair activated its weaponry with an ominous-sounding rattle and hum.

'Dolac, look, please… don't make…'

'We must obey Daedalus.'

'No, we mustn't! He's evil, can't you see?'

'Step away from that door, Marn.'

'I'm leaving, Dolac. Now.'

Dolac fired then, and Marn's chair erupted into scorching flames. Belinda shrieked and, in that instance, Marn fired back on his elderly mentor. He fired with much greater accuracy and Dolac was consumed in flame. He screamed and gibbered as his glass skin shattered and liquefied and his heart within roasted for a few seconds, crying out of its own accord.

'Help me!' Marn howled in his blazing chair. 'Get me out of this!'

For once Belinda found her nerve and grasped his slippery hands. With one determined wrench she yanked him out of the chair and she kicked it back down the corridor. It ran up against the wall and exploded. The corridor rocked and filled with acrid smoke. Marn weighed heavily against her and, under his instructions, she manhandled him through the now-opened doorway into the Corridor.

'You'll find a sled in there,' Marn whispered against her neck. 'Get us both inside it. Start it up. You won't have to give it directions. It will take us down the corridor… to the other end…'

As Belinda half dragged, half carried the Glass Man into the Corridor, the great door clanged shut behind him.

She found that they were on the lip of a sheer drop into a tube some twenty metres wide. The single wall around them was deep purple and blue, pulsing and glowing with life. It was like being inside the arteries of a colossal beast. She hated it.

But, just as Marn had said, there was a sled – a sleek three-seater bobsleigh-type craft – waiting for them at the edge of the queer precipice. The controls looked blissfully easy. She bundled him into the back seat and then clambered aboard inelegantly herself.

Marn had gone into some kind of shock as Belinda powered the sled's engine.

'I can never go back... I can never go back... I have murdered one of my own people...'

'That old get was asking for it!' Belinda yelled. 'He fired on you first, remember! Now tell me, before you pass out, where are we going?'

Marn was becoming feebler by the second. She could hardly hear his throaty voice above the roar of the motor. 'To the Ghillighast. The sled will take us to the domain of the Ghillighast.'

Belinda turned back to the controls. 'Are they friends of yours, these Ghillighast?'

The sled began to nudge forward, towards the vast drop in the tunnel.

Marn was saying, 'They are the greatest enemies we Valceans possess.'

And then the sled pitched forward and Belinda screamed as they gathered speed and momentum. The air itself started to howl as they plummeted into the Corridor.

Chapter Twenty-Two
It's a Place I Sometimes Go to...

It's a place I sometimes go to on a Sunday evening.

I don't tell the others. It's none of their business. I slip out of the house and across the park and I'm back after a couple of hours.

It's the kind of place you can go to and are welcomed with no questions asked. People recognise you and they are friendly, they pat your back, shake your hand, they take the pound coin that I always pop on to the golden collection plate at half-time with a grateful smile.

They gaze admiringly at my Edwardian finery. That's what someone at the Spiritualist Church once called my clothes. Edwardian finery. Until then I'd never realised what I wore was that old-fashioned.

Inside it is warm. Sprays of irises and lilies bedecking the altar. When one of the nice old couples who come here have an anniversary, they often donate a bouquet for the front of the church that Sunday.

It's a little tradition they have. I feel buoyed up by the atmosphere here, and it gives me a small measure of faith in something. I'm not sure what.

Something beyond the usual tread of the life we are used to. Something bigger. I seem to need that sense of the divine, or whatever. I like it when they get a medium on, spreading messages and tittle-tattle from the hereafter.

And there's always the chance, I suppose, that one day I'll get a message that's just for me. That one of my deceased loved ones will one Sunday consent to grace me with their presence. Whoever they are. And I suppose that's what I come here for too, to this small, whitewashed, warm and rather ramshackle church beside the park.

I'm a bit surprised it's still on tonight. One Sunday before Christmas, the worst winter on record. Three deaths locally - put down to desperate wild creatures come in from the countryside.

Three deaths! And the town is almost cut off from the outside world by snow.

Still the church manages to bring a medium in from outside, and there she is, in a hot pink tracksuit, waiting patiently in the pulpit as they conduct the more orthodox part of the church service and everyone nods their habitual hellos to each other.

I can't believe the whole congregation has braved the elements to be here, no different from any week. I suppose I did too, and I'm no more adventurous than the next person. Rather less, in fact.

Fitz has said I'm like a hermit most of the time. How Fitz would laugh if he knew where I went on Sundays. He thinks I'm off down the pub, or off on some dubious assignation.

There's a little fellow who gets up first to announce that they're still looking for performers for their Christmas show. 'Anyone with a talent, any talent at all, should see me afterwards.'

He grins shyly from the front, running a distracted hand through his moplike hair, which is obviously dyed black.

His wife runs this whole place, and she sits behind him in dark glasses and a voluminous blue frock. Her hair is teased up into the tallest beehive I've ever seen, though it's rather thin.

The little man goes on, telling us that Thursday night is for line-dancing lessons, to be held in the crypt where Healing-the-Sick goes on of a Saturday afternoon and where we will shortly repair for our cups of tea.

Then there is a speech by his wife about the two worlds.

She speaks in a low, rhapsodic voice about how our world is interpenetrated by the World of Spirit and it's nothing to be afraid of. They're only keeping a gentle, watchful eye on us, that's all. We shouldn't think of them as beings from another dimension, but as dear friends who long to see us again.

Then we all have to stand and the little man plays his guitar while we all sing, in ragged unison, 'I Believe in Angels' by Abba.

We all sit down while the visiting medium in the pink tracksuit does her thing. I'm quite used to this by now. I think nothing of it when she goes into her trance and her eyes flick back, showing their whites like two cracked eggs. I'm sitting right at the front as usual and I can see it all go on.

Straight away she starts picking on various members of the congregation and saying she's got messages. Nothing for me. It all goes over my head. We're not supposed to look round at the recipients of the messages, but I can't help it. I want to see their reactions.

There's a woman who lost her husband and the medium tells her he was glad she never buried him in the blue sweater she knitted for him, the one that didn't fit. Alive, he never had the heart to tell her he'd hated the thing. The wife gasps, as if slapped. It's proof, though, proof that he's out there, watching.

A policeman returns to tell his wife that she isn't to worry about the fellas selling drugs in her block of flats. CID were looking into it. They were planning a raid in a fortnight's time. She'd see. The violence would end.

And that man at the back, sitting bent almost double, he'd better get down to his GP's at once. It wasn't too late to get it seen to.

I was impressed, heart-warmed and, by the time her little show came to an end and we all shuffled out of our seats and towards the crypt, disappointed once again that I hadn't been told anything for myself.

Once down there, we queued, jostling good-naturedly for our tea in blue china cups from the hissing urn. It was a strange place to have tea and biscuits with people you only half knew. You knew them only to smile and say hello to, and because you'd heard what their dead relatives had to say to them. It was a curious kind of intimacy to have with someone.

The crypt had been partially converted into a hospital, with beds and tasteful curtains on runners, all of which could be drawn aside when the space had to be used for line dancing. There was an altar laid with a fresh white cloth and, on it, a whole series of rather cheap statuettes. This church had a less than orthodox iconography, come to think of it. They were very fond of the Virgin Mary but also, it seemed, of Princess Diana.

The little man whose wife ran the whole shebang joined me near the small altar with his cup of tea. He put the saucer, without a thought, straight on to the crisp white cloth. He seemed quite at home here. He was a dapper little fellow: he wore a black coat, chequered trousers and a spotted bow tie, which was askew.

'Forgive me,' he said in a rather melancholic tone, 'neither my wife nor I know your name. We knew your face quite well, because we've seen you come here week after week, but no one's managed to find out your name yet…'

'I'm the Doctor.' I smiled. 'Though I don't really heal the sick.'

'Quite,' said the little man, and munched on his garibaldi. Everyone else had plain biscuits. 'We were just curious about you, you know.'

I shrugged carelessly.

He went on. 'My wife, Marjorie, the one with all the hair –' at this, he giggled mischievously – 'has quite a talent herself, you see. Not for mediumship *per se*, but for spotting mediums themselves. She's rubbed shoulders with so many over the years, you see, something is bound to… so to speak, rub off.'

'I'm not sure I follow.'

'Marjorie says you have quite an aura about you, Doctor. She says you must have the knack. The talent. You must have a prodigious talent.'

Did I? It's quite hard to look at yourself and discover what it is you can do that others can't. I've always found it hard, anyway. I explained something of the sort to the little man. He shook his head.

'Marjorie says she can see great things in you.'

There was something about him, something insinuating and dark that I didn't like at all. 'Excuse me,' I muttered, and put down my cup and saucer and pushed by him, through the milling crowd of worshippers and nosy parkers, and started to make my way out.

On my way up the stairs, though, I walked straight into the medium herself, surrounded by her entourage. I bumped right into her, my nose centimetres away from her plump pink bust.

I looked into her eyes and they flickered.

Without pausing a beat, the medium flew into a trance.

She said, 'Iris will come to you soon and free you. No not free you, necessarily. Explain to you. She says you will say she's got some explaining to do. As usual. You'll not recognise her at first. But she's there for you. And it's about the Glass Men. It's about Valcea. You are trying to believe they are from a dream, but they're not.'

The medium grasped my wrists.

'They are real! They are realer than anything in this life you have now! And Iris will save your life. She promises that, when the time comes, she will pull you out of the way. You might hate her for it at the time, but she will save your life!'

I pulled my hands away from her and flung myself through her gaggle of sycophants.

'She put you here, Doctor. She's put you in this place far beyond the pale in order to save you! You, Doctor, you are saved!'

I pelted up the stairs, leaving them shouting behind me.

I fled the church to the freezing outdoors and the park beyond.

Chapter Twenty-Three
That's Another Directive You've Breached...

'That's another directive you've breached!' Captain Blandish yelled. 'No unauthorised beings, nonbeings, alien incursions, extradimensional spectres or intelligences to manifest themselves upon the bridges of authorised Federation vehicles...'

Daedalus groaned. 'Enough, please, Captain. I haven't come all this way to have you throw the book at me.'

'Clear the bridge now,' Blandish clipped. 'Skeleton staff only.'

'No one leaves,' Daedalus roared.

'Ehm...' said the Doctor.

'Yes, Doctor?' asked Daedalus pleasantly.

'You!' shouted Garrett at the Doctor. 'You're working with him! You were his accomplice all along!'

'That fits,' growled Blandish. 'It was only after the Doctor came aboard that we encountered the city, and –'

Daedalus waved his taloned fingers. 'Alas, gentlemen, much as I would like to be able to say I have the Doctor in my employ, I would never make so bold. He's a free agent, is the Doctor, and not one easily bought.'

'Too right,' nodded the Doctor.

'Where is she?' burst out Timon. 'What have you done with my Belinda?'

'*Your* Belinda, is it?' said Daedalus. 'Well, you'll be pleased to hear that she's currently hatching a rather tricky and hazardous plan. She has corrupted one of my people and they are at this very moment travelling down into the city of the Ghillighast in a rather misguided attempt at causing a revolution of some sort.' Daedalus gave a terrifying chuckle. 'Is your Belinda given to such acts?'

'They're doing what?' said the Doctor hotly. 'I never told them to...'

'Now, now, Doctor,' Daedalus smirked.

Blandish had become deadly serious. 'What do you want with us?'

'Simply to provoke you, Captain.'

'What?'

The Doctor had started marching towards the elevator. Timon pulled out his blaster. 'One step more and I shoot.'

'Where do you think you're going?' demanded Blandish.

'I'm going after Marn and Belinda,' said the Doctor in a steely tone. 'I don't know what they think they're doing, messing about with the Ghillighast. Now let me past.'

Back at the viewscreen, Daedalus was chuckling away to himself, enjoying all of this immensely.

'You can't fetch your TARDIS,' said Garrett in an even tone.

'And why not?'

'Because it's gone. While we were down there, in the City of Glass, it vanished.'

'What?'

'With your friends Compassion and Fitz inside it. I gather they got tired of waiting for you.'

The Doctor's eyes blazed with anger and he swore profusely. 'I've told them! I've told them again and again!' Then he rounded on the captain. 'This is your fault! If I've lost my ship and my friends for ever I'll –'

There was a sudden shrill bleeping from Garrett's work station.

'Ah,' said Daedalus with a broad wink as Garrett bent to examine his monitor. 'Here is a piece of information I think we've all been waiting for.'

Garrett digested the data on his screen and spoke rapidly to his commander. 'Sir, we can afford two reasonably large discharges of sonic energy at the city. Enough to disable it at any rate. We cannot destroy Valcea, but we might at least degrade its potential for utilising weapons of mass destruction.'

'Ha!' Blandish leapt out of his command chair. 'See, Daedalus?

144

We've got you beaten! We've got you at our mercy! I only have to give the order and –'

'Captain,' said the Doctor in a suddenly hushed and all too serious tone. 'You can't mean this. Surely you can't –'

'We're going to bomb them.'

'But Federation policy –'

'– is quite clear on matters such as this, Doctor. We either leave in peace, having not interfered in the indigenous situation at all, or we degrade their potential for causing war. In this situation I see only that we can take the latter course. Mr Timon, would you care to prepare to act on my command?'

'Oh, oh,' sighed Daedalus. 'Bliss!'

The Doctor ignored him. 'You're mad!' he cried. The others on the bridge looked rather shamefaced at this. Only Garrett and Blandish seemed fully intent upon destruction. The lights switched abruptly into red-alert mode. 'You're insane! You don't know for sure that Valcea has any weapons of mass destruction! You've no idea whether it poses a threat to the rest of Federation space!'

Blandish's tone in response was icy. 'It shouldn't be here. And its supreme commander is ruthless and evil and quite antithetical to our project.'

Daedalus snorted at this. 'Oh, how priceless.' He came to stand beside the Doctor. 'All I can suggest, Captain, is that you fire at will.'

The Doctor stared at him. 'Why do you want them to attack? Why would you encourage them?'

'What would you do now, Doctor?' asked Daedalus gently as the bridge crew of the *Nepotist* scrambled into attack mode, each of them working feverishly at their stations. 'What would be your usual response to these events?'

'I would stop them. I'd stop them doing this. Firing on an unknown world like this, on any world, is never the answer. It's so clumsy, so stupid. Civilians will be killed… Valceans who don't even know what's happening to them.'

'So you would prevent them from firing on my city?'

The Doctor nodded firmly. 'Indeed I would.'

Then that familiar, dematerialising, draining-away sensation started up around the Doctor and Daedalus once more. The bridge about them was becoming less substantial and real.

'I cannot allow you to intervene like that, Doctor,' said Daedalus. 'So I am removing you from the ship at this moment.' The elephant's voice seemed to come from all around as they faded slowly away. The crew of the *Nepotist* had slowed down and, as the Doctor watched, Blandish appeared to be giving the final order to fire. His mouth was opened in a rictus. Timon's hand was plunging slowly towards the lever, moving through the air as if through treacle.

'In the normal run of things, you would be there to stop them, Doctor. But I have removed you. I have changed this small portion of this small history. And how does that make you feel?'

The Doctor was transfixed by the voice, and by Timon's hand closing on the lever. 'Why are you doing this?'

'They have to fire on my city. They have to attack Valcea. This is the new order of things, Doctor.'

And with that, Daedalus whisked the Doctor away from the ship and took him back to Valcea, secreting him like a ghost would, subtle and blithe as a spirit, hiding him under his cloak, and the two of them arrived back just in time and not a moment before the *Nepotist* discharged its expensive bolts of sonic energy to shatter the City of Glass.

She had never driven like this before.

Maddy was a good driver, a careful driver. Her father had taught her in car parks on Sunday afternoons when she was seventeen. She had been driving for years. Never had she driven like this.

This was no kind of road. It was sheer, worse than ice. But it gave like fabric, buckling and sliding as the Morris Minor thundered its way through the corridor. It was like driving through silk.

And they were going up.

They were in a tunnel now, having negotiated the opening that Ian had pointed out to them. The mouth of this corridor had opened like the maw of a beast and swallowed them right in. For what seemed like hours now they had been driving up a sharp incline.

Into the sky, Maddy thought. Straight up into the sky.

She decided it would be better not to think at all, but to just keep driving and let someone else – Ian; he knew more about this – let someone else make the decisions.

But Ian was silent in the passenger seat, gripping himself with pain. He was as tight-lipped as Big Sue in the back. Big Sue was incredulous, appalled, on the edge of her seat. Ian was in pain. That was the other reason Maddy had to go on and drive and submit herself to this nightmare. Her son was in pain, awful pain, and this was the only way she knew to help him. He had talked about his father and how his father would help him.

But who was his father? As Maddy went into autopilot and thought she was getting the hang of driving in this curious atmosphere, she allowed herself to wonder what Ian was on about. It was the first time he had ever mentioned a father. Something in her, some possessive, jealous, motherly part of her, bridled at the idea of a father waiting for Icarus. He would take the boy off her. She would reunite them and then she would have to go home alone. And be alone again for ever.

It would all have been like a dream.

But the important thing was Ian's safety. In any case, maybe they would never make it home at all.

The thought struck Maddy that she would rather be dead than living alone again.

Then Big Sue screamed out, 'Maddy!'

Maddy woke herself with a jolt. Sue was grasping the headrest in front of her with both hands. 'There's a bend! Watch out! Are you watching? There's a bend in the road... in the tunnel!'

It sheared off at a difficult angle. Maddy reined herself in and pulled the car round. Its tyres ground into the silky walls of the tunnel and they were safe. They were safe on the floor of the corridor, still pushing on, the engine complaining the whole time.

But there was something on the road ahead of them.

'Get past them,' urged Ian feebly. 'Get past them.'

It was a tank of some kind. A squat black vehicle, bristling with tubes and pipes, and it had stopped dead in the middle of the corridor. As they approached in the Morris Minor, they could see figures clustered around this apparition. They were in some kind of armour.

'It's a road block,' said Big Sue.

'Let's get the bus back on the road!' Iris had cried.

She was a Valkyrie again as she started up the engine and the great red beast swung itself around on the treacherous snow. It leapt into life – an obedient beast, much nimbler a mover than it first appeared. Owner and vehicle were in accord once more and Iris urged her vessel on towards the Corridor she felt sure that the ladies and the boy had taken.

'What are they thinking of?' she cried above the noise of the engine.

'It must have taken a great deal of courage,' Compassion mused. 'People from this time can't be used to the sight of incursions like this.'

Iris tossed her head. She wasn't warming to this new person at all. 'I think you'll find, dearie, that this little era is awash with incursions. When I worked for the Ministry we…'

'Keep your concentration for driving,' Fitz suggested, peering over her shoulder.

'I beg your pardon?' she snapped.

'It might be safer', Fitz said hotly, 'to keep an eye on the road, rather than arguing with –'

'I can drive this thing in my sleep!' Iris shouted. 'And sometimes I do! Why don't you two belt up, and sit back there?'

Compassion looked at Fitz. 'I could put her to sleep. I could drive it myself.'

Before them, the coruscating maw of the Corridor was opening up, melting the snow around itself. It was almost licking its lips in anticipation.

Fitz shuddered. 'Let her get on with it,' he said. 'And we'll –'

He was yanked off his feet then, along with Compassion, as the bus hurled itself into the Corridor and put on a brisk burst of speed. The bus loved being in anything transdimensional. Iris was whooping with pleasure.

The Doctor was watching Daedalus as reports started coming in.

They were back in the ornate throne room of Valcea and every few moments the walls would tremble, almost buckle, with the aftershocks as the city absorbed blast after blast. It was quite an onslaught. The Doctor wondered how long before they were caught in a direct hit.

The Glass Men remained calm, trundling in their chairs up to Daedalus as he sat complacently in state. They reported on casualties in curt, expressionless tones and, from what the Doctor managed to overhear, the damage was extensive.

It was a City of Glass. Of course it couldn't withstand the kind of fire power the *Nepotist* could throw at it. Were the Valceans even considering the possibility of retaliation? He was amazed the word hadn't yet been brought up. He hadn't so far heard anyone suggest it to Daedalus. And Daedalus was taking the news of the ruination of his city with a wry, tight-lipped expression.

Each time there came the sound of another glass tower, at the other end of the city, bursting under sonic pressure, collapsing, splintering, crashing down, the Doctor shuddered. He was going to die here, with the rest, in shards.

He ran to Daedalus's side. 'You caused this! You purposefully brought this on!'

'Ah, Doctor,' Daedalus smiled. 'I thought you might want to talk again.'

'You're having them destroyed.' the Doctor was shaking with anger now. 'I want to know why.'

Daedalus stared at him, a curious smile touching his lipless mouth. 'You aren't used to knowing less than your opponent, are you, Doctor?'

For a second he was floored. 'What do you mean?'

'About the future. About possibility. Quite often you know all the implications, all the consequences. You like knowing enough to nudge things back on track, don't you? You know all about Time.'

The Doctor glared at him. 'What do you know, Daedalus? What have you found out?'

'There is a reason why I came to rule these people.' Daedalus paused as a particularly ear-splitting explosion interrupted. Much closer this time. There were cries outside the throne room. 'The Valceans have potential, you see. In their own small sector – in this region known as the Enclave – the Men of Glass have the potential to evolve into something quite dangerous.'

'And you've seen this?'

Daedalus nodded his massive head. 'In their own small space, in their own sweet way, they could become the Daleks.'

'I don't believe it.'

'You didn't believe it of the Daleks, either, when you were given the chance to avert their ascendance. You thought they might suddenly learn how to be nicer.' Daedalus laughed at him.

'You know nothing about me.'

'Someone told me about that adventure of yours. Someone told me you had the chance to put things right and that you never quite managed it.'

'Who told you that?'

'No matter. The important thing is, I've put a stop to what the Valceans might become. I'm having them destroyed now, before it all turns rotten. Me! I'm doing it!'

The ground was shaking violently now as Daedalus roared out his triumph.

'Doesn't that make you feel good, Doctor? To really put paid to the genesis of monsters? Isn't that really what you'd like to do?'

The Doctor was backing away from him. He made for the double doors as the pillars of rock and glass around him swayed and toppled and glass in shards and chunks started to drop from the ceiling.

'You're the monster, Daedalus,' the Doctor yelled. 'You are!'

Daedalus was shrieking now. 'Time has chosen me for her Champion, Doctor! I'm only fighting the good fight! And I'm so very good at it! Aren't you impressed?'

The Doctor fled from the throne room.

Chapter Twenty-Four
The Astonishing Thing is . . .

The astonishing thing is that even with the snow encrusted now, two feet thick and sealed with a coating of the finest, sheeniest ice, some of the flowers in my garden have survived.

When I step out there this morning I get a little jolt of excitement. A sudden rush of hope. Something, at least something, is defying and running counter to the prevailing, freezing wind. And if it isn't to be me, at least the garden might. Or certain flowers of the garden, even they might weather the cold.

I go out in my pyjamas, at first light, tugging the cord on the trousers tighter and watching my breath hiss out in clouds of instant crystals. The cold is exhilarating, this nip on the air.

I remember once being unable to feel the cold. I remember – when I was younger, somehow – being able to stride about in the ridiculous wastes of the tundra in my shirtsleeves, while everyone else was turning blue, swaddled in their anoraks and boots.

When was that? I remember digging with my bare hands, and then with an ice-pick, deep into blue arctic ice and recovering a seed pod, the size and shape of a brain, a dark-green brain that was wedged into the permafrost.

I remember taking a scarlet double-decker bus across a landscape of snow and endless ice and the cold hardly striking me as uncomfortable at all. Indeed, I remember rather enjoying the chill. But when was that?

It's all tangled.

When I dream, I so often see lines, doodles, scribbles... Timelines. And something has happened to them, or is happening to them still, or is about to...

Almost as if something shadowy, and terrible, has occurred to leave the lines pliable and open to influence. They are prey to the slightest touch... tender as the youngest vines on the trellis. Any gardener with half a will could surely take those vines, those frangible lines, and twist them, torture and graft them into the most fantastic patterns, the way I do, almost ineluctably, in my dreams. Or, tiring of that, of creating arabesques, they could go the other way. The lines could be untangled and made flat. Ordinary. Linear. Parallel and apparently unproblematic lines...

Still. My private Doctor gives me the pills and says that it will be all right.

I tread lightly across the silvered grass and the path that Compassion laid for me, but the frost is so heavy that my bare feet can't make any impression anyway. I note glumly that a good number of the plants are dead, after all – the honeysuckle twisted hopeless on the trellis, the wild thyme, of course, lying flat where we left it.

But it's then I look at the crumbling redbrick wall that separates us from next door, and the tangles and vines that cover it, matted and still a lustrous green. Passion flowers. Each flower is an exact circle, lashed with fine lime fronds. Like a kind of clock. Concentric rings of purple and green. A perplexing clock-faced flower. Very bad at marking off time evidently, for here it is, flourishing in the coldest winter on record. It is at the sight of these gorgeous, alien flowers that my hearts give a jolt of pleasure.

I remember something about passion flowers. Something specific and horticultural. A bit of general knowledge, which pleases me, too, because lately it's been as if I know nothing about anything at all. I, who used to be such a storehouse of impossible facts. Now I'm a well of endless fictions.

Anyhow, what I remember is this: the passion flower, delectable green and purple monster that it is, is plagued to death by caterpillars and butterflies of the most virulent type. The grub creatures trail over each of its spiralling vines quite systematically, munching and munching and munching. They

154

can shred the healthiest plant down to nothing in a matter of hours. They lay bright yellow eggs on the handy, healthy leaves. Bright yellow eggs shaped like pert breasts, complete with nipples. These spawn more of the parasites and so it goes on.

To defend itself, the passion flower pulls off a blinding trick. It develops yellow eggs of its own – sham eggs extruded like pimples from its leaves, to deter butterflies from spawning there. This spot already taken – look! I'm covered in a freight of precious eggs. So the butterfly moves on. Camouflage of a very specific sort. Clever old passion flower.

I touch the dark gloss of the leaves. Turn them over, tease out the tendrils, inspect my astonishing plants for this kind of subterfuge. And indeed, here they are: the counterfeit eggs. Eggs produced by the plant itself as an alibi.

Satisfied, I turn to go back to the house, where I'll start to make breakfast for the others in the kitchen extension. And I remember that today is to be a big day. Sally is coming for dinner, and bringing her batty next-door neighbour along to meet me. I have to cook, and before that I have to read at least some of Sally's novel. The thought of which doesn't please me. Something puts me off reading that manuscript.

Already it is starting to snow fresh snow.

What the passion flowers make me think is this…

When, at times, I'm feeling less than authentic, what I could be, really, is one of those counterfeit eggs. I could just be an extrusion of my own environment, pretending to be the real me, and by my very, unwitting presence, warding off the presence of the real, real, real me.

It seems more natural that way. More self-determined. Better than thinking someone else has made an environment for me, on my behalf, and popped me safely inside. I wouldn't like that at all. No. I've grown here naturally. That's the best way to think about it. I am a natural hybrid, that's all.

It's cold. Get in the house, Doctor, and get that kettle on. Get the bacon frying. French toast. Call Fitz out of bed.

Chapter Twenty-Five
Many Tales Are Told...

Many tales are told about the Ghillighast.

In the legends of most worlds they appear as mysterious, almost godlike beings who have harnessed great powers. Sometimes they are alluded to as benevolent, watchful creatures who, although possessed of great knowledge and skill and foresight, decline to intervene in the doings and misdoings of others. Elsewhere they are pigeon-holed as terrible meddlers, arch-interferers and general busybodies. Elsewhere again they are known as a scourge upon the Enclave. They are diabolical, engendering war, unpleasantness and pestilence in all quarters they visit.

Let us arrive on their moon a little ahead of the sled that carries Belinda and the Glass Man Marn. As their transparent craft glides and swoops and drops inexorably towards this barren satellite, let us skip gently ahead and enter into...

Ah, a rock-lined cavernous room full of robed and chanting figures. Tapestries and braziers and mystical symbols. A High Priestess and a sacrifice. The chanting reaching an eerie climax.

'Enough!' cries the High Priestess, and tosses back the hood of her cloak. She frees her voluptuously furred ears. They unfurl with an elasticity of which the venerable priestess and Empress of Ghillighast, Meisha, is justly proud. She sniffs the incensed air speculatively with her jutting snout and declaims to her assembled, batlike brethren, throwing open her robes and silken wings, 'They are about to arrive.'

The Ghillighast snigger and stir with expectation. Meisha realises that their marking the arrival of the strangers with a ritual like this gives the whole affair a festive quality, rather as if they had decided to throw a surprise party. And why not? These strangers and their advent were foretold centuries ago, when the

Ghillighast first attained their powers.

Her robed colleague Simaf has overheard this. Or rather, the import of her thought has been imparted to him.

'Perhaps this arrival of the strangers', he sends back to her gently, 'is the very reason we were given these powers in the first place.'

Meisha bridles at this. 'How dare you, Simaf!' she shouts, in the curious whinny she affects when angry. 'That is tantamount to sacrilege. And in the Chamber of Pesst, to boot!'

Simaf gives a suitably low bow in the direction of their altar, behind which is the graven image to which, the Ghillighast generally suppose, they owe their lives, success and everything – a bloated, multi-legged being hewn from stone, with faceted eyes and mandibles you would swear were about to twitch. 'Praise to Pesst,' Simaf says hurriedly.

'Although,' muses Meisha, not uncharacteristically changing her mind, 'you are right to stress the importance, the historical significance of the arrival of Lord Marn and the Lady Belinda.' She hops off her podium and surveys the rest of the Ghillighast, all progressing now, respectfully, out of the Chamber of Pesst and into the flame-lit tunnels, to await the arrival. 'We are very lucky to live in such times.'

Simaf echoes the mantra. 'We are lucky indeed to live in such times.'

Meisha nods approvingly. 'And perhaps there is a grain of truth in what you say. Perhaps all of Ghillighast history is geared to this moment. Everything we have accomplished, everything our forebears have attained, all of it was laid in place, ready for the moment our race greets the Man of Glass and the Lady from the Land of Nepotists. We know something momentous must happen then. All our written, prewritten history, tends to this evening. And after that; nothing. After that, history is ours to make up.'

'Quite,' says Simaf in a wheedling tone, hoping that this means he may profit from the venture in some manner as yet unseen.

'It has been a very great burden for our people, has it not, Majesty, to labour under two millennia of prewritten history? We shall be glad of extemporising, no? Freed from the shackles of foreknowledge, who is to say what the Ghillighast might achieve?'

'What?' Meisha is scandalised. 'You dare to utter such presumptuous nonsense in the Chamber of Pesst, in the presence of your Empress? This is blasphemy!'

Simaf quails. 'I was only saying, ma'am, that the time of choice is coming. A New Ghillighast, freed of the old ideology and…'

Meisha has turned away from him. 'Indeed. And perhaps you are right, in what you say. Perhaps. But you do well to remember what we have gained from the powers harnessed by our great forebears. The Three who ruled us at the beginning of time. The Three who bestowed on us our power over and above the Pesst…'

Simaf nods. 'And what of those powers, Majesty? Do they vanish at midnight? Are we to lose them altogether in the third millennium?'

'We shall see, Simaf,' says Meisha, striding with as much dignity as she can muster, from the room. 'We shall see. Come, my colleague. Let us bear witness to the Arrival.'

Simaf scurries after her.

'Tell me more about them,' said Belinda worriedly, as the bleak-looking moon in the tunnel ahead grew larger and larger. She had to shriek over the noise of the rushing wind, which felt like it had ripped almost every hair from her head. She was pleased Marn had taken control of the slim vessel and seemed to know where they were heading.

She glanced worriedly at his bloodless wounds but he had, she noticed, a curious steeliness about his expression and his whole body was tense. She wondered if the showing of weakness was taboo to the Glass Men.

'They are the Valceans' sworn enemies, of hundreds of years' standing. They seem to have mastered many black arts and magicks and that's why we can't be doing with them.'

'I see.' Belinda remembered her captain, Garrett and the ship's doctor, 'Forceps' Felixstoe, beaming down to a world where magick was the thing. That had been a terrible affair and none of them had been quite the same afterwards. Still, just at this moment, Belinda was feeling rather heroic, all in all.

'Also,' Marn went on, 'they are rumoured to be possessed of a great and mysterious power. Something to do with the very fabric of the universe. Something that lets them into the secrets that bind the whole thing together and which tells them the future.'

He was looking at the moon they were approaching with a stifled dread that even his glassy impassiveness couldn't hide. He's terrified of them, Belinda thought. She had to keep him talking.

'What is it, this mysterious power?' she asked, as the moon loomed hugely before them.

Marn shrugged and started to guide the sled towards what seemed to be a dark and hulking city on the landmass closest. 'Reports from various Valcean spies seem to suggest that their power resides in their ability to manipulate lice.'

Then the sled's engines cranked into noisy overdrive as Marn guided it skilfully to the ground.

They were lowering themselves with some grace into a dark and icy courtyard that was open to the sky.

It was only as the small sled actually touched the frosted stone and Belinda and Marn looked apprehensively out through the windscreen that they saw the welcome committee.

Twenty creatures were ranged around the vehicle, all of them bowing and scraping. They were each about a metre tall; each had wings and feltlike ears and was covered in coarse, dark hair.

'They seem friendly enough,' said Marn as he slid open the hatchway.

'Lice?' Belinda said incredulously. 'They mastered the fabric of the universe by manipulating lice?'

Marn nodded. 'Apparently. Lice know a thing or two, by all accounts. They are everywhere. Tiny but omnipresent. The Ghillighast are powerful, they believe, because they listen to the tiniest, most insignificant of life forms. It's just the kind of reverse snobbery you'd expect from them.' He nodded across to where a distinguished-looking creature with luxuriously furred ears and a resplendent cloak was waiting with her colleagues. 'She looks important. Let's talk to her.'

'Welcome!' the creature was bellowing through the frosty air of the courtyard. 'Welcome to the Ghillighast moon, Lord Marn and Lady Belinda.'

The two travellers looked at each other in some surprise.

He has always been the kind to take notice of the little things. The way these glass artefacts, or each of these shelves – bulbous, spindly, attenuated, gleaming – shiver and start to topple.

The minute calibrations; their insensate attempts to right themselves – despite the tremors, in spite of the explosions, the clamours, the pain in the City of Glass – to keep themselves preserved.

He could very well be fascinated by their endeavour and he could very well stay to watch each of them drop from its shelf and smash, as the windows cave in and cracks appear, as gashes prise themselves open in ceilings, floors and walls.

This is a city of windows. Valcea is nothing but windows, although not the most clear-sighted of cities. Many are opaque, tinted and opalescent – crazed like Tiffany glass. A place of refractions, distortions and not the easiest city to flee.

Not even when it is still – a place full of distorting mirrors, an Art Deco stab at a funhouse. Now a place of torture, of course, now that it's under siege. A place of jagged edges, composed of spiteful blades and knives, fractures and slivers.

Although a man prone to having his attention snagged by the smallest of things, the Doctor is forced to look to the much bigger picture. Luckily, another favourite topic of his. Jagging and piecing such jigsaws together.

Striving after coherence, clarity, patterns, or at least some sense of a drift, a tendency; an inkling of the same plan in the endless round of bartering between chaos and order. Oh, chaos and order. Old chestnuts.

Sometimes he longs for the days when he thought it was all like a game of chess.

And the City is still crashing down around his smarting, stinging ears. He is covered in cuts. He can taste blood. His clothes are shredded and torn and there are holes punched through his shoes.

All through the city of Valcea rise the screams of the Glass Men, ghastly, hollow, ululating cries that emerge in a curious harmony, as if they were dying of one accord, colluding with their sacrifices and submitting to this onslaught from space. From the *Nepotist*. From Blandish and his lot.

The Doctor's blood boils with fury. The Glass Men have given up, he thinks. And maybe they have no choice.

He is also the kind of person who likes to think the best of people. Could the Valceans really be anything like the Daleks, at any point in their history? The Valceans he has seen so far have been submissive and quiet. They act on orders. The only way they could fall to evil would be if they had a ruler, a ruler like Daedalus who could make them do his own malign bidding.

The Doctor doesn't believe a word Daedalus has told him.

He has come to the outskirts of the city. There are more Glass People here, milling about in their chairs, juddering along, their metal tapers brushing the ceilings. Shedding sparks with some alacrity. The Doctor dodges and swerves and apologises, passing between them.

Here there is greater variation in physiognomies: women, children, elderly people made all of glass. Different shades and types of glass: some cut in a more angular fashion so that the Valceans appear almost boxlike, others more fluid, as if made of molten glass and in the process of being finished off. All of them cry in the same ghastly voice as the chrome floors shudder and judder.

As the Doctor comes to the galleries where the entrances to the corridors are waiting – and to which the Glass People are trying to escape – the lights flicker and dim and come back on again for a moment or two before going off completely.

At last, inevitably, the power supplies have been stymied and cut. The energy that powers the Valceans' chairs via the ceilings has been suddenly sapped. And the Glass People are trapped, wedged, gridlocked in collapsing passageways.

In the chill, cramped dark their cries start to rise in pitch. They panic. Some even attempt to leave their chairs and try to make for the corridor thresholds on foot.

Almost there, turning back, the Doctor is appalled. Even with his better-than-average night vision he can see little in the dark pandemonium. He can see one or two Valceans lower themselves on to their legs and stagger towards him, towards the tall airlock doors. He can see the ruby red of their hearts giving off their own blaze of light and determined heat.

He sees the anguish in the glass faces, dimly lit red and blue, as they strive to flee. But their bodies are not built for escapes like this. Their legs can hardly withstand the weight of their bodies. There is the brittle, savage, snapping noise of bones cracking all around him. But sharper than bones, even more brittle.

The Doctor watches these first few brave souls, leaving their chairs, crash into shards on the metal floors. As they fall full length they burst apart, out of all recognition.

'What can I do?' the Doctor cries, above their noise and that of the City. 'How can I help you?' He sounds desperate, helpless. 'Tell me... Please!'

One of the Valceans closest to him says, not too loudly. 'There is little you can do. We aren't as resilient as you. You can fling yourself down into that corridor and come out safely at the other end, wherever that is. We cannot throw ourselves in the same way. If we do, we would shatter.'

'But... I must help you!'

She laughed. 'Nothing to be done, Doctor. It is... Doctor, isn't it?'

'Yes, but –'

'I met you last time. I am Kerna.'

The Doctor hadn't the heart to tell her that he had no recollection of having been here yet.

'Daedalus is sacrificing you all,' the Doctor tells her. 'He caused all of this. He's doing it for a reason. He wants to create chaos. I must...'

Kerna reaches out one cold hand and pats the Doctor's. 'You must get yourself away, Doctor. That is the best service you can do us Valceans. You have helped us enough in the past.'

'Have I?' He runs his hands through his hair. 'This time I've done nothing. Nothing. Now you've been destroyed.'

Kerna's voice went even lower. 'You must help everyone else. All the other worlds in the galaxy you inhabit. Daedalus is bringing them into war. He is destroying Valcea like this to bring them all into war. If you don't get out and warn them, Doctor, they'll all go to war, just as he wishes. He will have succeeded. You must go, Doctor, and do everything you can to prevent his plans from bearing fruit. He wants this war more than anything. To draw the Sahmbekarts, the Steigertrudes and Ghillighasts and Owl races of the Enclave into war with your galaxy. He mustn't succeed.'

'So that's what he's doing.'

'Don't let our sacrifice be for nothing.'

'Why didn't you all tell me sooner?'

Kerna was close enough to the corridor entrance to plug in the entrance codes. As she opened the circular door for him, she said, 'Shame, Doctor. A man like you knows nothing of shame. Of letting in the wolf at your door. You are a man of integrity. We let Daedalus in because of the promises he made us... We thought we were the most precious beings in existence and that

Daedalus would protect us. And now we must pay for our selfishness. Just go and do what you always do. Set about foiling these hideous schemes. And always remember Valcea.'

The door slid open and the Doctor took a last look backward. He passed into the outrageous blue of the threshold.

'Oh, and Doctor,' said Kerna. 'Give my regards, when you see her again, to Iris.'

Then she shoved him, with surprising strength, into the cool blue of the corridor. He dropped effortlessly into free fall and Kerna let the portal close after him.

Chapter Twenty-Six
It Was Mad, Really...

It was mad, really, with the weather being like it was.

The chances were that I'd get a little way out of town and then I'd get stuck in a ditch and frozen, or attacked.

But I had to see her.

I wasn't feeling too fit by then. Even walking had become a bit of a chore. But something, I don't know what it was, something reinvigorated and pushed me on, once I got into the countryside beyond the North Park.

Here, I was on the outskirts of town, and there was something that drew me – something to do with the sight of all that white and the trees black as mascara brushes receding into the silvery distance.

She lived alone in a house in a village. Not too far from our town. I used to walk this way, over the fields, to see her. I hadn't been out this way so much recently.

We hadn't heard much about this village since winter came on. If the town was frozen solid and people found it hard enough to get along there, what chance did the villagers have? I was ashamed to realise, stamping along beside the stream, catching my breath, leaning up against the black wet bark of a tree, that I hadn't given her situation much thought.

She could be dead.

Maybe not. Dead wasn't like her.

She'd be fine. She'd be sitting in front of the fire.

Same old girl.

I was freezing. I hadn't wrapped up warm enough. The little light that the day had garnered was beginning to vanish.

Not far now.

I wondered if the note I had left on the hall table would perplex Compassion and Fitz. 'Gone to check on mother.'

They never even knew I had one.

The house is coated in ice.

A clear envelope of ice as if no one has stirred within for days. Perhaps weeks. All the windows and doors are shut and no light glows welcomingly from within. I crackle and stir and trudge through the tangled garden, the grass at knee height. It hasn't been cut since I came out last summer to give it a mowing. Was that the last time I saw her?

I have my key.

The kitchen is dark. Bottles on the draining board – emptied, milk and gin. Cups stacked high in the sink. A cat dashes from a corner of the dark kitchen and sneaks behind the pantry door, staring at me. Something like a cat.

I come into the house like a burglar.

There is music in the house.

Dim, shut away, but still music, still jaunty, still signs of life. I follow it. Track her down to her study, here on the ground floor. Ragtime stuff. Jazz from the l920s.

At the end of the hall, her door. The hallway is warming. There are candles lit. My feet start to throb as the cold is drawn out of them.

Heads on these walls. Heads stuffed with sawdust, mounted on plaques. A lugubrious moose, staring appalled up at the staircase. A crocodile's triangular head. Truncated bits of creatures jut out all over these walls. My mother once had a dalliance with a hotshot taxidermist and these were his gifts to her. Birds and small mammals are posed and poised in glass cases. Even some creatures I barely recognise. Some that appear to have fur and feathers and scales. Hybridised creatures, their oddity notwithstanding, still finding themselves stuffed and mounted.

They give me the willies.

'Mother?'

* * *

Sequins, fringed shawls, feathers, beads.

My mother is dressed as a party girl from the twenties. She's a Flapper, a Scott Fitzgerald girl, a Louise Brooks brewing cocktails in the shaker I bought her last Christmas.

She's heavily made up: great black rings of kohl around her eyes, green eyeshadow. She's awash with cocktails and heady jazz. She's in a large wine-red armchair beside the gramophone and she's got her feet up on the overstuffed pouffe.

She's pleased to see me, but she can't get up.

'Jonny, Jonny, Jonny,' she drawls. Smoky Eastern European vowels. She's never shaken her accent one bit.

'Hello, Mother.'

She sits me down and gets to work on concocting me a drink. She's never believed that I don't really drink alcohol.

Mother can't get up to hug me. To whirl me around the cluttered room, dancing, as I know she would like to. She has a tartan rug over her lap. It slips slightly as she starts to talk more animatedly, tipsily, and, as it slides, you can see her tail. Her mermaid tail. I look down at the carpet in my usual, fretful embarrassment and see that tail's termination in her splendidly iridescent and unashamed fins. She swishes them in pleasure as she hands me my cocktail.

'What is it for, that you come to see your old mother now, Jonny? Are you in danger, in difficulty again?'

I tweeze the olive off the cocktail stick. Warming up again, my leg has begun to throb with pain. 'I'm sorry to say I am.'

'And your mother will help you. You come back to her in the end, no?'

'I don't come running every time, Mother. I do all right by myself. I look after myself.'

'It is true,' she muses. 'I wish that you did want your mother more often, Jonny.' She sighs and there is an extra hiss behind her as the gramophone needle clicks to the end of the 78.

'I'm not sure what you can do to help me.'

'Tell me. Tell me, Jonny.' Then her tail twitches and her hand goes up to her mouth. 'You have not been having your episodes again, have you?'

It strikes me then that she does care for me, after all. She really cares what becomes of me.

I nod. 'Almost the same as before. The dreams, the hallucinations... but something else.'

'But your Doctor... is he not helping you? He was recommended to me, that Doctor. He is the best. I was reliably told that he would be a good thing for you. And so handsome, that Doctor, the definite article in his blue ruffled shirts, his cloak and his velvety coats...'

'He's been giving me these pills to block my dreams and fantasies...'

'This sounds to me like a very good thing indeed, Jonny.'

'But these green pills make me worse, Mother. I fret and go over things. I see things like these spiders... this matriarchy of spiders on a world of cut blue crystal. I've seen velociraptors chasing me and my friends in the tunnels of the London Underground, the rails hissing and sparking with electricity. I've seen these things like giant foetuses, head to toe in venomous suckers, oozing poison, and they live underwater inside something shaped like a giant heart... and objects, dead, inanimate objects... talk to me.'

'Jonny, Jonny...' she hisses. 'You must stop this.'

'I know.'

'It is no good for you. The stress on your hearts...'

I remember my mother taking me as a boy to Harley Street. We saw another, very expensive, doctor. He had wild staring eyes and his speech was nothing but a string of *non sequiturs*. He prodded and poked and went, 'Aha!' and he went, 'Of course!' And he solemnly declared what we already knew: that I had been born with two hearts.

My mother, in her wheelchair, her mermaid's tail covered in a blanket, sighed and told the doctor from Harley Street that she hadn't come all that way and paid all that money to be told the patently obvious. She knew that her little boy was unusual. She knew that he was special. He could talk from birth. He had no navel. He had two hearts. He was a medical mystery, a prodigy, the seventh son of a seventh son.

We abandoned the medics from then on. The word 'doctor' was banned from our house. My mother determined that we would hide our curious selves away from the world. Her fish's tail and my uniqueness. We would keep these aspects quiet. She hired me a private nurse and a schoolteacher. We called him Badger.

'Are you in love?' my mother asks archly.

I shake my head irritably. She always wants to know. Even when I have been in love, or infatuated, I've never let on.

'I'm in some pain,' I admit. She takes in a breath as I show her my leg. The moleskin of my trousers is split. I had to cut it with a knife because my calf muscle has bloated and grown so much. I'm like Oedipus, clomping along with a gammy leg to see Mother. She looks appalled.

'What is this you have done to yourself?'

I can feel something stirring and moving inside the dense muscle and sinew of my leg. It feels as if something is nestling inside there, hidden, secretive, growing. A parasite nurtured within my flesh, burgeoning and waiting to come out. I tell her this, my voice low, tense.

She looks at me, her face etched with concern, her eyes gleaming with fascination and horror. She always knew something unique was going to happen to me. It was in the stars and the charts from the very beginning.

And now things have come home to roost.

Chapter Twenty-Seven
In the Corridors...

'In the Corridors,' said Compassion suddenly, 'it's not as simple as you might expect. You can't simply ride in and chase after people. They loop, they cross over, they furcate and double back. It's a huge cat's cradle of cross connections and strands. You could end up chasing after your own shadow for ever.'

'Great,' muttered Fitz from behind them.

Iris locked the bus on to automatic pilot with a grunt. It was a much better driver than she was, anyway. 'You seem to know an awful lot about it.'

'Yes. I do.'

Fitz tutted. 'Compassion knows about all sorts of things.'

'Well,' said Iris, a good deal more brightly than she felt. 'She's a good person to have around in an emergency.' Actually, she was thinking the exact opposite.

Iris could have wished for more supportive companions as her vessel careered its hectic way through the twisting, silk-ruffled corridor. She hadn't a clue where they were going. Following on after the ladies in the Morris Minor now seemed a rather foolhardy thing to have tried.

Fitz had sat himself down on the *chaise-longue*, as if waiting for her to come up with something, as if he had every faith in her. Which was flattering, if not terribly useful. He had explained to Iris that he came from the 1960s – one of her very favourite eras, naturally – but she couldn't help wishing that he was someone with a bit more nous about him.

Face it, though, she thought glumly: who really would know anything about Corridor mechanics, or about the unique properties of the Enclave, anyway? It was, after all, a very small principality, tucked away from the universe at large, and mostly it operated by its own idiosyncratic rules.

The Doctor might know.

So where was he? She'd rung him up ages ago. And then these two turned up in his stead. He was off having fun somewhere, up to his ears in somebody else's adventure. He just never listened to her these days. Ever since Hyspero and their rather terrifying adventure there; the affair of the Scarlet Empress and their encounters with the golden bears, the ghostly djinn and the alligator man; and then all that business in New York and Paris with the lost manuscripts and assassins running about... and... She sighed heavily.

The truth was, he didn't trust her any more. She had abused her position as one of his oldest and (dare she say it?) most beloved of compatriots; she had ensnared him in her own shady plans once too often. Of course, it was all in order to save her own bacon, but he'd obviously taken the hump. He'd decided that mucking around with Iris Wildthyme was far too risky.

And so he had sent these lackeys – this lazy, shabby boy and this frosty, confrontational girl – in his stead.

He can't be bothered with me any more, thought Iris mournfully.

Then there was an urgent bleeping from the dashboard. Iris wrenched her eyes away from the (admittedly fabulously gorgeous and perplexing) silk of the Corridor's interior and dashed to the controls.

'Life signs,' she said quickly and flicked on her scanner. The picture was rather distorted and crackling.

It showed the tunnel ahead.

A flock of white creatures, wings spread, unencumbered, were heading their way in ragged formation.

'It's those owls,' she informed the others. 'They attacked the mall. Now they've come after us again.'

'Do you know?' said Fitz. 'Knocking around with you is absolutely no different from hanging around with the Doctor.'

Iris cawed with laughter, jumping back into the driving seat. 'Well, we both have fantastic adventures,' she conceded. 'But he's a bit of a wuss, compared to me.'

Compassion nodded to the murky screen. 'They're almost here. Are they dangerous at all?'

Iris flashed her a grin. 'They're appalling. But I'm sure you can deal with them, dear.'

'Has this bus got any weapons?'

'I used to have a harpoon gun.'

'A what?' gasped Fitz, looking nervously at the scanner and the rapidly approaching owls.

'A harpoon gun. Came in very useful. Unfortunately, I had to leave it behind recently, when I had to make a swiftish escape –' she wrestled with the steering wheel, she'd decided to try a U-turn. '– from Skaro. That really was a hair-raising business. Oh, the Daleks can't stick me at all. Right! Evasive manoeuvring! Watch this, kiddiwinks!'

The bus rattled and shook as she pulled it round at full speed. Its top deck swayed and threatened to overbalance at any moment. All around them the insubstantial fabric of the Corridor convulsed as if it had swallowed something nasty and alive. Iris grappled at the wheel and the bus itself protested at her manhandling, but she steeled herself and gradually, painfully, brought it round.

'We're going to break through the side!' cried Compassion. 'You're going to breach it!'

'Exactly,' said Iris, through gritted teeth.

The owls were at the windscreen abruptly, all in one white plunging rush of feathers and claws. They were at all of the windows at once, clattering with talons, butting the glass with the great solid domes of their heads. It was almost as if they thought they could pick the whole thing up between them and bear it away in their claws. As the bus swung round they grappled for purchase and shoved their faces in at every window. Everywhere the passengers could look were their huge, baleful green eyes. All they could hear was the screeching and the keening of owls.

Iris accelerated once more and the tunnel began to bulge outward; the blue walls stretched and started to split.

Compassion shook her head. 'You're doing it. You're breaking through.'

Iris bellowed in triumph as the Corridor punctured and burst outward. The bus trundled on at top speed...

...into another Corridor, tangential, implacable, welling endlessly before them.

'Now, Iris!' shouted Compassion. 'Get past them! We can outrun them in this, surely.'

But the windows down the side of the bus chose that moment to cave in under the pressure of the owls' onslaught.

Suddenly Iris's TARDIS was full of the creatures. Taller, broader, more powerful than men, standing two-footed and proud with their massive wings unfurled and frosty, brilliant white; they were too large for the interior of the bus.

They bore down instantly on the terrified occupants.

The Doctor quite enjoyed free-falling like this.

There was no sense of pressure, nor of immediate impact. No rush, no danger. Just miles and miles of blue. Time to think. Time to sort things out in his head.

Mustn't let himself get depressed.

But he'd managed to lose everyone. The TARDIS, Fitz, Compassion, Belinda, Marn, the whole of the City of Glass. He'd let Blandish and the *Nepotist* attack Valcea and he'd left Daedalus to his own devices and out of his sight. He hadn't even managed to contact Iris. And he'd left the Glass People of Valcea to be almost utterly wiped out.

What will you do for an encore, Doctor?

He had to start pulling this situation round.

He was falling and falling, Alice-like, into the unknown.

And then the tunnel buckled round and he found himself dropping lightly on to what seemed like some kind of floor.

Good. Progress. At least he could get to places under his own steam now. Pretend he had some kind of purchase on events. Standing upright was a good start.

He walked, tugging his tattered clothes straight and thinking things through.

He walked for some hours without seeing anyone at all.

The Corridors led on and on and he hoped they weren't infinite.

This could be how it all ends, he thought gloomily, with me leaving the galaxy on the brink of war and I'm stuck walking for ever in infinite corridors, unable to get out and help anyone. He couldn't imagine a crueller fate. This was like walking every corridor he had ever visited all at once.

Fitz felt himself roughly seized about the shoulders and yanked through the rapid blurring and pounding of wing beats. As he was pulled out into the maelstrom of the Corridor he passed out gladly.

After him came Iris, dragged from her driver's cab and, kicking and screaming, borne aloft between two of the massive predatory birds.

Compassion had secreted herself in the stairwell of the bus. She had crawled over the priceless, rucked-up carpet, and over the smashed, fallen furniture and bric-a-brac and she had managed to hide herself away from the attention of their attackers.

She watched, holding her breath, eyes narrowed, from the gloomy recesses of the stairwell to the upper deck, as the owls swooped out and off with their captives, as simply and as ruthlessly as they had come.

Soon there was not an owl to be seen. Nor a trace of Iris and Fitz. Only destruction throughout the downstairs of the bus, and feathers and shards of glass everywhere.

And the bus was still plunging heedlessly, madly into the new Corridor Iris had rashly opened up.

Compassion slunk back out of her bolt hole and stole down the length of the bucking and bouncing bus.

She took a deep breath and sat down to the controls.

Big Sue and Maddy could only stand by helplessly and watch as the Morris Minor exploded into flames.

They were held shackled in manacles and chains. Surrounded by massive, hulking warrior women with tusks and horns and layers of golden armour. The ground underfoot was shifting and hazardous and the two of them were held upright only with the help of their bindings and the remorseless grip of the creatures who clasped them.

They stood, appalled, in the shadow of the woman's immense craft and stared as Maddy's dirty white car was engulfed in flame.

One of the warrior women was training the end of what looked like a hose pipe on to the vehicle. Once the car had been reduced to cinders and there was no chance at all of the ladies using it to escape, the warrior woman snapped off the nozzle of the hose and the livid flame cut off.

It's a kind of fire engine, Big Sue thought. Except they use it to burn things up. She looked up, gazed around at the hulking brutes who owned this fire engine, at their tusks and dewlapped jowls, their piggy eyes. What powerful women, thought Big Sue, half admiringly.

Maddy was thinking about how her father had bought her the Morris Minor in the last year of his life. How he'd cashed in his Post Office savings account, knowing he'd never get a chance to use the money himself now, and bought her the car as a surprise. 'Now you can go where you want,' he'd said weakly. 'You can go much further afield than your poor old dad ever did.' And that was true enough. Maddy didn't have a clue where she currently was. But she snapped herself out of this reverie. The others needed her. They'd all been captured by these warthog-type women and someone was going to have to do something productive. Speak to them, bargain with them.

The Steigertrudes were led by the largest of their number. She was called Emba and she was every bit as confused as her captives. She swung her massive, grey-tufted head around and stared at the Corridor again and back at her crew members. One minute they had been plain-sailing quite happily through the known and familiar expanse of the Enclave, the next they had arrived here, in this horrid, enclosed space. They had been prevented from continuing with their vital mission. (What mission? Why, their usual, relentless mission.) And Emba had determined that anyone they came across would have to be captured and interrogated. But not burnt. Burning could wait. There were things to be sorted out before any of the Steigertrudes had fun again.

Emba turned her attention to the boy.

He was struggling feebly between the two golden-armoured women who held him. He was quite different from the other two prisoners. He was a native of the Enclave, Emba was sure of that. He had to be. He would know what was happening to them all. Just the way he thrashed and protested in the Steigertrudes' grip alerted Emba to the fact that this boy had something to hide.

'He keeps saying he has to get back to his father, ma'am,' Karlotta blurted out just then.

'My father,' yelled the boy. 'He'll destroy all of you if he finds you've kept me prisoner!'

A smiled touched Emba's fleshy grey lips. She drew them back to reveal her stumpy tusks. 'Oh, yes?'

'He wants me to go back to him.' The boy started struggling again. 'All of this… Everything that's happened is because of me. He wants me back.'

At this, the bigger of the captive women nudged her companion. 'Is that true?' she hissed.

179

Maddy shrugged helplessly. 'I don't know. I never knew he had a father.'

'Tell me, boy,' Emba rumbled massively. 'Who is your father?'

The young man's face glowed with a sudden, almost fanatical zeal. He threw back his head and spat at them: 'Daedalus! That's who! The ruler of all the Enclave, if he has his way. And if you keep me prisoner like this and he –' He convulsed then, with a terrible cry. He twisted once more in pain, his eyes flickered back and he went quiet and still.

'Ian!' the younger woman screamed, seemingly wanting to run to him.

'Get them into the Engine,' growled Emba. 'We've got to keep moving. If the boy is correct, this could put us all in a very interesting position.'

'Captain,' said Garrett abruptly. 'We must stop the bombardment. If we continue, the engines will –'

Blandish jolted out of his trance. Once more every pair of eyes on the bridge of the *Nepotist* was upon him. They were waiting for his next order. He blinked. Where had he been? What had he been thinking of? How long had he been simply staring into space?

What was more – what had been happening all around him? He looked at his handy chronometer. Ninety minutes had elapsed. And then he looked at the viewscreen and gasped.

Almost half the City of Glass had disappeared. What remained was blackened and smashed. Only a few turrets and domes were still a proud translucent silver.

He spoke in a hoarse whisper. 'We've destroyed them.'

'Negative, Captain. We have merely acted upon your orders and degraded their potential and purported arsenal. Rather successfully.'

Blandish flicked a curt glance at his second-in-command. He couldn't believe Garrett was sounding so cold-blooded. 'What about Daedalus? Did we get him?'

'We have no way of knowing that at this point, sir.'

Timon broke in, furiously. 'Of course we don't. And we know he can just transmat at will. He was here and then he was gone! Of course he'll have saved his own neck.' The security officer sneered. 'All we've done is murder the Valceans... and Belinda, too. She was down there. She...' He broke down at this, just as the lift doors swished open and 'Forceps' Felixstoe, the ship's surgeon, came thundering on to the bridge, barking in a broad Norfolk accent, 'Bob, what the hell are you up to? You've bombed the living daylights out of –'

Blandish was about to start defending himself when Garrett's voice cut through them all sharply. He was over at Belinda's communications station, listening to an incoming signal.

'Captain – we're being hailed. This seems urgent.'

'Put it on screen.'

When the viewscreen shimmered and the crew glimpsed what had replaced the image of the ruined city, they all gasped. It was a lizardlike being on a bridge quite like their own. It had a vast head, peering down into the camera, and a massively disproportionate jaw, which bristled with tiny, savage teeth. Its body was spindly and covered with battle armour. It glared down from the viewscreen as if it were looking directly at them.

'I am the Commander of the Sahmbekart fleet you may or may not, in your foul bloodlust, have noticed occupying the space around the City of Valcea. Yours, Captain, is an act of war and aggression against the collected peoples of the Enclave. You may consider yourself as the sole instigator of the hostilities which will now, of necessity, ensue.'

And with that, the creature shut off his channel, to reveal a view of the impressively large Sahmbekart war fleet, ranged like piranhas in the bleak space ahead.

Largest was the commanding vessel: a salamandrine horror lit ghastly orange in honour of war. It was nosing its way purposefully towards the *Nepotist*.

Chapter Twenty-Eight
Never Had Belinda...

Never had Belinda had such a fuss made of her.

When the *Nepotist* had returned triumphant, battered, beleaguered, bruised, to Earthspace from Deepspace, after its original knockabout five-year mission, everyone connected with the Federation had gone mad, extolling and feting Blandish and his doughty crew for forty days and forty nights.

Belinda had missed the whole thing. She was holed up in her cabin with a dose of something alien and nasty and she missed the whole hoo-ha.

'Belinda's in her cabin with a bug,' Blandish, Timon and the others would explain at the various glitzy celebrations to which they were all invited. 'So she won't be joining us.'

When, later, Belinda heard how her absence had been explained, she could picture herself as seen by these Federation dignitaries: not incarcerated, beset by terrible germs, but locked in the lascivious clutches of some pop-eyed beastie with multiple legs she had managed to pick up somewhere *en route*.

And when, some years after the original mission, the *Nepotist* crew had been invited to re-form aboard the beloved and refurbished ship and there was a round of farewell cocktail do's to relaunch their journeying, Belinda was late and missed them all. She was nursing her ailing mother in Motherwell.

She'd only just made it to the *Nepotist* in time for warping back into Deepspace, where the ship was due to maintain and police the discreet barriers between alien factions.

So Belinda, despite all stories to the contrary, was no sort of party girl.

Except now, today, upon arrival on the arid, arcane Ghillighast moon, she was being made to feel as if she were someone special. Being made in the sense of coerced and bullied – but it was pleasurable all the same.

The way these peculiar, coarse-haired creatures addressed her, the way they skittered and bounced and hopped around her, flapping their leathery wings in glee, made her feel something of a legend.

In a rowdy procession that was hastily attempting to assemble itself into something more solemn, Belinda and Marn were led into what the alarming-looking but gracious High Priestess she now knew to be called Meisha called the Chamber of Pesst. It looked like a gloomy old place, decked out with altars and statues and rancid-smelling candles. There was a great big insect thing hewn from black stone, given pride of place.

It all gave Belinda the shivers, but she submitted to the ritualised and now silent hospitality of the batlike people and she even downed in one greedy gulp the goblet of foaming liquor that they offered her. Marn seemed alarmed at this and refused his own.

Some of the High Priestess's robed fellows had begun to chant again, in curiously high, whinnying tones and, from where she was sitting on a stone throne, Belinda was starting to feel a lot like visiting royalty.

Marn was back in his wheelchair but, divorced from the intricate network of energy currents that kept the Glass Men motorised on Valcea, he had to depend on being pushed about the place. This had made him seethe with annoyance.

'We seem to be flavour of the month,' Belinda whispered to him.

'Something is wrong.' He was quite tight-lipped and had been so throughout the ceremony of their arrival.

'Oh, live a little,' she suggested. 'They've given us drink and now they're putting on a little show, look. Singing, dancing.'

The High Priestess Meisha was back before the horrid hunched-over insect statue and she was joining in the incantations with a particular zest and brio.

'We praise Pesst for millennia-old promise and prophecy

fulfilling. We praise Pesst for esteemed visitors into our midst delivering…'

'She's singing to that insect thing,' hissed Belinda.

Marn nodded stoically. 'I told you. They worship lice. They believe the lice in their hides give them insight into the very workings of the Enclave.' He shuddered and Belinda could even see the glass of his flesh ripple with disgust.

'Lady Belinda,' Meisha suddenly called.

Belinda was startled. 'Um. Yes?'

'You will come here to undergo the final stages of our history.'

Marn nudged her. 'Good luck.'

Belinda, as she stood, was woozy all at once from the draught she had recklessly necked, and misgivings began to creep in from all quarters of her mind – scampering and tiptoeing on bats' feet and flicking bats' wings as they came. 'What do you want me to do?'

Meisha seemed surprised that the woman didn't appear to know what her own contribution to the end of Ghillighast history entailed.

'Why, you are to be the Bride of Pesst!'

Iris and Fitz were waking groggily on a different world.

The sky of the world at the end of the Corridor through which the owls had instinctively transported their unconscious prey was a smoky orange and umber. The land was craggy and dry and, this far up into the mountains, untainted by snow. The owls dropped the two of them into the bowl of a dried-up, crusty, congested volcano and then left them.

They flew screeching back into the tumultuous clouds and Iris and Fitz were left to regain their wits in a completely alien locale.

And they were not alone.

When Iris sat up she found that they were surrounded by beings who must once have been human. They were dressed in filthy rags and furs, all of them matted and blackened with blood.

She could only assume that they were the skins of the owls' other prey. These human creatures' hair and beards were overgrown and tangled and they all had a wild look about their eyes. They grunted and shrieked at the appearance of the newcomers.

Here we go, thought Iris irritably and jumped up on to her feet and brushed down her scuffed catsuit. She stretched with a yawn, shook out her mass of honey-coloured hair, fished a compact mirror out of her bag, checked her make-up and produced her slim, rather elegant blaster.

Then she nudged the rumpled Fitz fully awake with the toe of her stacked-heeled boot.

'Get up, Fitz. We've been left on the Planet of the bloody Apes.'

Fitz groaned and feigned losing consciousness again. She took his arm and heaved him up on to his shaking legs.

'Let me die,' he groaned. 'Just let me die.' He seemed shaken by the perilous flight to this place. 'I've never been so scared in all my life.'

Iris tutted, as if being picked up and flung through interstitial barriers and through interdimensional Corridors was all in a day's work for her.

'Where are we now?'

She shrugged. 'Looks to me like somebody's larder.'

'Oh, great.'

Fitz really looked a mess, she thought. She'd had more glamorous male assistants in the past.

'You know, Iris,' he said. 'When I said being with you was the same as being with the Doctor, I was wrong.'

She was distracted, watching a fracas breaking out among what were presumably the alpha males of the pitiful ragged bunch of primitives surrounding them. 'Oh yes, dear?'

'Being with you is like being in a sodding B movie.'

Iris's eyes gleamed. 'Bless your heart.' Then she raised her elegant blaster and fired six rounds of high-intensity energy beam (pink, the deadliest, prettiest setting, she thought) into the broiling sky above them.

'All right, you lot. Listen to Auntie Iris.'

The tattered creatures turned to her suspiciously.

'Now. You pre-verbal, pestilential darlings are going to do exactly what I tell you.'

There were stirrings of revolt from among the group, but most were content to listen and stare at the lady in the catsuit with the thing that shot hot pink.

'Me and my little boyfriend here need transport. Back into the real world, where the real adventure is going on. We need to get away from the owls…'

'Owls! Owls!' moaned the primitives. They looked up at the sky in terror.

'You're just frightening them,' said Fitz.

Iris had noticed the horses tethered up to stakes in the centre of the expanse. 'Hors d'oeuvres, look. They'll come in handy.' Then she addressed the rabble again. 'We're getting out of here. Untie those horses for us!' She let off another pink discharge, more as punctuation than threat. 'Look, does no one around here talk?'

As she said this, a figure hitherto unnoticed stood up from among the filthy crowd. Her hair was just as wild and tangled as the others', but it was bleached and she was wearing ski pants and a ripped anorak.

'Don't listen to her!' the wild-looking woman yelled. 'She caused all of this! It was her who got me into this!'

Iris's eyes widened. 'Nesta!' she cried.

'Kill them!' Nesta yelled. 'Or she'll bring the owls back!'

The ravaged half-human creatures began to advance on Iris and Fitz.

'Iris,' said Fitz. 'You really know how to make pals, don't you?'

It was some time before he realised that the Corridor wasn't forcing hallucinations on him.

The Doctor could almost swear that images and shapes he saw

187

were almost real. They looked architectural, as if the Corridor itself were forming itself into a city around him.

Buildings six storeys high, crenellated domes and roofs and bulging archways, each of them sly with darkened, inscrutable window slits. Out of some broken panes flapped ragged velvet curtains, all of blue.

Clock towers bonged out irrelevant hours and there were steps, hewn from frangible azure stone that promised to lead everywhere and nowhere.

Alleyways and ginnels, walkways, vennels and hidy-holes. It was all quite literal and palpable and all of it blue. No other colour presumed to flaunt itself in the city that crammed itself like *trompe-l'oeil* into the Corridor.

The Doctor progressed in his halting fashion across the rough violet cobbles and came to a slimy jetty and the lip of a rank canal, a lip of dense water, Prussian blue and surging, that pushed up to the stone of the jetty and bared its freezing fangs to nibble and chew.

The water wasn't quite frozen; it moved with a kind of sluggish grace. But it was ornamented with icebergs, the visible crowns of which were as large as whole rooms.

The Doctor discovered a waiting gondola at the jetty, tethered like a bull in a field.

Gingerly he clambered aboard and grasped the pole, mindful of the treacherous blue mildew (like mildew on cheese, he thought) that riddled the stone.

He punted himself surely, strenuously, into the dead centre of the freezing canal. A vista of bridges and bridges and bridges of every possible shape opened up, or rather narrowed in, to his vision. It became clear that he was still in the Corridor after all, and he still had a long way to go.

The gondola glided swiftly under the indigo eaves of bridges and the Doctor found he was shivering, and slightly damp.

Chapter Twenty-Nine
Belinda's Mother . . .

Belinda's mother, ailing for some time, wrapped up in woolly blankets, sipping hot tea splashed with whisky, refusing to let her daughter leave. Telling her if she left today, she might miss the moment her mother died and how ever would she live with herself after that?

Belinda in a quandary, fetching and carrying for her mother in Scotland. Knowing that her crew were assembling once more elsewhere, and soon the day would come when they would hightail it again for the deepest recesses of space and danger. All the while her wrist communicator beeped and vibrated against her pale skin and, as she lugged shopping bags home on the bus, she tried to ignore it. Her lover, Timon, too, would be up on the *Nepotist*, running final checks on the weaponry. Lovingly restoring the old girl. And Blandish would be at the helm again, reassuming the mantle of supreme commander and relishing the idea of revisiting his glory years. All their glory years.

Home the same as ever. The flat above the wet-fish shop her parents had run – for centuries, it seemed like. The whole building permeated by the smell, the back yard full of cats and the lopped-off ends and goggling heads. The scales that stuck everywhere, even upstairs in the flat, in the carpets, the furniture, the sheets and even in her mother's limp and washed-out hair. Her mother never even saw her shop now, wedged as she was into her chair. She left the mongers she employed downstairs to carry out the ancient business.

How Belinda despised that fish shop. She always had. She had run away to space in the first place just to avoid having to take it all over...

And now Belinda, stuck at home in Motherwell, with space

exploration just a dream again. As it had been when she was a girl – before the first time she escaped.

It was while she was trapped here, gazing longingly at the night sky once her mother was asleep, that she remembered her dreadful fear of sea fish.

It was while she watched the small, lightweight crafts busying about in the peachy, indigo night sky over Scotland, that it all came back to her, peremptorily, bafflingly. The thought that, at one time, any kind of fish, anything tentacled or scaled that could not breathe air, scared the living daylights out of her.

It was as if she were experiencing some curious moment of premonition. Her skin felt clammy and cold. She was Ophelia, dredged underwater, fronds and netting pulling her down. She could feel the fins and scales of fellow fish brushing eagerly past her – and she could hardly breathe at those cool touches.

Was it because she felt as if here, hidden away with her ailing mother, she was drowning? A communications expert out of touch with the world? A woman who had visited… oh, so many worlds and satellites in the past barely leaving the street she had been born in? Was it this claustrophobia that reactivated her fear of anything aquatic?

Belinda determined that it was.

Each night as she sat tiredly, rubbing her eyes and watching the stars, Belinda felt herself become even more fishlike. Fish-blind, cold-skinned, loveless, limbless, out of her element. And so busy, tending to that mardy and mawkish old dear downstairs. So busy she felt she had to grow tentacles to accomplish everything she must.

The rising gorge of her panic: *I am turning into a squid! If I stay here I shall become, irrevocably, a squid-woman!* It was this mounting alarm that made her sense of self-preservation kick back in. She found she could ignore those last-minute recall signals to the *Nepotist* no longer.

And she signed herself back aboard. She had her mother put away. She sold the business and sacked her mother's staff of mongers. And she left Scotland behind for ever. And, soon enough, she found herself aboard the *Nepotist* once more.

Chapter Thirty
After Six Years of Treaties...

'After six years of treaties and meetings and creeping around the policies and foibles of ministers from every planet in our ken.' Blandish was furious.

'After negotiations and barterings and beseechings! After helping out with local troubles and providing the strong arm of Federation law in distant outposts and armpits of the universe! This is what it comes down to!'

He flung out one fist and pointed savagely to the viewscreen behind him, on which the vicious pointed crafts of the hostile Sahmbekart fleet were arrayed.

'All-out war! And because of one mistake – one lousy mistake – and we're not even sure what caused that yet! How were we to know we were so close to Sahmbekart space? How were we to know what the Sahmbekart even were? *No one* knows what they are!'

Garrett was at his shoulder and he put in, mildly, 'Captain, perhaps you ought to moderate your speech for the official record.'

Blandish was stung. 'I'll say what I like, mister. And I'm not forgetting your part in inflaming this whole affair.'

Blandish turned to face the camera, which was still recording his message for his Federation superiors. 'In short, members of the Federation of planets, we have become somewhat ineluctably embroiled in a situation which has blown up in our faces.

'We appear to have... instigated a war with the combined races of the Enclave. A pocket galaxy of which we had no previous knowledge whatsoever. The Captain and crew of the *Nepotist* can by no means be held responsible, now or in posterity, for what ensues.'

He stopped and coughed and adjusted his tunic. He nodded. 'Send that as it is, Mr Garrett. Oh, you might edit out your small aside and my reply if you fancy yourself working for the Federation ever again.'

The captain marched smartly back to his command chair.

'Very good, sir,' said Garrett and took the portable camera that one of the ensigns had been training on Blandish.

As soon as Garrett was sure that no one was looking, he wiped the message surreptitiously and stowed the device away.

By then there was something else to distract them all on the bridge of the *Nepotist* – besides the captain's bristling ire and the war fleet on the screen.

With a trumpeting bellow of scorn, Daedalus had manifested himself once more in their midst.

He flexed his talons and said, 'Now, who's been rather rash, then?'

The interior of the huge engine, or tank, or whatever the burly, armoured women chose to call, in their own parlance, a vehicle that ran on twenty-three wheels armed with thrusting spikes – was very much smaller than either Big Sue or Maddy expected.

Once they were installed and bound in a corner of the greasy, sweltering vessel and the rest of the warrior women had clambered their ungainly way in through the aperture in the roof, there was very little space to spare.

'I can feel myself suffocating,' said Big Sue, who had stopped using the buses recently because of her claustrophobia. As soon as she had glimpsed the interior of the Steigertrude craft her heart had quailed.

'Deep breaths,' Maddy told her, her thoughts elsewhere. She was gazing with interest at the array of rather clunky devices operated by the warrior women, by which the engine seemed to be guided.

Soon, under the gruff commands of the leader, Emba – uttered with such authority that her wattles shook gravely as she gave them – the engine started to wend its formidable way down the corridor, stamping and snorting and crushing the blackened remains of Maddy's Morris Minor under its metal tyres.

Then they picked up speed, and the gargantuan women worked busily at the controls, pressing everything that lit up gold and whizzing every dial round as far as it would go.

Working in such a constrained space, they were all virtually sitting on top of one another, but they seemed to have perfected a curious system of working, whereby they reached over and around each other to get to the relevant controls, muttering a ritualised series of excuse-mes and thank-yous as they got on with their somewhat humdrum duties.

It was strange to see such creatures behaving with such dedicated and seemingly natural courtesy, Maddy thought. Despite everything else, and being scared witless, she was fascinated by her first glimpse of an alien species. Second glimpse, really, if you counted the owls, but she was trying to forget those things, and what they had done to poor Nesta.

For the moment the ladies had been deprived of the company of Ian. This still gave Maddy some cause for concern. She wanted to know what the leader, Emba, found so fascinating about her son, and what bargaining chip he obviously represented in her own scheme of things. Where were they?

A few moments ago Emba had been standing in what appeared to be her customary place, in the centre of the tiny control room, with the boy tucked under one massive, protective arm. But now both were gone.

Maddy looked about wildly and strained at her bindings.

Big Sue nudged her and shook her head. 'Hairpins,' she whispered. 'That's what we need. And, luckily, my wig is stuffed to the gills with them. There are more hairpins keeping me together than we'll ever need. Help me get them out.'

As Maddy leaned in to extricate the possible means of their escape, one by one, with shaking fingers, the screen of every warrior was showing the whorling blue of the Corridor ahead.

But still the engine trundled on, convinced of its ultimate confrontation with whoever lay at the heart of this venture.

Emba had secreted Ian off to a separate chamber, two rooms above the central one.

It was darker here and, as Ian blinked and looked about, he could see it was a kind of treasure trove. There were caskets and trunks brimming with jewellery and statuettes. They shimmered in the meagre light. Against the walls rested pictures in flaking golden frames, scabbed with mould. Books and manuscripts were heaped and rolled in corners and maps were strewn with criminal abandon.

'Where is this?' he asked.

'Somewhere quiet to talk,' said Emba. 'My own private storehouse.'

'For treasures and artworks?' Ian tutted and smiled, looking suddenly much older than his years. 'You surprise me, Emba. Isn't this the very opposite of what a Steigertrude commander is supposed to do with her life and resources?'

'What would you know about it?' she snapped, so hard that her wide, vicious teeth clashed loudly and her tusks gleamed horridly at him.

'I know enough. I know that this is a Steigertrude fire engine and that your race is pledged to trawl the Enclave in perpetuity burning up artworks of any kind. You're known for it. Art criminals. Everyone knows that about the Steigertrudes. Civilised worlds wait in fear of your visitations to galleries and libraries and installations. You're the scourge of the more cultivated regions of the galaxy.'

Emba tossed her head. 'Huh.' Then she rounded on the boy again. 'For an Earthling, a mere stripling, you seem to know an awful lot about us.'

'As you've guessed, I'm nothing of the sort.'

Emba gave a conspiratorial and quite ghastly grin. 'So long as you're not one of those children who, thinking they are some sort of "Homo superior", jaunt about the place in their one-piece spacesuits and go righting wrongs for the Federation.'

Ian laughed. 'No fear, there. My name is Icarus.'

'And do you approve, Icarus, of my little hoard?'

'I don't understand why you have all of this. Steigertrudes pride themselves on their militant philistinism.'

'Call me unique. Not even my crew realise what I have accrued. From every burning accomplished, I have rescued one item. What you see here are the salvaged remains of a thousand and one terrible missions.'

'Well done. What do you intend doing with it all?'

Emba licked her lips. 'Taking it to your father. I hear Daedalus often has his head turned by such trinkets.'

'I've heard the same.' Ian's eyes gleamed. 'So you will return me to him?'

'If you can prove to me you are who you say you are.'

Ian grinned at this. 'I can now. Now that my growing pains have ceased.' With that he began to shuck off the sweater and the shirt Iris had provided him with.

Emba watched in fascination as he revealed his slim, boyish torso and, as he turned, he demonstrated his new wings.

They were bright blue and sticky with newness as they flexed and tested themselves out, the muscles twitching, longing to flex the feathers bristling, parting themselves.

'Is this proof enough?'

After several hours the Doctor had picked up what he liked to think of as an expert rhythm and he was punting competently and quite contentedly, through the canals. Then something made him look up and stare at the next humpback bridge in particular.

On it a large red double-decker bus was coming to a halt.

The Doctor had never been so pleased to see it in all his life.

'It's Iris!' he cried delightedly.

He clambered unsteadily to his feet and yelled, 'Iris! I'm here!

I'm so pleased to see you… You've no idea!'

But when the familiar hydraulic doors of Iris's vessel slipped open it wasn't Iris who stepped out on to the bridge and looked over the side to the Doctor.

It wasn't Iris standing there with a gun.

It was Compassion.

'How does it feel, Captain?' Daedalus whispered, gurgling in pleasure. 'How does it feel to be the cause of this oncoming storm?'

'How do you think it feels?'

'Pretty bad, I would have thought.' Daedalus reared and started to pace through the brightly lit chamber of the *Nepotist* bridge.

Ensigns picked up their clipboards and pens and scattered as his swaying bulk approached them, but they were to him as were his own vermin that scampered through the folds of his ornate robes.

'I should be very cross with you, Captain. You have virtually destroyed my home and all of my adopted people. You have laid waste to the small fragment of a world I could call my own. And as for the Glass Men themselves, why, I think we could just about call that genocide.'

Garrett stepped forward. 'Your people? You dare to call them *your* people? You are a parasite. You move from world to world, adopting new races to patronise and subordinate… You couldn't have cared less for the Valceans, and you were just the same on my world, when –'

'Enough, Garrett,' snapped Blandish. 'Enough.' He turned back to the huge Daedalus, who stood, amused at their bickering and outbursts, almost bent double under the low ceiling of the bridge. 'Look. We've got a situation, Daedalus. And, whether I am to blame or you are, it doesn't matter now, least of all to that fleet out there. If we don't get on with dealing with those lizard things and get some backup from the Federation, then we're all finished, right?'

'Agreed.' Daedalus smiled. 'So what do you want to do?'

'I want you to leave us alone and stop interfering. I want you to go back to your world and let us try to sort this out.'

'Captain…' Daedalus chuckled and spread his massive hands, his monstrous nails glinting in the antiseptic light. 'You only had to ask.' He started to fade out of existence. 'Good luck with the Sahmbekarts. You think I'm bad. The Sahmbekarts are the wickedest bastards the Enclave has to offer.'

Blandish ignored him, and swung round to address the bridge crew. He wanted cloaking devices, force-shields, full weapons alert and damn the expense; he wanted backup from the Federation. He wanted full speed ahead and avast, me hearties. In short, with the prospect of a battle before him, Captain Robert B. Blandish was cheering up.

Emba led Ian/Icarus back into the hurly-burly of the control room of the Steigertrude tank and everybody gasped.

He stood in the middle with his wings stretched to their fullest extent and it was already so crowded in there that his perfect sapphire wing tips brushed each of the warriors in turn. He beamed with pride.

Maddy and Big Sue dropped the hairpins with which they were agitating the archaic locks and bolts of their shackles and gasped too.

'Ian…!'

Big Sue coughed. 'I knew there was something about him.'

Ian lowered his wings slightly and stood before his adoptive mother as if in apology. 'I have a destiny, Mother. There is something I have to do.'

Maddy had tears in her eyes. 'I think I understand.'

'You took care of me for a while, and I'll always be grateful for that. But I have my father waiting for me. My father granted me these wings. He needs me.'

There was something going on among the Steigertrude warriors at this point. Their attention was taken away from the boy and his mother and they were intent on their viewscreens. Emba rushed to see what they had discovered.

The scene outside was changing. Something was resolving and materialising out of the apparently endless Corridor blue.

'But who took you away from your father, Ian?' Maddy asked. 'What happened to you?'

'I was kidnapped,' he said bitterly. 'As a fledgling. I was taken by a race my father has pledged to destroy. A race of vermin so powerful even he himself is afraid of them. They are the Ghillighast. And I am to be instrumental in their destruction.'

'Destruction?' Maddy was confused. 'But Ian, you can't...'

Emba roared out over them all, 'We have arrived! We have found our way out of the chaos! We have arrived on Valcea!'

Everyone was craning to see the City of Glass on the screens.

When it loomed up, however, it was a scene of almost utter desolation.

Ian howled and thrashed his wings. 'No! Father! It can't be true!'

With the ragged semihuman horde in the bowl of the volcano acting in one accord under the deranged instructions of Nesta, Iris had no option but to act quickly.

She disliked weapons almost as much as the Doctor did, but it seemed that, during every escapade in which she found herself embroiled, they came in extremely handy.

As the pitiful primitive wretches advanced murderously on her and the horrified Fitz, Iris coolly levelled her blaster and winged Nesta, the cause and linchpin of this situation.

Nesta let out a shrill bleat of rage and collapsed backward on the calcified rock. Her hirsute minions paused in their rampage and looked startled at this.

Nesta gritted her teeth and spat, 'Don't look at me! Get them! Get that skinny bitch in the PVC!'

The shaggy prisoners started in on Fitz and Iris again. Fitz swore.

'I can't shoot them all,' said Iris quickly. 'I'd never be able to live with myself.'

'It's them or us,' hissed Fitz, backing away with her. 'Look at them. They're barely human. What have they got to look forward to in life? Being eaten to death by gigantic owls!'

'And the most enlightened of their number is poor old Nesta!' agreed Iris, shaking her head.

'Shooting them would be a mercy,' Fitz grumbled. Someone threw a rock – a hunk of magma – and struck him in the chest. He staggered and Iris grasped him.

'Quickly,' she said, 'those horses. Get the two least decrepit ones and untie them. Can you ride?'

'No.'

'Bugger it. Do it anyway.' She brandished her blaster. 'I'll hold this lot.' With that she started firing off a series of deft pink reports, which angered the primitives only further. Nesta was up on her feet again, bellowing.

'You let the owls carry me off, you cow!'

'What could I do, Nesta?' Iris yelled back. 'And look, I came after you! I'm rescuing you!'

'Don't give me that!'

Some of the closest of the rabble were within touching distance of Iris now. Their overgrown nails, claws almost, raked the air to get at her.

She bit her lip and fired on them. Two hit the ground and the rest surged over them, trampling their scabrous bodies in the orange dirt.

'Fitz, hurry!' Iris screamed. 'Or it's going to be a massacre!'

Fitz was pulling at the ropes that tethered the mangy-looking horses. The creatures were nervous and protesting – he had to watch out where they were kicking. He chose two that seemed strongest and fittest though they certainly weren't Earth horses.

They were stringier and more lithe and they were covered in glittering purple scales on which he rubbed his hands raw trying to pacify them.

At last the ropes were untied and he managed to haul himself with some alacrity on to the back of one, clinging on to the other's greasy rein.

'Iris! I've got them!'

He dug into the creature's flanks with his heel and the thing spurred into action. He was much higher up than he'd thought and he clung to its shaggy mane for some kind of support.

'Not before time, lover boy,' said Iris grimly and, firing one last blast at the horde, took possession of her own horse and mounted it in one swift leap.

'Jesus,' said Fitz admiringly. 'That must have taken some practice.'

Iris holstered her blaster in her boot with a smile. 'Tell me about it, sweetheart.' Then she slapped her mount's hide hard. 'Come on! There's a track leading to the side –'

An all-too-familiar keening and screeching filled the sulphurous air. It echoed around the interior of the mountain in a wild spiral, as the owls circled above, dropping lower and lower into the dusty bowl.

The primitives were cowering and moaning in terror.

Iris was swearing profusely.

'It's distracting them, anyway,' Fitz shouted. 'Show me the exit. While they're busy we can…'

But Iris was already riding off, leading the way.

With some effort Fitz got his own horse to follow, as the first of the owls ravenously swooped into the volcano's heart.

Chapter Thirty-One
Before She Knew It...

Before she knew it, all the ceremonies pertaining to her own betrothing to the great god of the Ghillighast, Pesst, were over and done with.

Belinda didn't think she'd come out of it that badly, considering.

The Ghillighast had danced around her for a while, waving incense and making her drink more of that rather intoxicating and not unpleasant brew. Then they had garlanded her in exotic-smelling local blooms and there had been some more singing.

Then a whole group of Ghillighast wheeled in what looked like an ancient carriage clock, on metal wheels no less, and it sat in the centre of the chamber, the size of a small cow. A sacred clock. The room fell silent as it counted down the last few seconds of something or other.

It turned out to be the last few seconds of the Ghillighast millennium.

'More singing! More dancing!' cried Belinda, somewhat drunkenly, in her new capacity as goddess.

Even given this rank, they still shushed her as the clock's hands met at what looked like midnight and it chimed in the beginning of a new era.

The clock face opened like a tiny door and one hundred golden clockwork bats tottered out. They sang in shrill, prerecorded voices, of all the glories to come for the Ghillighast race.

Then they took to the murky air, on tissue-thin wings of gold leaf, fluttering about the head of each entranced observer.

Suddenly the Ghillighast were hugging each other and the Priestess Meisha came to kiss both Belinda and Marn on the lips. Marn gagged and Belinda tried her hardest to be polite.

When there was some measure of order again, Meisha said, in jubilant tones, 'And so begins the new era for the Ghillighast. We are free at last of predetermined history… and we have a new queen for Pesst.' She turned grandly to Belinda, 'And what would you have us do to mark this new beginning, Your Majesty?'

Belinda glowed pink. 'More dancing!' she repeated. 'More singing!'

'No!' said Marn, feeling more enthusiastic than he had for ages. The import of the recent ceremony and the dispersed miniature golden bats had suddenly hit him and he realised what it meant for the Ghillighast to be free of their history and detached from their usual, almost supernatural insight.

It meant that they were eminently pliable.

'Wait,' he said, when he was sure that every pair of glistening eyes was upon him. 'We have more vital things to accomplish here than merely celebrating the new age.'

'Yes, Lord Marn?' asked Meisha, still according the Glass Man due respect, even though Belinda was the important one.

Simaf, her suspicious aide-de-camp, was at her side instantly, whispering, 'I wouldn't trust the Glass Man, madam. He is still what he is. He is still a Valcean, even in the new era…'

'Nonsense, Simaf!' chortled Meisha. 'In this millennium, there are none of the old antagonisms! All is swept away! What you say is tantamount to blasphemy!'

Marn took his advantage. 'We must mark this turning of the celestial gyres by going to Valcea. We must use the Corridors and go to my homeworld.'

'Why?' scoffed Simaf. 'So your precious brethren can wipe us out entirely? So you can lead us into a trap?'

'Simaf,' warned Meisha.

Marn was shaking his head. 'No. Valcea has been almost totally rendered asunder by the machinations of our foolish leader, Daedalus.'

The chamber rang with the loathed name. Each of the presiding Ghillighast hissed and spat the word.

'He has brought disaster down on my people – and, as perhaps the last one in a position to fetch help, I beseech you all to come with Belinda and me to join forces with the Glass Men and bring Daedalus to his knees!'

The Ghillighast roared their approval at this, drowning out entirely whatever view their betters might have on this matter. Marn grinned wolfishly.

'I have your agreement, madam?' he asked Meisha.

'We must consult our Queen Belinda.'

Belinda was staring at them blankly. 'Hmm?'

Marn glared at her. 'Tell them, Belinda. Tell them we have to go back to Valcea.'

She wrinkled her nose. 'Oh, not there again.'

Marn couldn't believe it. 'It's your only chance of seeing your ship again, your people!'

She shrugged. 'It was a rubbish job anyway.'

Marn's voice went steely. 'Belinda…'

'Oh, very well, then,' she conceded, giving a surprisingly effective regal wave.

The Ghillighast shouted their approval again and Meisha cried, 'Fetch the dogs and the sleds! We prepare for action immediately, on this the very cusp of our brilliant new age!' She swung round on Marn. 'And you can find this Corridor that you say will deliver us to Valcea?'

'I can indeed, ma'am.'

Meisha was exhilarated at the idea of at last bringing the age-old antagonisms straight to the home of the Valceans. She was less forgetful of the past than she was outwardly feigning. 'Then we embark within the hour!'

She hurried off to make arrangements for the dogs and sleds.

'Well, thanks a lot, Marn,' grunted Belinda. She hefted the flagon of brimming liquor. 'I might as well finish this off if we're going out in that bloody cold again.'

Marn said, 'You want to see Timon again, don't you?'

'Timon!' sighed Belinda. She had almost forgotten her lover. Her eyes grew misty and she nodded and gradually sank into a doze as the preparations went on around her.

When Belinda woke, she and Marn and all of the Ghillighast were in transit, across shining, luminous fields of ice, on robust wooden sleds pulled by huskies.

As the small boat glided directly under the bridge he reached up and clasped the stone and tried to heave himself up on to it. He wasn't terribly successful and depended on Compassion grasping his hands as his own grappled for purchase. 'Thanks.'

He grinned and steadied himself.

Compassion stared coolly at the dishevelled Time Lord. She slipped her gun away.

The Doctor tried to start again. Compassion's appraising silences could be disconcerting and he found himself covering them up with bluster. She wasn't the most sociable of companions. He thought she may be rather shy.

'Well, I'm certainly glad to see you,' he said. 'And the trusty old bus! The number twenty-two to Putney Common! When did you meet up with Iris, then? She's a card, isn't she?' He faltered. 'Where *is* Iris by the way?'

'She's dead,' said Compassion. 'She was taken off screaming by some giant owls. The same thing happened to Fitz. They were probably eaten.'

The Doctor's face fell. 'What happened? I mean...' He took a hesitant step. 'They can't be dead! Iris couldn't... How did you escape?'

'I hid on the bus. They overlooked me.'

The Doctor became businesslike. 'We're going after these owl things. We're going to find out what's happened.'

'I wouldn't bother,' said Compassion.

'You certainly *don't* seem very bothered.'

'There isn't any point,' said Compassion. 'As far as I can see, what we should do is find our own TARDIS again. Iris had taken us off after some women and a boy, looking for these civilians who had gone off and lost themselves in the Corridors. It was a very foolhardy plan. We should find the TARDIS and leave.'

The Doctor was depressed by her attitude. 'Where did you leave the TARDIS?' And then he interrupted himself with, 'And how did you operate her?'

'I don't know.'

And what's more, he thought, how did you even find me here?

Wasn't it a tad convenient that she should just swan out of the ether in a red double-decker? He found he was staring at her earpiece again, which glinted in the blue twilight of the Corridor. He knew that thing put her in touch with all sorts of unfathomable frequencies. But then perhaps the TARDIS had alerted her, tuning itself to the Doctor's biorhythms in the Corridors, good and trusty, ever-vigilant companion that it was?

Even if not, he decided perhaps he should tinker with that contraption of hers, so it was the TARDIS's own signals that had dominance over any others she might be quietly picking up. A kind of friendly filter. If she was to travel with him, he wanted to be sure she was on his side. And with the TARDIS's help, he was sure she could become an all-round better person and happier in herself.

Compassion was bold before his scrutiny. She turned and led the way back on board Iris's bus.

It seemed that everyone was converging on Valcea.

Or what remained of Valcea. The crust of land that was only, really, part of a world, that ringed the ruined City of Glass.

A new night was coming down on the Valcean remains and with it came the promise of war.

The *Nepotist* charged its engines and its weaponry, preparing to engage with the Sahmbekart fleet that bristled and shone with malevolence all around it in the murky atmosphere of the Enclave.

In the Corridors, stretching and warping and radiating out from the City of Glass, where ten thousand sparking forms lay dead and dying, forces were gathering to converge on this final battleground, from which would spring conflict that Daedalus was sure would spread throughout galaxies that even in their outermost quadrants dwarfed the confines of the Enclave.

Daedalus sat in his wrecked and shattered stateroom and concentrated on his further plans. With only a few surviving favourite Valceans surrounding him, he drew tighter the web that would urge the denouement on.

He sent Corridors deeper, deeper into the galaxy foreign to him, lashing them like tripwires, like grappling hooks, into the paths of unwary races on the other side, knowing how intrigued, how curious they would grow.

And how, slowly but surely, they would find themselves drawn into his web.

He sent them out, unfolding them across space like invitations; through time, too, to the locations he had memorised from the journals and diaries of a traveller he had once known.

Corridors extended to far-flung worlds with names like Telosa, Skaro, Wertherkind, Sonturak. And it was Daedalus, not the *Nepotist*, who alerted the Federation to the possibility of war on their doorstep.

Fitz found his admiration for this woman growing, even in the midst of their flight from the heart of the volcano and the ransacking owls.

With the shrieks of the ragged primitives – as they were seized up and eaten – ringing in his ears, he kept his mind on pursuing Iris and her horse up the perilous track to the lip of the volcano.

It took every ounce of his energy to get his own mount to follow in the right direction. He watched Iris's back and her golden hair bouncing on her shoulders and tried not to think of the carnage back in the dusty arena they had left.

But what a woman. What a fantastic bird.

He wondered, when all of this was over, what she'd say if he... well, not made a move exactly... but suggested that he... well, not swap allegiances exactly... but asked if he could join her on her bus... off into whatever startling adventure she was off to next. And then, as time went by, she might think more fondly of him... who knows? She might already think he was sexy. He caught himself thinking such lecherous things, and grinned to himself even as he felt himself choke up. Perhaps the TARDIS hadn't done such a bad job of putting him back together.

Up they came to the very lip of the volcano, the apex of the dead mountain and they could see the sterile landscape stretched out before them for hundreds of craggy miles around. Geysers blew and glaciers crept in the crotches of mountain ranges in every direction.

The pathway led back down the sheer side of the mountain and Fitz felt his bile rise and his head whirl at the sight of the gradient they now had to deal with.

'Depressing, isn't it?' beamed Iris cheerfully. For a second he was sure she was giving him the glad eye.

'I don't think I'll make it,' he said.

'Yes you will, my sexy little fella. Come on!'

Iris plunged her horse down into the hazardous decline.

Fitz's heart jumped several beats at her epithet and then he persuaded himself, just as swiftly, that she talked to him like that only to get him to do exactly what she wanted.

Now they were on the other side, they could hear nothing of the owls or the pathetic remnants of human beings they had left behind. Fitz was glad to block them out of his thoughts and stop himself from feeling guilty.

They thundered down the blackened mountainside and his brains were becoming addled, he was sure; they were turning into mincemeat, into scrambled eggs, by the jogging and thudding and the pounding of hooves on diamond-hard magma.

Could he leave the Doctor's company for this woman?

What would the Doctor say?

He couldn't imagine never seeing the Doctor again. There was so much they hadn't said and done, and since Sam left…

He'd never said goodbye to her, either.

If he left the Doctor now… And who was to say he hadn't already? He felt a nasty pang, somewhere in his gut, and suddenly he could see the Doctor's face before him and he remembered how he had laughed when Sam told the story of her erstwhile infatuation with the Time Lord.

But Fitz could see how it might work. All that power and intelligence, that charming intensity… Even if he was raving mad.

Fitz swallowed hard. He was the one who was raving mad. He was in the midst of the most ridiculous danger, horse-riding down a mountainside, probably about to die and, in the final few minutes of his life, what was passing through his mind? Not the greatest, most fulfilling moments in this life – but a consideration of his chances of getting laid by Iris… and even of getting laid by the Doctor. What was it about Time Lords? What had really happened to his poor old head?

He tried to keep his mind on the horse-riding.

Iris shouted back at him, hair streaming in the smoky air: 'There's some kind of rock formation coming up. Look! The ground flattens out, but we'll be in a kind of…'

Maze. The word was maze.

As soon as they got themselves, breathless but safe, to a less steep incline they were wedged into walls of filthy, sooty rock, a narrow passageway that only just let them and their horses through.

It was a labyrinth of petrified lava and they were rattling quite blithely into it, losing themselves in its obscurity.

And then there was something worse to add to Fitz's growing list of grievances.

They hadn't left the owls behind after all.

Their shrieking cries heralded them as they flew straight over the mouth of the volcano, and came whistling down out of nowhere, to pick the fugitives out of their maze.

'Iris!' yelled Fitz. 'They're coming after us!'

Iris just spurred on her horse ever harder and led the way left, right, left, left, right again, plunging ever deeper into the heart of the maze.

And Fitz just had to follow, watching the froth on the lips of his exhausted horse fleck pink with exertion.

The *Nepotist*, it turned out, had actually used most of its power reserves in the demolition job it had unleashed on the City of Glass. So when it came to dealing with the Sahmbekarts the best it could do was muster a force-shield and sit waiting for the worst.

Tai-Nur, the ship's engineer, shouted out through the intercom, above the horrendous noise of the engines, that he was giving the best power he could. He couldn't give the captain any better.

Blandish threw himself back into his command chair and rapidly weighed up his options. He glared irritably at Garrett, who seemed fairly unperturbed, as ever, by their predicament. But this was worse than anything they had faced in any of their missions. Five years exploring the furthermost reaches of the galaxy and several subsequent years policing the dangerous barriers between empires – none of it compared to this.

The *Nepotist* was a sitting duck and there was little they could do to defend themselves.

Where was the Federation backup? They hadn't even made contact yet. They couldn't be that far away, could they?

But this was a strange and unknown space.

The presence of these Corridors, etched in mesmerising blue on the viewscreen, shifted the usual perceptions of time and space into unforeseen dimensions. Really, none of them knew what they were dealing with yet.

But the Federation should have been in contact by now.

'Garrett?' In desperation Blandish turned to his second-in-command. 'What can we do?'

The other members of the bridge crew looked askance. Never had they seen their Captain without a plan or a scheme up his sleeve.

On the viewscreen, the vast and demoniac Sahmbekart mother ship loomed up.

Then it fired off its opening salvo.

Impact was virtually instantaneous and, even with the toughest, least penetrable shields up, the *Nepotist* rocked in its orbit, sending everyone aboard flying across the room.

Blandish leapt to his feet. 'Garrett!' he shouted at the impassive science officer.

There was a second blast then from the Sahmbekarts and the *Nepotist* lurched again, more violently.

Tai-Nur's voice crackled over the comm. 'The shields are going, Captain... we...'

Garrett marched straight up to the command chair.

'It's quite easy. We use the *Nepotist* itself. We take ourselves out of the firing line and we do the most damage we can.'

'How?' Blandish whispered. 'How do we do that?'

Garrett was inhumanly cool. 'We switch off our shields. And then, quite simply, we crash through the Corridors. We take the whole lot with us. And then, finally, we crash-land on Valcea.'

The bridge crew were silent at his words, until the ship was hit again, and the last tatters of their force-shield were stripped off them like tin foil and the Sahmbekart moved in easily, so easily, for the kill.

Chapter Thirty-Two
Even Aboard the Bus...

Even aboard the bus it wasn't plain sailing.

The Doctor drove on through the Corridor and gradually the buildings pressing in around him grew larger and more ornate.

They lost sight of the blue canal and the landscape was taking on a different aspect – a mismatched one.

It was a weird *mélange* of alien architectures, as if these were buildings snatched at random from all times and places and reassembled in haste to line the bus's route in sinister fashion.

The Doctor drove on relentlessly, refusing to be deterred from the route he had determined would lead him back to Valcea.

He drove with an air of mock cheeriness which clearly irritated Compassion, who was watching him narrowly from the gangway. He could feel her presence at his back and wished she would make more small talk. But no. She wasn't that kind of girl, he knew.

He fumbled through the loose cassette tapes in Iris's glove compartment. 'She usually has quite a selection. Shall we have some Shirley Bassey? Abba?'

'No,' said Compassion.

'Dusty Springfield!' the Doctor cried, and jammed the tape into the deck. As Dusty swept into 'I Just Don't Know What To Do With Myself,' he went on, ignoring his companion's simmering silence: 'When I was exiled on earth in the 1970s, I met Dusty Springfield once, you know. She was hired – incredible though it might sound – privately by UNIT to go undercover in Memphis. There'd been abductions and whatnot. Anyway, I was called in and met her. She'd been kidnapped herself by then and I had to free the poor girl. She was lovely. Quite charming.'

He was shouting over the rattle of the engine, glancing over his shoulder now and then and tossing his hair out of his eyes.

Suddenly Compassion lost all patience with him.

'Doctor, you're babbling at me.'

His face fell. 'I am?'

'It happens when you get nervous or overexcited. It's very distracting.'

He blushed. 'Babbling? No one else has ever complained,' he lied.

'You ramble on about nothing when there are more important things to discuss.'

'Ah.' He grinned and tapped his nose. 'I don't think you've cottoned on yet to the incredibly sophisticated way in which I operate.'

'Yes I have. It's wasteful and ostentatious.'

'Right.' With a sudden burst of energy he pulled the bus into an emergency stop, switched off the music and jumped out of the cab.

'You, madam, are stepping out of line. You've not said a decent word to me yet since you... um, rescued me. In fact, I'd go so far as to say you rarely have a decent word to say to anyone at all!'

Compassion tutted. 'I'd agree with that.'

'But that's awful!' He grabbed her elbows and found himself shrugged off. 'You have to give people more time. Look at Fitz... He's really not Kode, you know. He's a new man – well, his old self, I suppose.' He sighed. 'If you tried a little harder, I'm sure you'd see he's all right, actually... he's a good man...'

'He's dead anyway. I told you. And that woman. Iris.'

The Doctor shook his head firmly. 'I don't believe it.' He smiled. 'See? I've got intrinsic faith in my friends.'

'Then you, Doctor,' said Compassion, 'are a fool.'

He paused, fixing her with a cold glance that she found she couldn't shake.

Very slowly he inclined his head towards hers, until their noses were only an inch or so apart.

'I would suggest, Compassion, that you make just a tad more effort with your social superego. Your manners are appalling.

And what's more, I should like to point out just how tactful I am being in not demanding to know, right here and now, exactly how you found me.'

It was a second or two before she could even find her voice. When she did, it shook very slightly.

'I don't know what I did, Doctor. I don't know what happened at all…'

He nodded grimly. 'That's what I thought.' Then he went back to the driver's seat, turned Dusty back on, and they started off again.

The maze was becoming tighter and tighter. Fitz felt, as they stumbled and careered through the ash and slag, kicking up clouds as they went, that the walls of blackened volcanic rock were pressing in ever tighter and that soon he and Iris would be crushed.

Heedlessly Iris pressed on, slowly now, then galloping fiercely, and all the while the cries of the savage circling owls echoed above them.

'Iris!' he yelled over the choking fumes. 'We're causing a dust storm! They're bound to find us!' He could only imagine how conspicuous they would be from the air.

She reined her horse in. 'You're right.' And she jumped off again, slapped the creature's rump, and let it pelt off, back the way they had come. 'That should distract them.'

Fitz did the same and carefully unwound his borrowed scarf. 'Hey, we could use this to… like, if we unwound it… we could use it to find our way through the labyrinth.'

'It's been done before. I've seen the Doctor get through more scarves than Salome does fans during a dance. In fact, I saw Salome doing a fan dance with one of the Doctor's scarves once upon a time. Anyway, that old laying-a-trail ruse never comes off.' She set off again on foot. 'Come on.'

'I'll be bruised head to foot in the morning,' said Fitz ruefully. 'I never thought riding was such hard work.'

Iris snorted. 'You've never been riding with me before.'

'Quite.'

She turned on him with a raised eyebrow. 'Let's get this straight, sonny Jim. Any more of your double entendres and I send you home this minute.'

'I wish you could. Anyway, what do you mean, double entendres?'

'You know. You've been flirting away like mad with me, from the very first moment we met.'

She hurried on, pacing easily through the narrowing passageways. Fitz felt through his pockets for his Woodbines and tried to keep up. 'I've done no such thing!'

'Pretending to be the Doctor and all. Oh, I know your game, my lad.'

'And?'

She whirled around to find him grinning and lighting a bent cigarette. She took a step towards him.

'And you, sweetheart, don't stand a chance.' She flicked dramatically at her hair.

'Oh no?'

'I'm out of your league.'

'Aren't we all travellers in the fifth dimension together?'

She laughed. 'What do you want, some interdimensional version of the Mile-High Club? We aren't the jet set.'

He smiled. 'I think that's exactly what you are.'

'Flattery.' Iris darted forward and kissed him suddenly, grasping his unshaven face smartly in both hands and forcing her tongue into his mouth for the briefest of instants. Then she let him go.

Fitz turned crimson and coughed.

'Don't tell the Doctor.' She grinned.

An owl screeched almost directly overhead and Fitz found himself dragged bodily, by Iris, around the next twist in the ravine.

'Come on!' she cried, as if it had been him holding them up.

The owl screeches became louder, almost deafening.

The birds were upon them now.

And as the two fugitives rounded the last corner they saw that they had arrived at the dead centre of the maze.

Here there was steam and a pool of black mud, popping with sulphurous fumes. In the middle of this expanse, like a trophy, was a vast green egg, gilded in gold and platinum.

And, guarding it, were the owls, massed and resplendent in ivory.

Iris swore.

From behind them came the owls that had pursued them through the maze. They soared straight overhead, mission accomplished, and joined their mates.

'They've got us now,' said Fitz, gulping, as each pair of baleful eyes turned to stare in the newcomers' direction.

From the private journal of Captain Robert B. Blandish

Where are the empirical laws of physics?

Call me prissy, pedantic if you like, but I do like to know where I am.

How can races and worlds a million light years apart be brought into the same arena like this? My Science Officer Garrett points out, not for the first time, that any alien technology, sufficiently advanced, will look, to the uninitiated, like magic. Well, I say: bullshit. We all live in the same universe, don't we? So we all have to operate by the same physical laws.

We *do* all live in the same universe, don't we?

Even when we all went to that crazy alternative mirror dimension, years ago, where we found all our identical evil twin counterparts, even then things weren't that different. The world still made some kind of sense.

I don't think we've ever been anywhere as messed up as this.

As soon as we fired on the crackling loops of energy that were apparently Corridors, radiating from Valcea, which, according to Garrett, were Corridors stretching themselves through space and time, the place all went to hell.

The Corridors buckled and whipped around, lashing themselves against the hull of the *Nepotist*, as if they were alive, like tentacles, and resisting the ship as it drove at them. I wanted to snap those bonds. I wanted to see what happened. I don't know what it was with me, but I still wanted to cause more damage.

But the more damage we tried to cause, the more we pitched the whole might of our vessel against the Corridors, the more we became ensnared.

It seemed that they really were alive, to some extent. Like creepers and vines they lashed themselves on to us and we were caught in the cat's cradle of this luminous tangle.

The Sahmbekart fleet hung still in space, holding their fire power for now. A relief.

At least we had baffled them with our foolhardy attempts to cause more chaos and they had desisted from firing any more. We couldn't have taken much more of an assault.

But when we had caught ourselves up, ravelled ourselves thicker in the Corridor, what did the Sahmbekart leader do but contact us again?

His vile image reappeared on our screen and he oh so politely asked for permission to come aboard.

I granted it.

And so it was Garrett, Timon, 'Forceps' Felixstoe and myself waiting in the demat chamber as the Sahmbekart supreme commander had himself scintillated aboard the *Nepotist*.

He arrived standing up in one of the tubs.

He was far more frightful in the scaled and gleaming flesh than he had been on the screen. His jaws seemed so much bigger. You could see the constant stream of saliva coursing between his broken teeth.

And his legs were a shock. Each of the two was twice the thickness of his torso. He also had a tail, which swished impressively behind him as we led him down the corridor to the chamber where, we had determined, we would talk this thing through.

'I would prefer to talk on your bridge, Captain Blandish,' he said, quite politely. 'And from there I may keep an eye on my fleet. Reasonable, yes?'

He turned one of those gimlet eyes on me then, and I, involuntarily, gulped. I agreed. 'Just so long as we can come to some amicable agreement.'

The Sahmbekart shrugged as I showed him to the elevator. I noticed how small and puny his forearms actually were.

'I am not here to bargain with you, Captain. I am here to tell you what is to happen to you. You are in no position to bargain with me.'

And then he fell silent as the lift took us whizzing back towards the bridge and my fellow officers and I were squashed against the walls by the bulk of his saliva-damp legs.

Extract ends

The Ghillighast had erected a kind of pagoda, all of pale-pink silk, for their honoured guests to sit in.

It was placed on silver runners at the head of their procession across the ice fields and the sheer impenetrable, unending night.

The dogs ran for hours, their muzzles frosted and bearded with ice, and now and then they would let out the most ghastly moans and ululating howls. They howled at what they thought was the moon, but they were confused.

These past few days, there had been an increasing number of moons and Corridors in the sky above Ghillighast, as had there arrived more and more ships, emerging like the newly born from the Corridors. The sky was looking almost congested.

In other sleds, the Ghillighast sat hunched up, staring keenly into the way ahead, their vestigial velveteen wings folded up around them like shawls.

The High Priestess Meisha rode alone as usual, seated on the back of a wolf, which pounded along, kicking up plumes of snow.

'Something very bad is happening,' Marn said worriedly, as he drew aside the pink drapes and looked up into the hectic night sky.

'I shouldn't worry about it,' Belinda said, sitting back on the cushions. 'What can we do?'

'We can fight.'

'Who?'

Marn's eyes were gleaming again. 'Daedalus. He's behind this. For hundreds of years the races of the Enclave hardly bothered each other at all. Now he's stirring it all up.'

They entered the Corridor.

The wolves and the huskies and the dogs howled louder.

The fire engine was rolling impressively over the remains of the outer walls of Valcea.

There was a terrible sound of breaking glass as wall after wall went under the metal wheels.

Inside, the occupants held their breath. It was as if their vessel was too heavy for the city to hold any more. It creaked and groaned under their mass.

As they listened, the Steigertrudes and the ladies and Ian could hear the cracking and splintering and the groaning of glass.

Emba turned on Ian and demanded, 'Where is your father? Where will he be hiding?'

'The throne room,' said Ian, without thinking. He could hardly remember being there. He barely remembered anything at all before being taken away by the Ghillighast. His earliest memories were of their chilly, dirty moon and living in caverns, kept there like an animal.

But there was still the glimmering of a memory: his father's throne room in the very heart of this city. He could almost see it.

And his father?

He remembered tusks, a powerful, rank, bestial smell. And a booming voice.

He gave Emba the nod. Told her to head for the heart.

Chapter Thirty-Three
The Bus Is Rattling...

The bus is rattling so much.

This is because the end of the Corridor is nigh. This should come as some consolation, for the disturbance, the kerfuffle, the discomfort of it all will be over soon.

But the travellers on the bus don't know yet that they have almost escaped from the Corridor.

In a final constrictive effort the Corridor is wondering how it might go about keeping these travellers and their bus lost up its own voluminous sleeves. How to ensnare them further and for ever; gollopped and gobbled up in its huge and awkward peristalsis.

But the Doctor is no fish-bone to be choked on!

Both his hearts jump up in horror at the idea of being eternally swallowed in an anomaly such as this – no matter how diverting it may be.

He revs the engine of his borrowed bus. The fabric of the Corridor itself shivers pleasurably at his stubborn resistance, his trickiness, his unwillingness to be contained by it...

And the Corridor plots and schemes in its own not entirely vacuous manner.

It wonders how to keep him here.

As does the bus. Iris's ship has been with her for so long, and she with it, that it thinks along much the same lines as she does.

When the Doctor is aboard, Iris is happy.

And so is the bus. It is as if the master were home again. The bus feels like Nelly Dean, hovering at the hearth at Wuthering Heights, waiting for Mr Heathcliff to come home – with all the attendant awkwardness of their relationship.

So while the Doctor is here aboard, as he has been again and again through all their many and sporadic lives, the bus is reasonably happy and pleased with itself.

As pleased as it can be with its mistress missing and presumed to be dead.

As the bus enters a new phase of Corridor – a murky stretch, a cavern, a moist, unnerving space – Compassion sits still and tries to compose herself.

It seems that every muscle of which she is in possession is twitching.

Her legs cramp up, her fingers spasm.

Is it something to do with this place, or something else? Nervously, she plays with her hair.

The bus rattles fit to burst.

The bus rattles as if someone were determined to shake it until the interior dimensions come loose and peel and fall away from the external, robustly buslike exterior. Compassion knows that, given that this is a TARDIS, this isn't actually that impossible.

She feels as if something had come loose inside her and were rattling around.

She starts to feel she isn't even inside her own body any more.

The Doctor is on his feet, hands on the wheel, staring out at the new stretch of tunnel.

'I can't drive through there.'

Compassion goes to look through the smutty windscreen. At first she can make out nothing in the cavern.

The Doctor gently pulls the bus to a stop, and kills the music.

Then he whooshes open the door and leads them both out on to a floor that gives, surprisingly, underfoot.

A sapphire heart-shaped cavern, and it is occupied.

From ceiling and walls depend coils and fleshy tubes. They twist and ravel and from them hang weighty objects, slightly larger than ripe melons.

They drift out as if there were no gravity in here, though the

Doctor and Compassion remain on the ground with the bus.

'What are they?'

The Doctor looks grim. He looks ashen.

He nods to make Compassion look again, to look harder.

Then she realises that the tubes she sees are twisted and coiled like umbilical cords because that is exactly what they are.

And from the end of each floats a baby.

Each hugging itself, head lowered, eyes shut.

There are perhaps ten thousand bright-blue babies afloat in this room.

As the Doctor steps tentatively into the chamber, one tiny blue fist closes on the calf muscle of his left leg. He feels those tiny fingers squeezing tight on his flesh. He cries out and the hand relaxes.

But the fingers have left a mark. He can feel it.

Chapter Thirty-Four
Existential Angst is an Embarrassment, But...

Existential angst is an embarrassment but...

If I were to get stuck in the blue Corridors - toddling up and down ad infinitum - where is it I'm actually stuck? In blue vortices for ever, shot from one end to the other, never able to re-enter real time?

That sounds to me like never getting back to real progression - even regression - ever again.

You know how Shirley Bassey sings themes to James Bond films, but she's never actually in the film itself? All we get is her voice, warning girls to watch out for Mister Goldfinger, et cetera, et cetera... But she herself is never fool enough to become embroiled. Well, that will be me. I'd be in a title sequence only. I'd never get to be in the actual story.

I will be the voice of the frame.

Exempt from plot!

But me - I'm a mover-shaker, aren't I?

I am implicated, I interfere, I tamper and transgress. That's always been my role. I am a man made to make Old Enemies and blissfully we cross and recross one another's helter-skelter path; our reunions and run-ins infinitely recurring and all of it takes place within some kind of real time. Exemption's no fun.

Never to be in my own adventure!

No more episodes for me!

Oh no!

But even then there's a kind of implied adventure, isn't there? And it would be about how I inveigle myself back into the functions of story. How I break out of a crippling stasis. And I can see it all now.

But - horrors - the thought of this for ever.

Me, merely gracing an endless title sequence.

As if archived, canonised. A dead Cultural Artefact in a museum of flotsam, jetsam, trash. Unreinventable.

Stories all ravelled up and done with. As if novelty were the key! And I were not free just to rewrite, remake, replay, repeat! Ha!

Gracing an endless theme, though – end credits, title sequence – never to impeach again.

> *impeach:*
> to accuse of a crime
> to challenge or question
> to entangle

Safe for ever!
What if that's how I've ended up?

And his companion for this seemingly last, endless, safe adventure was called Compassion. She was one of the least companionable of his many assistants. Was she called Compassion because she was abetting this stasis? The thought did flit through his troubled mind. Perhaps she was one of those saving him from himself.

Chapter Thirty-Five
Iris Made Fitz Come...

Iris made Fitz come and sit cross-legged with her around the fire she had built.

He was reluctant, still thinking the owls were going to pounce at any moment and rip the pair to shreds.

But Iris talked him round and said that nothing like that was going to happen at all. They just wanted to talk.

Under the shadow of the huge, ornate egg, Iris set to work on the fire with her pistol.

Soon it was crackling away busily and warming them through. She started to talk breezily about other occasions she had gathered round the campfire with friends, on other outings, and then she asked Fitz how many cigarettes he had left.

The sky was a broiling purple now. Night had set in with a vengeance, and the mountainous land was chilled right through.

The owls gathered once more and their leader arrived and settled before Iris and Fitz wearing a cloak which, he claimed, sported the feathers of every species of bird in the Enclave. It was this that enabled him to speak to them.

Iris shrugged. She'd heard of odder things. 'Go on, then,' she urged.

The owl blinked its baleful eyes and, with everyone's eyes upon him, began.

'There are two eggs belonging to our race. The story goes that they were entrusted to us, when we were quite young, by our god. They were never to leave our grasp.'

'Your god?' asked Fitz. Iris nudged him.

'A great white bird,' said the owl solemnly, 'who, when the galaxy was half its present size, roamed everywhere looking for somewhere safe to bury his eggs. They were not to be hatched. They were simply to be watched until their time came. If they were hatched early, there would be calamity, and we were to murder the offspring.'

'That sounds a bit harsh,' said Iris worriedly.

'For generations we owls have mulled over the meaning of the white bird's instructions. Now we think, for the most part, that there was only a metaphorical truth to the warning. We were simply to look after the eggs.'

'Where did the white bird go?' asked Fitz.

'No one knows,' said the owl. 'We only know him as the great white bird who began time.'

'I see.'

Iris bit her lip. 'And someone stole one of the eggs?'

'That was the reason we left our world. We are not an aggressive race. We prefer to remain here, going about the task we were given in the first place.'

'Who stole it?'

'Daedalus,' said the owl. 'The self-styled king of Valcea.'

Iris blanched. 'Daedalus, you say? But –'

'Years ago he sent out the first of his Corridors and arrived with the evil Glass Men who are under his thrall. What chance did we stand? We had to watch as he marauded on to our world and took one of the eggs. The other we hid, deep inside the volcano.'

Fitz looked at Iris. 'Do you know this Daedalus?'

She pulled a face.

'The egg has hatched,' said the owl, stirring its cloak of feathers. 'This much we know. To taunt us, soon after, Daedalus sent us the shattered remnants of the shell. The mucus inside was still fresh.' Then he looked at Iris, and, with only a touch of accusation, said, 'You have seen the offspring.'

'I believe I have, yes. Ian.'

'Ian?' said Fitz. 'That young lad?'

'When we attacked you in the place with the glass ceilings and the fountains, it was him we were seeking. You prevented us.'

'I thought you were going to kill all of us!' said Iris. 'You didn't exactly explain yourselves. You just attacked.'

The owl was unperturbed. 'Our real enemy, against whom we must join forces, is Daedalus.'

'Yes,' she said slowly. 'I think you're right.'

'We fly to Valcea, this very night.' The owl drew itself up to its full massive height.

The damage was less extreme the deeper into the Valcean city they travelled.

Here there were only pillars fallen, walls hanging in shards, metal grilles fallen in.

There wasn't a single Glass Man to be seen. They had all retrenched somewhere, left to lick their wounds.

The Steigertrude tank rolled on through the shards and debris.

When they came to the roomfuls of glass statues and *objets d'art* they stopped. A kind of primal instinct overtook the women.

They clambered out of their engine and unspooled the hoses. They couldn't move on till they had reduced the precious glass objects to molten pools.

Maddy watched in dismay from inside.

Big Sue was saying, 'It's barbaric.'

'This is your city, then… Icarus?' said Maddy.

'All of it ruined,' said Ian. He gathered his wings about him. He looked at the controls of the engine.

A slow smile, one Maddy had never seen before, stretched across his face.

'We can leave them,' he said suddenly, realising that Emba and the others had left them unguarded.

'Help us out of these chains and things!' Big Sue commanded, but Ian didn't have time.

He leapt at the controls he had watched the Steigertrude women operate so skilfully and the engine burst into life.

Outside, Emba felt the hose jerk and pull and she turned with a roar.

'Those idiots!'

The engine was starting to rumble towards the wall.

The other women shook themselves out of their reverie of righteous art censorship, and turned to look in horror as the glass wall collapsed and the tank rolled through.

The roof began to cave in. Chunks of masonry and glass dropped into the hall.

Emba shrieked at them to fall back, to drop the hoses and run. She saw two of her fellows fall under the weight of debris before she, too, fled.

And then the tank was gone.

Remorseless, Icarus headed deeper and deeper into the Glass City.

Behind one wall were paralysed Glass Men, waiting for the power to come back on. They let out barely a cry as the tank rolled over them, and stamped them into shards.

The supreme commander of the Sahmbekarts looked out on his fleet with some satisfaction.

Behind him he knew the Federation crew were watching nervously, knowing that he held all the cards.

His was the power to call off all hostilities now.

He could pacify his fleet and his people; he could tell them the Federation meant no harm.

He could explain that the whole situation was, as Blandish had told him, and as he believed it to be, due to the machinations of Daedalus of Valcea.

But he wasn't going to.

This was his chance.

For years the Sahmbekart people had been aware of the worlds beyond their Enclave.

And the Enclave was much too small for the Sahmbekarts.

For years they had monitored the radio transmissions from beyond their space and gradually they had become aware of what a big place waited out there. Somewhere they could go to plunder, one day.

And now it had come to them.

Here was a chance to take on the representatives of the wide universe beyond with impunity. And these representatives were no match for the Sahmbekart fleet.

It was delicious.

'Will you talk with them?' Blandish asked quietly. He was sweating. Beads stuck out on his forehead. He was a repellent creature, decided the Sahmbekart commander. Hardly a worthy opponent. But he would be the first of many.

'I promised no such thing,' he told Blandish.

And then he did an astonishing thing.

He yawned. Right in front of the captain he opened his massive jaws and yawned.

But he was gargling at the same time, and flames burst from his mouth and with a kind of sneeze he spat them into the air before him.

He generated a column of vicious flame before the startled eyes of the bridge crew.

Then he did another and another.

And within the brief columns of flaming light materialised Sahmbekart warriors, in full dress armour, armed with lasers.

By the time Timon and the Federation guards could even gather what was going on, six of the lizards had appeared. They in turn began spitting flame around the place, so that the number of creatures increased exponentially by the second.

The commander laughed. 'Do you mind, Captain, if I invite my friends along? And then you can tell them yourself?'

There was a squawk of the intercom then.

The chief engineer's voice managed to squeal something about Sahmbekart docking on to the *Nepotist*; the ship was being boarded and invaded.

And then his voice cut out.

The commander clashed his jaws with glee and told his

minions to round up the bridge crew.

They had triumphed.

'What are they?' Compassion stared about her. 'Are they real?'

The Doctor nodded. 'It's no illusion. Nothing in the Corridors is unreal. Everything has been brought here from somewhere, from some time. But it's all without rhyme or reason...'

They were still staring at the chamber of floating babies.

'We have to pass through,' said Compassion. 'Whoever put these here are depending on your soft-heartedness. They want to keep you here for ever.'

'So what do you suggest?' snapped the Doctor. 'That we roll right through in the bus? Squash them flat?'

'We don't even know what they are. They're nothing to do with us.'

'We have to leave the bus.'

She shook her head. 'It's the only bit of protection we have.'

He took her arm and pointed at the room. 'Look – there are babies growing out of the walls, the ceilings, the floors... We can't just ride over them.'

'Then do what you should have done before.'

'What?'

'Her bus is a TARDIS, isn't it? Use it like one. Dematerialise. Come out the other end. Take us to Valcea.'

Compassion stalked back into the bus.

He followed.

'You've no idea how erratic this thing is. I found out last time – and we're in a region of great instability. We've no idea what the Corridors will do.'

But Compassion was already at the controls as he closed the doors behind them.

Before he even knew what was going on, she was plunging the dematerialisation switch.

One minute they were charging and howling through the

windswept blue of the Corridor.

The next, the dogs had dragged them into a white glass space, crazed with fractures and filled with the sound of distant explosions.

Meisha screeched in exultation. 'We've made it! Praise be to Pesst for bringing us safely to Valcea!'

The dogs pulled their sleds to a halt and stood panting as the Ghillighast stared in some awe at the cathedral-sized space around them.

Belinda poked her head out. 'Back again.'

Marn was appalled. 'There is little left of my city. This was our most sacred building.'

Behind them the blue Corridor sealed itself and vanished with barely a whisper.

The High Priestess Meisha was barking with triumph.

She had seen something none of the others had seen yet.

At the far end of the shattered cathedral, in a patch of pearly, spectral light, a glass pillar had fallen and, pinned beneath it, bleeding but still alive, lay the great leathery body of Daedalus.

One of his tusks had snapped. (Oh, how like Ganesh! God of the broken tusk! Daedalus was ever alert to his own status as iconography.) He was breathing stertorously, glaring at them with contempt. His hide had turned an ashen grey.

As Belinda helped Marn out of the pagoda and back into his chair, and pushed him across the rubble-strewn floor, she watched the Ghillighast gather around the fallen king.

'Help me out!' he started to bellow. 'Help me out immediately!'

The Ghillighast shrieked with laughter. One or two picked up slivers of glass and pricked at his hide to see him bleed and what colour flowed fresh from his wounds.

He moaned piteously and flapped his taloned hands. 'Let me out and I will give you this world. The Ghillighast will rule her unimpeached.'

Meisha was unimpressed. 'Daedalus, we already do.'

* * *

Blandish, Garrett and the rest of the bridge crew were shepherded into the captain's oval office.

They were locked in and forgotten about as the lumbering creatures ran amok on the bridge and throughout the ship.

There came the sounds of slaughter as the Sahmbekarts thinned down the crew numbers, but the prisoners in the oval office knew that they, at least, would need to be kept alive for now.

They were the ship's pilots. Only they could take it back to the worlds beyond the Enclave that the Sahmbekarts so coveted.

Garrett was overcome with misery and remorse.

'We should never have agreed to arbitration.' He glared down at his Ship's Kitty and, in a moment of rare anger, flung it to one side. 'It was an expensive decision.'

Timon was even more bitter. 'We gave in. We should have gone down fighting. While they were firing on us, we should have given it all we had. We should have flung ourselves at the mother ship. Taken them with us.'

Blandish seemed curiously quiet. They looked at him and suddenly they knew he had hatched a plan. Just like his old self.

He hurried around to the other side of his desk and flipped open a hidden panel.

'The Sahmbekarts don't know about this. I had this installed after the first five-year mission. How many times before that did we need something to override the main controls? How many times was our bridge taken over by hostile alien forces?'

He was grinning now, full of bravado once more.

'Forty-seven times in all,' said Garrett.

'Exactly!' cried Blandish. 'And we always came through, didn't we?' Then he started tapping and typing busily at the buttons on the hidden controls. 'We *always* come through.'

'What are you doing?' asked Timon.

'I'm taking your cue. Since you're in the mood for a kamikaze mission, I'm giving instructions to override the bridge. I'm telling the *Nepotist* to crash-land – on Valcea!'

It was Belinda's voice that startled them all then. Hers was the prerecorded voice that spoke, with chilling calm and precision, counting down the moment of impact for sixty seconds.

'Everyone,' said Blandish, with a rakish, somewhat hysterical grin, 'brace yourselves.'

Chapter Thirty-Six
I Was Panicking Over Dinner...

I was panicking over dinner.

The potatoes had turned mushy at the parboiling stage. And then I was diverted by noise in the hallway.

Fitz was greeting our guests.

They were swaddled up in winter things, coated in fresh snow.

Sally was breathless and pink-faced, beaming, glad to be here, brandishing a bottle of expensive red wine.

Under her other arm she carried that strange dirty dog of hers.

With her stood the fattest, oldest woman I had ever seen. She wore about twenty layers of coats and cardigans which she enlisted the gallant Fitz to help her remove.

Fitz stifled his laughter as he helped the old woman with her endless layers and hung them on the hatstand in the hall.

'This is my neighbour, Iris,' said Sally brightly.

And the old woman fixed me with a roguish look. I didn't like it at all. When I took her hand it was scratchy and dry.

She looked like *Baba Yaga* in the old Russian fairy tales my mother used to tell me on long snowy evenings like this one.

The long snowy evenings we had been stuck in for weeks.

Baba Yaga flew about the world in a mortar and pestle, and she lived in a shed on chicken legs. Her home could run about the place.

She wore a cloak woven from the feathers of every bird in the world.

This old Iris took ages to let go of my hand. Behind her Fitz was dying to laugh.

'And so you are the Doctor,' she cackled. 'Sally has told me a surprising amount about you, young man.'

'Has she?'

'You have a very great destiny,' she said, eyelashes fluttering, as if she were in a trance. 'Or a very great past. Which is it?'

I gulped. 'I must go and check on dinner.'

I made Fitz show them into the dining room and told him to persuade Compassion – never at her best in strange company – to be sociable and nice.

I heard Iris asking about the lizard and the angel fish in our tanks.

Sally followed me into the kitchen. I didn't hear her until I had my head inside the oven.

'Don't mind Iris. She likes to go on all mysterious.'

I was balancing the roasting dish, carrying it spitting to the bench, where I set to work carving the meat into delicate slivers.

'I feel like I've seen her before,' I said.

'Perhaps you have.' She pinched a bit of meat. 'Melts in your mouth,' she smiled. 'You always could cook.'

'I saw my mother this week.'

'How is she?'

I shrugged. Sally and my mother had never approved of each other. Each convinced that the other was about to take me away.

As I started transferring the meat to the warmed plates, Sally said, 'You haven't said anything yet.'

'What about?'

She looked hurt. 'My book. That I gave you last week. You've had a whole week to read it.'

'You know I'm not a fast reader. My concentration has been all over the place.'

She pulled a face, disappointed.

'And…' I went on, straining vegetables over the sink, 'with the weather like it's been…'

'What's the weather got to do with it?'

'Everything's been… like a struggle for survival recently. As though we were slipping into a second ice age.'

'And that stops you reading a book by your oldest, dearest friend. Who really needs your opinion.'

Whoops. I'd hurt her feelings.

As I started arranging things nicely on the plates she was poking away at something on the kitchen table. A leather-bound volume on the oilcloth.

'At least you're reading something,' she said, sounding even more hurt.

'That's Fitz. He found it in the attic among my family's old stuff. I'm not reading it. Honest.'

She flipped through the ancient pages.

'The *Aja'ib*. Hmm. "Chapter One Hundred and Ninety-Seven... In Which Our Hero Knocks Down the Bridges Into the Citadel To Allow The Green Men To Conquer, Little Knowing That The Grey Men Are Not Far Behind.".'

She flicked again. '"There were seventy elderly sisters in that ghastly mountainous realm and they set out with some trepidation one horrid night to destroy the filthy remnants of that man they most despised, the man already dead, whose head was made all of cracked glass, so that his brains, bruised, dashed, already sent mad, could be seen pulsing within." ' Sally looked at me. 'Sounds like rum stuff. "In Which Pale Shadows From Another Land Impersonate Everything Familiar to Our Heroes".'

'Fitz likes that sort of stuff.'

'Hmm. Maybe *he'll* like my book.'

By the time the hostess trolley was loaded and Sally helped me push it through, we found that Compassion was lighting the candles on the table.

Fitz was drinking.

'Where's Iris?'

'Fitz upset her,' said Compassion.

'What did he say?' I was furious. The tone was all wrong.

'He said her bus in the street outside was an eyesore.'

'Her bus?'

Sally nodded. 'She drove us here.'

'Where is she now?'

Compassion rolled her eyes. 'Up in the bathroom. Sobbing her heart out.'

Chapter Thirty-Seven
Now The Great Beast...

Now the great beast was shackled and slumped in the corner of what had once been his throne room, his stateroom; the glass cathedral in which once he had sat resplendent, passing out his querulous commands, and watching the games that he had demanded for his own hellish amusement.

Now he sat defeated, hunched over, examining the jagged edge of his broken tusk with his talons.

He seemed almost oblivious to the Ghillighast as they skittered about his city.

Meisha had settled herself on his throne and flung the odd taunting word in his direction, but he didn't respond.

Marn the Glass Man watched on in horror. Belinda couldn't understand her friend's attitude.

'But you hate Daedalus,' she said. 'You wanted to see him fall. And he has! Without us doing anything. He has just given himself up.'

Marn looked at her gloomily. 'What makes you think the Ghillighast will be any better?'

Belinda shrugged. 'They seem rather decent to me.'

'You know nothing about them. There's no telling what they'll do now that... now that my people are extinct.'

'Not quite extinct, Marn. You're still about.'

'There is only me!' he moaned. 'Daedalus didn't know what he was doing letting the humans fire on the city. He has wiped us out for sure.'

Belinda was kneeling down by his chair, whispering conspiratorially. 'If there's one thing I've learned from travelling with Blandish, it's don't reckon on the ending before you get to it. Anything might happen yet.'

'Don't mention that man's name to me.'

'You blame him for attacking Valcea?'

'Of course I do.'

Belinda shook her head. 'I don't believe Blandish would do such a thing. Honestly, I don't. For one thing, Timon would never let him... and Timon controls the weaponry aboard the *Nepotist*.'

'You don't understand, Belinda,' said Marn wearily. 'Daedalus can make people do what he wants. He has a brain the size of a wheelbarrow. He can control you without you even knowing it. Make you see what he wants you to see, say what he wants you to say. How else do you think he got most of the Glass Men to do what he wanted?'

Belinda blanched. 'So... even captured like this, tied up, and defeated-looking, he could still try to...'

Savagely Marn nodded. 'Of course he could! Don't let him fool you!'

The pair of them stared across the shattered rink of the floor to the bowed-down, bulky green figure now sitting at Meisha's feet.

Belinda thought she saw the elephant's eyes glinting with something other than abject misery.

'So... he could be messing about with our minds now, and we might not even know it?'

'Exactly,' said Marn firmly. 'We have to be on our guard. Hallucinations, everything.'

Belinda gulped.

Meisha was speaking now, addressing those excitable Ghillighast who weren't already exploring the city and gathering spoils.

'So this is how our history recommences. In glory and victory and the effortless sacking of our enemy's city. Thanks be to Pesst and his delectable bride, the Lady Belinda.'

All of the Ghillighast applauded and chattered at this and, once more, Belinda found herself at the centre of everyone's attention.

But then she saw the elephant's eye burn with a peculiar malevolence and she started to feel herself change.

'Belinda!' Marn was shouting. 'What's happening to you?'

Belinda was feeling rather hot.

Around her the Ghillighast were gibbering in terror.

They ran about the place, encircling her, heedless of the shrieked commands of their equally startled High Priestess.

Belinda had no idea what was happening to her. She felt too warm, and itchy somehow and, in a way she couldn't quite define, she felt *bigger* all of a sudden.

The Ghillighast stared up at her in horror. Even Marn seized the wheels of his chair and attempted to manoeuvre himself backwards.

To all intents and purposes the Lady Belinda had been transformed into a squid.

Her clothes had dropped off her and her skin had turned tough, rubbery and mauve.

And there was a great deal more of it.

Now she had numerous lithe and densely muscled serpentine legs and they struck out in all directions, terminating in deadly flippers the size of sleds, so that she squashed one or two Ghillighast stone dead on the spot, even before she was aware of the very nature of her transmogrification.

Her two eyes were huge now, almond-shaped and like two rocks of amber; there was a desperate pleading in them – and she looked at Daedalus in his chains, to get him to free her, but he was still.

Belinda flailed her new limbs and the remaining columns in the throne room trembled precariously.

'What has become of the Lady Belinda?' shrilled Simaf, clutching hold of his mistress's wings.

She shook him off. 'How am I to know?' She stared in horror. 'It's all the doing of Daedalus! It must be!'

'What do we do, madam?' asked Simaf. 'Shall we kill her?'

'*Kill* the Bride of Pesst?' screamed Meisha. 'Why, that is

blasphemy, Simaf! No… it is Daedalus we must slaughter! And do it now – before he causes worse disasters to befall us. We were fools to let the monster live even this long! Guards!'

Meisha regained some measure of composure when her most loyal Ghillighast guards advanced then, bearing their tiny but deadly silver daggers.

They saluted her calmly, as if nothing untoward was even going on around them, and then they advanced on the crouched figure of Daedalus.

'Slaughter him!' Meisha howled. 'Tear him to pieces! The Ghillighast will never live peacefully here on Valcea, or anywhere else, until Daedalus is killed!'

So the Ghillighast rounded on the apparently helpless elephant.

And Belinda, equally helpless, thrashed around her purple limbs.

Hers was a gurgling, oceanic lament, an endlessly salty caterwaul.

Marn tried to calm her and turned, breathless, to watch the killing of the hated Daedalus.

At last, under the manic, shrieked commands of the haggard bat queen; the Chiropteran High Priestess, Daedalus was about to die.

Marn licked his dry glacial lips and watched.

The Ghillighast raised their daggers to strike.

And with a tremendous wheezing groaning sound – like the aeolian harp of Hades itself – a crimson double-decker bus materialised smartly, stubbornly before them all.

'It's really happening,' said Garrett dully.

The room was now very hot. Blandish leapt up from his desk chair. It was metal and, like the walls around them, starting to scorch.

'We're really destroying the *Nepotist*,' said Garrett. 'After everything. After all our years together. This is it.'

Blandish looked almost jubilant.

'And we've given ourselves a fighting chance. We destroy the commander of the Sahmbekarts, and give the fleet something to think about. We do what we always do – we save the day.'

Timon didn't look impressed. 'And kill ourselves in the process.'

The noise was unmistakable now. A keen roar of protest from the engines beneath them. Blandish hardly dared think of what he had committed his beloved ship and crew to.

He knew the engines would already be cracking under the stress and he knew the engineers down below would already have died a terrible death.

But the Sahmbekarts couldn't do anything about this. They were stuck with the ship as it went down.

They might survive the crash-landing, but they stood only the same chance as Blandish and his fellows.

He would show them that he meant business.

The heat and the noise became unbearable. He knew that the bridge crew would have started slipping unconscious to the ground as the lights shorted out and the room began to shake.

Blandish found himself laughing uncontrollably as he himself sank to his knees and the room rocked, and the door slid open abruptly, to reveal the bridge beyond and the chaos out there.

The Sahmbekart commander filled the door frame. Over the tumultuous noise he screamed, 'What have you done?'

And then nothing.

Once more Iris was aloft.

She tried not to look down through the entire voyage. If she looked she would pass out for sure, and this was one of those times when passing out was not a good idea. Instead she looked across at Fitz, in the clutches of his own owl, and he seemed all right.

He was a brave boy, really, she thought. All the owls had come on this flight. They knew the way through the tunnels. Of all the

247

races of the Enclave caught up in the blue Corridors, the owls seemed the most proficient. They seemed to scent, instinctively, the way to go.

She looked backward as they emerged, at last, from the swirling blue of the Corridor, and into the frigid air high above Valcea.

She drew in her breath at the sight of the owls bringing up the rear.

It was an impressive sight. It took twenty of them, or thereabouts, to carry the gleaming green egg between them. Since they were all coming on this assault on Valcea, they had brought their precious relic with them for safekeeping.

Iris looked back at the country ahead and gasped once more.

She gasped at the snapped shining pinnacles, the shattered glass turrets of Valcea.

And then there was an explosion that buffeted them and made the air around them, even this high up, shudder and distort.

Some distance away from the city there was a searing light.

She could pick out a trail of fuel and a scorch mark on the night sky.

And in the frozen tundra there was a pall of smoke, a wad of black fuel and drear steam.

Something had crashed straight on to the fields of ice.

'What was that?' she yelled across to Fitz as the owls made their determined way down to Valcea, beating their powerful wings against the turbulence.

Fitz looked shaken. 'It was the *Nepotist*!' he cried. 'Didn't you see it? It fell out of the sky…!'

The Doctor had stumbled out of the bus and started gabbling almost immediately.

The assembled party gazed at him in amazement, seeming unable to ignore him or get on with what they were doing.

The Doctor took everything in his stride. The Ghillighast and the creature who appeared to be their leader or Priestess, and the prostrate, defeated Daedalus. He paused when he saw the Glass Man Marn and recognised in the globular, astonished eyes of the giant squid the stricken expression of the erstwhile Belinda. He rallied himself and decided to make the most of having everyone's attention. There was still time to save the day.

'I'm always doing this. I'm sorry. I'm interrupting again. It's funny, though. It seems that whenever I'm in Iris's bus, the old thing drops me in the most hectic and embarrassing spots. Nothing like my own ship, which makes a habit of landing me on the outskirts of things, so that I usually have a long walk to get to where the action is. It must be that Iris is terribly lazy or impatient or something. But anyway, here I am again, back in the thick of things. And goodness! It seems like I've got some catching up to do!'

At this he gazed up at the distraught serpent that Belinda had become. 'Hello, Belinda, old thing,' he grinned. 'You've grown a bit!'

She flailed around at this. He patted one tentacle to calm her and winked. 'I'll sort it out. Don't you worry.'

He whirled on one heel, saw that Daedalus was about to be executed and rushed over.

'Oh, am I in time to watch a decapitation? I've never cared much for that kind of thing. I've always thought there were more interesting methods of dealing with people like this.' With that he snatched the silver blades out of the hands of every one of the Ghillighast guards. It was one single, easy movement and the bats were hardly aware he had done it until he was absently stowing their weapons away in his capacious pockets.

'Mind you,' he said, 'when I say "people like this", you realise of course I really mean "villainous scum". Because that's exactly what I think of you, Daedalus.'

The others jumped back then, as the elephant opened both eyes and fixed the Time Lord with the most vicious of looks.

'Yes,' said the Doctor. 'You can give me the evil eye all you want, but I still think you're a… well, you're a… swine!'

'And who are you?' a voice asked imperiously.

The Doctor turned to face the Priestess. 'I might be any number of things. And who, exactly, are you?'

Meisha's eyes blazed with fury. 'This is not how our new history is supposed to be.'

A single shot rang out then, and everyone turned to see Compassion, standing by the bus and brandishing her weapon.

'Nobody move,' she said in a steely tone. 'Anyone makes a move towards the Doctor, and they're dead.'

He clapped a hand to his head. 'Compassion, that really isn't necessary. I'm really doing fine without –'

At this point there was another new arrival.

The tall twin doors into the throne room crashed inward and teetered on their ancient hinges before dropping to the floor.

Everyone turned to stare at the Steigertrude tank as it lumbered up to the end of the room.

The Ghillighast Priestess seemed completely lost by now. 'And what is this?' she asked.

Daedalus himself seemed shocked by this apparition. He stood up, stiffly, groaning, casting off his shackles with almost no effort.

There was something strange in his look.

As if something were happening that he hadn't counted on.

He spoke hoarsely as the Steigertrude engine drew to an arthritic halt.

'It is my son! My son has come for me!'

Even the Doctor was baffled now. 'Who?'

Chapter Thirty-Eight
He Was Astonished To Find . . .

He was astonished to find himself alive.

But Blandish had always known his was to be a glorious destiny.

He had always known, from his earliest years in the Federation training corps, that his was to be one of those names that would stick in the annals of starfaring history.

And so he was alive to fight another day.

The room was on a slant.

He was lying on the moist corpse of the Sahmbekart commander.

He struggled to his feet in the dark and kicked the body for good measure.

Good. But there might be others around. He had to be on his guard.

Who else was alive? 'Garrett?' he hissed. 'Timon?'

Timon spoke up and, as the captain's eyes became accustomed to the new, rather dreary light coming in from somewhere, he saw Timon struggling through the heaped dead and unconscious bodies towards him.

'We made it,' said Timon quietly. 'But who else did?'

They found Garrett then, his head split open, lying face down over the desk.

His own expensive brains were spilled all over his captain's paperwork.

'Anyone else?' asked Blandish hoarsely.

Timon hunted around for a moment, but he knew it was hopeless. 'It's only us.'

'I thought . . .' said Blandish, and covered himself. Made his tone hard again. 'I thought so.'

He began to pick his way out of the slanted room, back

towards the bridge.

Timon followed and it seemed this was where the light was coming from.

The translucent ceiling of the bridge was cracked completely asunder and the frosty light of Valcea was peering through. They could climb out and on to the surface.

'You thought a lot of Garrett, I know, sir,' said Timon, as he watched his captain gaze up at the crack in the ceiling.

Blandish dragged his command chair over so it was under the hole.

'More than that, Mr Timon. We never spoke of this. No one realised this in all these years. We never talked about it much. But Garrett and I were lovers from our first assignment on this ship.'

Timon's jaw dropped.

Blandish seemed to be controlling himself by an immense effort of will.

'Shocked, are you, boy? You shouldn't be.'

He braced the chair with the fallen body of one of the massive lizard warriors, and prepared to hoist himself up through the ceiling and outside.

'We loved each other. We may not have shown it publicly. Not like you and Belinda. But we did. And now he's gone.' For a second Blandish seemed to lose control. 'We were supposed to die in battle together.'

He was up on the surface of the ship now, and reached down to give Timon a hand.

'So, you see, I've got nothing to lose now.'

Timon struggled up through the cracked hull of the *Nepotist*. 'I see, sir.'

Then they were both out in the night sky, overlooking the shining miles of ice.

Blandish pointed at the ruined glass city, a mile or two distant.

'We caused that. And because of it, because of us, there is bound to be war. What say we go and deal with Daedalus once and for all, eh?'

* * *

The Doctor stood back and let others take centre stage.

He was as baffled as Belinda, and Marn, and the Priestess by the appearance of the trio that stepped out of the Steigertrude tank.

There was an old woman, pulling her wig and hat straight, bundled up in a sheepskin coat.

A younger woman in glasses, and a rather beautiful boy with livid blue wings stretching out around him and his chest bare.

It was the boy that the room was staring at.

It was the boy that the suddenly restored Daedalus addressed: 'You came back to me, after all.'

'I received the call,' said Icarus.

'You were on the Earth?'

Icarus nodded. 'This woman took care of me. She treated me as her own.'

Daedalus looked at Maddy. 'Then she shall be rewarded.'

Big Sue and Maddy were both staring at Daedalus.

They could hardly believe what they were seeing. They were struck dumb.

'Have you nothing to say, Earth woman?' Daedalus asked.

'But...' Big Sue stammered. 'It's a bloody elephant!'

Icarus interceded. 'I promised these women that, if they brought me here, Father, to you, they would be rewarded with their youth again. It is what they most desire. Another chance.'

Daedalus grunted in amusement. 'Don't we all?'

Then he clenched and unclenched the talons of both hands.

They shimmered and glowed with light.

Big Sue and Maddy found themselves doing precisely the same thing.

Sue turned on Maddy: 'What is he doing to –'

'Of course,' said Daedalus mildly. 'Their minds will be wiped. They will recall nothing.'

And then, standing where the two women had been, was a single figure.

It was Maddy thirty years younger.

253

She was fifteen. She was dressed as Maddy still, but she looked like a whole other person.

She looked confused and on the brink of tears. In her arms she held a squalling baby wrapped in sheepskin.

Daedalus addressed her directly. 'I am sending you both back home. This moment. The child I give you, Madeleine, in exchange for my own child. On the condition that you name her Susan.'

The girl Maddy nodded quickly. She was scared. 'Yes, sir.'

Icarus stepped forward. He kissed the girl on her cheek. 'Goodbye, mother.'

Maddy stared at him hopelessly. As if she could remember his face but couldn't place his name.

And then Maddy and Big Sue faded away.

Icarus turned to his father. 'You will get them home safely?'

'For my son,' laughed Daedalus, 'anything.'

Meisha had been watching all of the proceedings narrowly. 'He is your son? Your true heir?'

Daedalus nodded grandly. 'He is indeed.'

'Then you shall both be our prisoners. And we shall execute you both!'

Daedalus threw back his gargantuan head and laughed. 'What do you think the Ghilligast are, Meisha? Do you really think they are destined to rule the Enclave? Is that the glorious destiny left to them?'

The High Priestess stood resolute. 'I do believe it.'

Daedalus wearily shook his head. 'You should have listened to the vermin you routinely consult, Meisha. You should have listened more closely. Because the Ghillighast themselves are just so much vermin themselves. You're nothing! You're not fit to rule your own moon, let alone anyone else's world! You're finished and useless! I only let you live so close to Valcea because you amused me. Do you really think you can threaten me now?'

Meisha had tears standing in her eyes. 'But this is the time of the Bride of Pesst… This is her apotheosis…'

'Ha!' cried Daedalus, with a magnificent shrug of his trunk. 'I think you'll find this is no one's apotheosis but mine!'

As he was laughing fit to burst at this, the Doctor was backing away towards Compassion. He had noticed something no one else had.

'Get back into the bus,' he warned his companion fiercely.

'What?' Compassion wasn't used to being told what to do.

'It's safer on the bus!' he urged. 'Now, go!'

'But…'

He tutted, and pointed up at the wrecked ceiling above.

Compassion saw the owls arriving *en masse*, an immaculate formation of perfect white plumage.

They rose up above the ceiling of the palace of Daedalus and then, inexorably, they crashed through the remains of the glass.

'What…?' bellowed Daedalus and looked up to see the owls descend.

The Doctor and Compassion turned and pelted towards the bus.

The owls filled the air of the throne room. With them they carried their precious egg.

And Iris and Fitz.

Chapter Thirty-Nine
The Throne Room Was...

The throne room was silent now.

Until the huskies started barking.

Up till now they had been slinking in the shadows, puzzled, frightened, out of their depth as their masters the Ghillighast went about their business in this strange new world.

But now the huskies started howling and barking and they longed to rush in and attack the newcomers.

The owls were standing in the centre of the floor, perfect, huge, gazing impassively at the occupants of the room. There were thirty of them and their egg sat protected, a great green-gold jewel, in their midst.

They ignored the protests of the dogs and fixed their gaze on Daedalus, the bleeding, battered king of this world. And his son who, raising his own azure wings to protect himself, began to back away, knowing that it was for him that they had come. Suddenly the boy grew defiant.

'Kill me if you must. If the compulsion
is so great,
if the force of your mythology
of what is bred
in your hollow bones
leads you to desire
my desecration;
the bursting of my gizzards
the shredding of my wings;

then do it
act out your history
figure your mission out
upon me.'

'In the bus,' said the Doctor again.

'You aren't the kind to run away,' said Compassion.

'I don't care,' he snapped. 'Get aboard.'

Then he turned back to the frozen knot of figures and bellowed.

'*Iris*! Here!'

From among the owls emerged a tall golden-haired figure in lime-green plastic. She threw back her head and laughed.

Beside her was Fitz, somewhat cowed by recent events.

The Doctor turned on Compassion with gleaming eyes. 'I told you they were alive.' She shrugged. 'You don't know yet', he said, 'how we do things round here.'

While the owls were still taking things in, getting their bearings – solemnly gazing at the Ghillighast, the shattered remains of the stateroom, the elephant and finally, finally, with their huge eyes burning in terror at Icarus – the Doctor seized his chance.

'Run!'

Iris and Fitz pelted across the chrome floor, skidding on snow and broken glass, towards the bus.

They tumbled inside, with the Doctor bringing up the rear.

Iris seized the antiquated controls and, with a few sharp jabs and wrenches, plunged them into the vortex.

The Doctor stepped back in horror. She had taken them out of time.

He hoped she knew what she was doing.

'Why are we here?' asked Compassion, as she gave the swirling continuum outside a scornful glance.

'We're buying time,' said Iris. 'We can pop back when need be. I've bookmarked the exact moment. Don't worry.'

Fitz was back on the *chaise-longue*, fishing out a bottle from the drinks cabinet. 'I've had more than enough. Why don't we just sod off for good?'

But there was no answer.

Iris seized the Doctor and gave him a rough bear hug. A

surprisingly powerful one for such a svelte woman.

He coughed and found himself responding.

'It's been far too long,' she said. 'But I knew you were here.'

'Hmm,' he said, through a mouthful of honey-coloured hair.

'I just know when we're embroiled in the same adventure. I can feel it in my water.'

'Hmm,' he said again, trying to shake her off.

'You just took so long getting to me! I had to get to you!'

'Quite. What were those owls?'

'Ah.' She relinquished him at last and started to explain about the giant egg and its connection to the boy Icarus, and how the owls were pledged to protect one and destroy the offspring of the other, and how she and Fitz had hitched a ride, and how Daedalus was the father of the angel boy, and how the boy had been secreted on the Earth and...

'Why don't we just have one of our little mind-melding thought-transfer Time Lord telepathic conference things?' she asked brightly, flexing her fingers and brushing her hair back from her temples.

The Doctor shuddered. 'It always feels as if someone's rummaging through my sock drawer.'

'Good,' she said. 'Then I can see what you're hiding in there.'

With that, she clamped her fingers to his forehead and he had no choice but to reciprocate.

Fitz and Compassion looked on as the two of them silently apprised each other of their recent respective doings. Compassion looked faintly nauseated.

At last the two of them broke off contact.

'Of course,' said Iris to Fitz, 'we don't really have to touch each other to make contact. It's just that the Doctor likes running his fingers through my hair.'

The Doctor looked grim. 'So we're in quite a pickle.'

Iris tossed her head. 'The whole Enclave is in a pickle. And it's all down to Daedalus!'

He looked irritated. 'So while I was stuck in the Corridors, you've been busying about causing even more trouble! Bringing the owls to Valcea, of all things! How is that supposed to help?'

'I had to get here somehow,' she said grumpily.

'But I'd almost sorted the whole thing out! Daedalus had got Icarus back – that was all he wanted really, I'm sure of it. He'd just stop all of this nonsense – and then the Federation people could have come and taken him away.'

Iris shook her head. 'The *Nepotist* has crashed itself. A kamikaze mission. You know that.'

'I could have prevented that! I could have saved Blandish… all of them… I could have sorted it out…'

'No, Doctor. And don't even think Daedalus would have stopped at getting his son back. That was hardly the point.'

'Well, now those owls are there, they'll rip him to shreds! And that's your fault, Iris! You've caused that!'

She sighed. 'As I said. I've bookmarked that point. It doesn't have to happen.'

'That not the way I do things.'

'It's how I do them.'

They were at loggerheads.

'Doctor, Iris…' began Fitz placatingly, taking a swig of brandy. 'Why –'

'Shut up,' Iris snapped at him. She went on: 'Daedalus wants this war to happen. He knew that if he caused enough trouble within the Enclave, he would get it to draw the attention of the rest of the universe. A universe which had, hitherto, been completely oblivious to it. He wants that kind of unpleasantness.'

Compassion put in, 'Why should the rest of the universe be so interested in a little cul-de-sac like that?'

Iris snorted with impatience. 'Because the Enclave is part of the Obverse. It would be terribly valuable for all sorts of reasons. You've seen how things work there. You've seen the Corridors. Obverse physics could have a profound effect on our – on your – universe. It should have remained a secret.'

'Obverse?' The Doctor frowned.

Iris smiled sadly. 'Yes, I've not told you much about that before, have I, Doctor?' She started to move back towards the cab of the bus. 'The Obverse is my home.'

'Obtuse, more like,' muttered Fitz.

The Doctor was confused. 'Are you saying you're not who you claim to be?'

'That and more besides!' laughed Iris. 'Now, shall we get back and wrap up the end of this thing?'

Although a squid, and having to learn to cope rapidly with a whole new way of being, let alone thinking, Belinda found a surprising amount of continuity between her usual and her present form.

She had watched the arrival of the owls with some perplexity, and then the fleeing of the Doctor and the others into the bus.

Her heart had hammered inside her chest at the thought of their abandoning her to this chaos. Her new, powerful heart, thudding away in panic as the bus vanished. She had stared at the spot as the sound of dematerialisation faded away.

Then the owls rose as one and started screeching again. It was as if the bus's disappearance had freed them into action.

They attacked the boy Icarus.

They fell upon him, shrieking.

He disappeared under the blur of wings.

There was a storm of white plumage and then scarlet.

Daedalus howled.

The Ghillighast were frozen in horror and their dogs were silenced and stilled.

Chapter Forty
Iris Had Come Down...

Iris had come down at last, looking rather blotchy and red.

But she had rallied through their first course and began to regale her audience with stories about parapsychology, which she absolutely believed in.

The mind could play some funny tricks, she said.

Then, gamely, between courses, and picking over the shredded remains of the duck carcass, she moved on to cryptozoology; a much-maligned science, she claimed. Bigfoot was absolutely real, too. *And* she's had first hand experience of loch monsters and alien incursions of all kinds.

Fitz excused himself and went out into the back garden to smoke.

On the way he picked up the *Aja'ib*; which had become a sort of talisman to him.

In the garden he inspected the herb garden again and found that Sally's dog, banished out back, was eating the wild thyme.

'Hey boy; stop that. Stop!'

The mangy dog looked up at him quizzically.

'What did Sally call you again? Something tautological, wasn't it?'

The dog coughed wearily. 'Canine. It's purely descriptive. Nothing tautological about it at all.'

Fitz's mouth dropped open. 'You can talk.'

The dog rolled his eyes. 'Why should that be such a surprise to you? Look at that book you're reading.'

'This old thing? It's all fantasy.'

'Yeah, yeah,' said Canine.

'But it is! Look at the things it talks about. All of it is meaningless. The Shaft, the Obverse... the Enclave. Those terms make perfect sense in the book... but not in the everyday, the rational world outside this book.'

'Oh?' asked the dog, sounding rather withering. 'Listen, Fitz. Learn to think of all these things as stories. And stories can't contradict each other because, in the end, they're all made up. Nothing can take precedence then. All right?'

'I'm not sure I know what you're on about.'

'Well, you reckon the world you live in takes precedence over the world you're reading about. So you've established a hierarchy, yeah?'

'Of course! I'd be out of my tree not to!'

The dog was looking sceptical again. He gave a kind of shrug and started nibbling the herbs once more. 'Maybe. But think how happy you might be if you didn't have to make those choices about what you should invest belief in. Here in the Obverse you can think of it all as a kind of fugue.'

'Fugue?'

'Hmm,' said the dog, chewing. 'No contradictions anymore. Every story holding equal sway. It means there are always alternatives. And it means no natural ending.'

Fitz took his last drag on his cigarette and ground it out on the window sill.

'I don't believe it.'

'No?' asked the dog.

'No. One reality has to be more valid than the other. It has to be realler.'

The little dog laughed and said, 'Well... what if you found out that the one you're in was the less real one? What if you found out that you yourself are less than real?'

Fitz laughed and looked at the moon.

'You're one hell of a dog. Do you know that?'

'Oh, yes,' said Canine primly.

Chapter Forty-One
After I'd Had A Few Drinks…

After I'd had a few drinks and managed to blot out my panic over dinner and also the nagging pain in my leg – which seemed, at times, to be reaching an almost unbearable pitch – I decided to come clean with Sally.

Around the table, the others fell quiet as I turned, rather blearily, towards her and said, 'I did read your book, you know. Every bit of it. I read it twice. I stayed up four nights running with it. Sat up in bed, afraid to go to sleep.'

She looked shocked. 'Then why did you lie to me? Back there?'

'I don't know.' I cried out then, as the pain dug in harder. They all looked at me.

'Are you all right?' Iris frowned.

'It's my leg.'

She glanced under the table. 'You should see a doctor.'

I needed to explain to Sally.

'It's very hard, when someone you know writes something. Especially when it implicates you. And you have to say what you think. I mean, what if it wasn't what you expected… or you're disappointed? Or it's actually really good and you can't depend on your own ability to say why you think it's good and you come across sounding all insincere?'

Sally smiled. 'I just wanted to know what you thought. I wanted your honest opinion. I'd respect that.'

I went on.

'I was afraid to go to sleep because of the dreams I'd been getting. But the dreams I'd been getting were just like your book. How did you know, Sally? How did you know what went on in my head?'

The Men of Glass with their ruby hearts, the Scarlet Queen of

265

Jam, the Mock Turtle, the Bearded Lady, the savage owls, the angel boy, the demoniac elephant – all of them from my dreams.

The ones I was meant to suppress.

Even the twin confrontations at the close of both halves of the book, in the equivalent throne rooms at the heart of Hyspero and Valcea – even these oddly mirrored denouements were all too familiar.

And, above all, Iris. She had been the biggest shock of recognition.

'I made it all up,' said Sally simply.

And it was Iris who tipsily replied, 'Darling, there's no such thing.'

Chapter Forty-Two
As The Doctor Waited...

As the Doctor waited for Iris to take them all back to the precise moment they had left, he already knew what he had to do.

The owls. He would persuade them not to kill Icarus.

Icarus and his father would be sent back to the Federation. Daedalus would stand trial.

The Enclave would remain secret.

He would find out what the Obverse truly was.

He would find out where Iris came from.

He would find out where Daedalus had come from, and how Iris knew him.

He would engineer some way for the Ghillighast, owls, Steigertrudes and Sahmbekarts to return peacefully to their own, secret worlds.

He would never let Compassion out of his sight again.

He would tell the owls to look after their remaining egg. To never let it hatch.

He would have to look into the destiny of Icarus.

He would find out what bearing he was meant to have on the universe the Doctor knew.

He would find Blandish.

He would...

'We're arriving,' said Iris, plunging the dematerialisation switch.

The Doctor took a deep breath, watched the swirling mists dissolve, and turned to tell his companions to wait aboard as he went off to solve everything.

He paused first, however, to see that the throne room appeared around them in precisely the manner it was meant to.

He waited for the glowing light of that chamber. The smashed glass and the assembled alien species. The owls and bats and giant squid.

Instead, outside, were winter woods.

Black trees.

Silvered snow.

Howling wind.

He turned, speechless, to Iris.

'I'm sorry, Doctor,' she said.

Blandish and Timon had arrived in the outskirts of the ruined City of Glass.

'This is a real kamikaze mission,' Blandish said. 'We're going the whole hog.'

'What do you mean by that?' asked the weapons expert.

'I mean, I am activating the weapon that I've never tried before.'

'You don't mean…'

Blandish nodded grimly. 'I don't see why not.'

As they picked their way through the rubble, they were approaching the Steigertrude women, who were still looking for their stolen engine.

'What are they?' asked Timon, appalled.

'As dead as the rest of us,' said his captain, who had slipped into a very peculiar mood.

Emba stepped forward.

'I suggest we join forces,' she said reasonably. 'And find the heart of this city and seize it.'

Blandish shrugged. 'It doesn't matter now.'

Emba looked at him curiously. 'What kind of soldier are you?'

'The Federation will be sending ships soon. So will the Draconians, the Daleks, the Martians, the Sontarans and Cybermen. Everyone will be coming here. We don't stand a chance. And neither does the rest of the universe while this city is still here.'

'Then,' said Emba. 'We must burn it,' said Emba.

Blandish nodded. 'Agreed.'

* * *

They agreed this just as the same thought struck the transformed Belinda.

And she knew that, if Blandish had in fact escaped and survived, he had the perfect means to bring all this to an end.

She was one of the few crew members of the *Nepotist* to have the privileged knowledge. The knowledge of how exactly Blandish was armed.

He could tick himself down to annihilation. Any Federation ship's captain could. It was seen as a necessary precautionary measure.

The captain's spleen had been replaced, at the outset of his career, by a tiny warhead.

As this memory drifted through Belinda's mind, the captain was making the necessary adjustments to activate the timer.

And as he led Timon and Emba and Steigertrudes into the wrecked City of Glass, he was ticking very quietly.

The Doctor hurled himself out into the black wind.

Iris followed with the others.

He howled out of rage and frustration.

'You did it on purpose! You stopped me helping everyone!'

Compassion looked curiously at Iris. 'Did you?'

Iris shrugged. 'There was no way I could *really* get back to that exact moment. He should have known that. I saved our necks. Isn't that enough?'

She shouted over the noise of the wind at the Doctor. 'Is that enough?'

'No!' he roared. 'I could have done it! I could have stopped this war!'

Iris shook her head. 'No. You can't always win. It had to go on.'

'It did not! I was there! I could have made them –'

'Doctor,' said Iris, moving towards him. 'It is inevitable. The universe and its Obverse. You couldn't impose yourself between them.'

He looked at her, his face twisted in horror. 'I don't know what you've done.'

Iris shook her head. 'It's your TARDIS you should blame, lovey, not me. You think it's coincidence it keeps plonking you right in the middle of all these dimensional disturbances encroaching on your precious Earth?'

'What are you saying?' the Doctor demanded.

'I'm saying your own ship knows more than you do... It knows what's going to happen, what *has* to happen. It's doing the rounds, it's been trying to prove itself wrong – but you *mustn't* go back to the Obverse, Doctor. You simply mustn't.'

The Doctor stared at her. 'I don't even know who you are any more.'

Iris shrugged. 'I'm just glad I could save your life. All our lives. That's enough for me.'

The Doctor pulled away from her.

'I wish I'd let you die on Hyspero.'

She gasped. 'You don't mean that.'

'I want to go into the Obverse,' he said.

'You can't.'

'You know about it. You can tell me how to get there.'

'I can't.' Iris looked away from him. 'Not yet.'

'You *have* to tell me, Iris.'

'I don't. You can't go there yet.'

'When, then?'

'Trust me, Doctor. I've sorted it out. I've sorted it out so you don't have to go there...'

'Fitz! Compassion!' he shouted. 'We're leaving!'

Fitz came hurrying up. 'How? I mean, where are we?'

The Doctor pointed through a gap in the dark trees.

Fitz looked through.

There was a sharp hill, drifted with snow.

Further afield lay the lights of Tyneside.

The angel statue, aglow with orange.

The shopping mall, blazing with late-night shopping lights.

The car park, packed to bursting.

And, closest to them, in all this regular hubbub, the TARDIS. Solid, blue, waiting for them.

'How did you know…?' he turned to ask the Doctor.

'I'm going now, Iris,' said the Doctor quietly.

She nodded. 'One day you'll see. There are things we really can't get in the way of.'

'Perhaps one day you'll care enough to explain it to me,' he said, in a very level tone.

Iris was fighting to stop her eyes watering. 'I will. You know I will.' She laughed bitterly. 'Gods, if you don't know already, you ought to. Doctor, one day you'll sit and listen to me, and I'll tell you the whole lot. Everything. One day you'll stay with me long enough.'

He looked her up and down. 'Iris… I don't think I want to stay with you that long… not just yet.'

He turned away from her and led his two companions through the black trees.

He turned his back on the bus and its lights blazing aboard and Iris silhouetted in their glow. She waved once but he had stopped looking back.

He led Compassion and Fitz through the trees and down the sharp, snowy hill, to the car.

'Why did you ever trust her?' Compassion asked him. 'She caused all of that. She made that war inevitable.'

He fished around in his pockets for his TARDIS key. 'It's just like I said. I've got to look again at the people I trust. I never used to be so… gullible. Pliable.'

Compassion looked stung at this.

They had to climb over a metal fence to get to the TARDIS.

Fitz tried to make the Doctor smile, passing his old scarf over to help him.

'I hate the feeling that Iris knows something I don't,' said the Doctor, as they walked up to the ship. 'It's like something hanging over my head.'

Compassion's eyes narrowed.

Fitz spoke up as he followed them into the vast, dusty, darkened console room.

'Don't you wish... sometimes... we lived a quieter life?'

Chapter Forty-Three
My Mother Warned Me...

My mother warned me about nights like these.

She was a mermaid, so she knew all about existing in more than one world.

Nights like these leave you prey to the demands of numberless worlds.

They sparkle and gleam and try to seduce and lure you into places you'd only dream about otherwise.

They tell you that this town isn't the only one where you might live.

Fitz and Compassion went off blearily to sleep.

Sally went to check that her dog was all right, had a quick word with him, and a fag, and then passed out drunkenly on the sofa.

Iris pulled a rug over her and then announced that she was going off for a midnight walk, as she often did, and would I care to join her?

It turned out she was a naturist. Her idea of a midnight walk in the snow was to throw off every last stitch of clothing in my hallway and go galumphing out into the night starkers.

I was appalled.

Her old woman's body looked so much thinner than I expected under all those layers.

She stood on the welcome mat and I hardly knew where to look.

At least the alcohol had soothed the pain in my leg a little.

And it made me less likely to wonder what the neighbours would say about a naked grandmother leaving my house this time of night.

'Why don't you try it?' she grinned rakishly. 'Cast off your Edwardian finery, Doctor?'

And before I knew it, she was helping me off with my green velvet coat and my waistcoat.

I was folding up my moleskin trousers and pulling off my cravat. We were giggling like school children. Off flew my shoes and my socks. She stood back as I shucked the rest of my things and folded them neatly. I looked up blushing and she smiled.

At last we were ready.

She opened the front door and let in the freezing night. Up came my goose pimples. She turned to smile at me again, still egging me on.

I was covering up my nakedness with both hands and then decided, oh, hang it – and strode out after her.

The cold drew us out of the house and the door slammed behind us with a resounding note of finality.

Here we were, ploughing through the snow.

Suddenly, gloriously free.

'See?' she said. 'Don't you wish you'd done this before?'

We walked into the park.

Strange how warm I started to feel.

She stopped and looked down at my leg.

She was staring at my swollen calf muscle.

It was quite a sight.

The flesh stretched obscenely.

'Something is growing in there,' she said, simply.

'That's what I've been thinking.'

'It needs letting out.'

'How?'

I thought she was mad.

Then I realised how mad I must be, to come out with her like this in the night.

She reached up into the branches of the dark tree next to us.

She snapped off the sharpest, most jagged icicle she could see.

'What are you doing?'

She bent with a grunt, at my feet. She seized my leg.

'Iris…'

And before I knew it, she had plunged the diamond-sharp icicle into the flesh.

I watched, curiously detached, as the scarlet blood ran freely straight on to the blue snow.

There was an instant release from the pain.

She murmured, tearing open the swollen muscle, and my flesh inside looked like peach flesh, parting neatly down to the clean pit of the bone.

And there, nestling in the warm meat, was a tiny blue body.

She touched it and it moved slightly.

It started to make a noise.

Iris tugged at the tiny creature inside my leg and, with one deft movement, tugged it free.

There was a slight sucking noise as it came away.

Then it was in her hands.

'He comes from the Enclave,' she said. 'A space filled with corridors in which he was free. A space between two worlds. He has to stay free to move between worlds.'

I clasped my leg.

'We'd better get you home. And I can stitch that leg,' she said. 'I'm a dab hand.'

The wound wasn't so bad.

I was just glad it was over.

I wanted to know what she was holding in her hands.

She showed me.

She opened both palms to reveal the tiny thing lying there.

It was a very small baby boy, all of blue.

As he dried in her elderly skin, his wings were shaking loose and fledging out.

I didn't know what to say.

She stepped back and held her hands aloft.

'Off you go,' said Iris quietly.

And the blue boy ruffled his wings experimentally.

As both Iris and I watched, breathless, my child took off and soared up into the black sky.

Twenty Questions

1. Was it completely fitting that Belinda was transformed into a giant squid, thrashing her newly granted tentacles as the captain of her ship stormed into the throne room on Valcea?

2. Or was it an ad hoc, impromptu, arbitrary change of form, perpetrated by a Daedalus embittered by his own metamorphosis, a Daedalus who laughed aloud in glee as Captain Blandish informed the assembled rabble that they were all about to die?

3. Or was it all to do with Belinda's eventual, heroic status as commander-in-chief of the defending armies on the frontier water worlds during the final push that the worlds of the Obverse made on the Enclave, and was she destined to find a new element?

4. And did Blandish's personalised weapon really go off as devastatingly as he had planned, destroying what remained of the throne room at the heart of the City of Glass?

5. Or did it merely set off a bizarre and unforeseeable chain reaction which splintered and shattered the transdimensional Corridors, causing them to mutate beyond anybody's wildest dreams?

6. And did those fractured conduits open up even further complex channels into known and unknown universes, so that even more spaces were jeopardised and even more races were sucked ineluctably into the bloody fray?

7. And was it so unforeseeable? Did Daedalus already know that the captain of the *Nepotist* was bound to seek to detonate his

secreted device? Did Daedalus set the whole plan in motion, everything dependent on Blandish's incendiary internal organ?

8. Did Daedalus rule supreme in the chaos and did he lord it over the ravening hordes?

9. How did he deal with the first new arrivals – the first being, naturally, the Daleks – who entered the space of contention, the threshold between thesis and antithesis bristling, buzzing, swivelling with fury?

10. Did the Steigertrudes and Ghillighast, led by Emba united with Meisha, form an army between them to defend the Enclave and maintain its fragile integrity?

11. At what point did the Doctor arrive?

12. And in which incarnation?

13. Was it really several, as many sources claim, and was it a tale as the legends have it?

14. Did Iris forge an alliance between Cyber factions and insect races and lead an assault on the homeworld of the first of the unknown races to emerge, hungry, from the Obverse?

15. Did Iris ensure that the earlier, merely eighth, Doctor was safely out of the way, on purpose?

16. Did she know what a can of worms had been opened?

17. Had she already been there and seen the outcome?

18. Did she live, like Merlin, backwards through time?

19. In the end, did she remove her Doctor, because she knew what must eventually become of him, or simply because she couldn't bear to see him there on the battlefield again, again, again and over again?

20. Did she want to prevent her Doctor from seeing what really did happen next?

paul magrs and jeremy hoad
norwich, spring 1999